WHEREVER Nina Lies

LYNN WEINGARTEN

Point

To sisters who love each other no matter what

Library of Congress Cataloging-in-Publication Data

Weingarten, Lynn.
Wherever Nina lies / Lynn Weingarten.—1st ed.
p.   cm.
Summary: Two years after the disappearance of her older sister,
sixteen-year-old Ellie goes on a quest to find her.
ISBN-13: 978-0-545-06631-0 (alk. paper)
ISBN-10: 0-545-06631-X (alk. paper)
[1. Missing persons—Fiction.   2. Sisters—Fiction.]   I. Title.
PZ7.W43638Wh 2009
[Fic]—dc22
2008021527

12 11 10 9 8 7 6 5 4 3 2 1   9 10 11 12 13 14/0

Printed in the U.S.A.
First edition, February 2009

Interior illustrations by Vicky Newman
Book design by Christopher Stengel

Acknowledgments

Thank you so very much. . .

To Liesa Abrams, Andrea Byler, Tigerlili Cavill, Mary Crosbie, Diego Hernandez, Melanie Altarescu Jafar, Sarah Lee, Greg Matherly, Micol Ostow, Christopher Prince-Barry, Lizzie Schechter, Christina Sfekas, Jill Santopolo, Daniel Shaw, Bob Smith, Siobhan Vivian, and Elise West for helping me with this book in a variety of ways, some that you know about and some that you don't. You are very special and very precious and of course very, very pretty!

To my fabulous agent Lydia Wills and her assistant Alyssa Reuben.

To Abby McAden and Morgan Matson, for being so smart and fantastic to work with. And to Cheryl Weisman, Christopher Stengel, and Elizabeth Parisi at Scholastic.

To Vicky Newman for her gorgeous drawings.

To Cheryl Weingarten and Donald Weingarten for being my mom and my dad! I love you both very much!

And to my brilliant, funny, and patient editor (and friend) Aimee Friedman. I am so happy to have gotten to work with you on this. Thank you for being so incredibly lovely at every step of the way.

one

The guy walking toward me is good-looking in an obnoxious way, like he'd play the hot jerk in a TV movie about why drunk driving is bad or how it doesn't pay to cheat on the SATs. He's got these big wraparound sunglasses on and a shiny black short-sleeve button-up shirt filled out with the kind of insanely sculpted arm muscles a person only gets when they spend most of their time lifting weights in the mirror and grunting at themselves.

"Hi," I say. "What can I get for you?" I've been working here for a year but I still find it funny when I hear myself ask that, it's like I'm a kid playing a game about working at a coffee bar, instead of a sixteen-year-old person who actually works at one.

The guy stares at the chalkboard behind me. "Can I haaaaaaaaave"—"a sugar-free skim iced chai."

"A sugar-free skim iced chai," I say. And I try not to look over at Brad, who I can feel watching us through the glass pastry case he's washing.

"Hey, Ellie!" Brad calls out. He's using his best "casual" voice, which is about an octave higher than his regular one. "Isn't this such a *coincidence*? How we were just talking about sugar-free skim *iced chais* and how good they are? And now this customer is ordering a *chai*? What was that funny thing you were saying about them? About sugar-free skim iced *chais*?"

I feel my face turning red. The thing that's fun about Brad is that he'll say pretty much anything to anyone; this is also the thing that makes me want to throw a muffin at his head sometimes, one of those scary-huge ones that we sell here for five twenty-five.

I turn back to the guy and make an exaggerated shrug, like, "Who is this nut? And why is he cleaning the pastry case?" But the guy isn't paying attention to any of this, anyway—he's too busy checking out his reflection in the back of the espresso machine.

I make his drink and hand it to him. He watches the muscles in his forearm as he pays, and then turns around to leave, he makes it almost to the door, but then turns back at the last second and marches toward the counter. He's holding his clear plastic cup up to his face. "This doesn't taste like skim." He jiggles the cup around. He stares at me, then down at the cup, then back at me. "You gave me a different kind of milk, didn't you?"

He's taken his sunglasses off. The skin around his eyes is too tan. And weirdly wrinkly. He makes this intense eye contact for a second, like I've been lying to him, but now that his glasses are off, I'll finally have to 'fess up.

"Nope," I say. "That was definitely skim."

"You're positive about that?" He keeps the eye contact a second too long and then holds the cup up above his head, looks at the bottom of it, as if that's where all the fat has deposited itself.

"I'm positive," I say. "I can make you another one if you want."

The guy just stands there. "No," he says. And then he raises his eyebrows. "But I think we *both* know what you're trying to do here." He stands there one second longer, staring, and then finally turns and walks out the door.

I wait two beats after the doors close, then I turn toward Brad. The moment our eyes meet we burst out laughing. "Oh. My," Brad says. He stands up, holding the spray bottle and rag to his hip. "I thought he looked kinda cute when he first came in, but I should have known his big, shiny glasses were hiding a face full of insaneness." Brad shakes his head slowly. "Arms like that do not come without a price."

"Um, speaking of insaneness?"

"Yeah, but *I* was doing it *as a favor*! If he had been anything resembling a normal person, my craziness would have been a great conversation starter!"

Brad puts the bottle and rag under the counter and then looks at his bright watch. "Okay, sweetness, you're off soon, so before you go, I'm just going to run to the back and restock.

If anyone comes in who I might think was your soul mate, make sure to tell him I said that he should give you his number!"

"Ha-ha," I say.

"I'm serious," Brad says. "Your very own Thomas could be just around the corner." I roll my eyes. Thomas is Brad's boyfriend who he met while working here. Thomas was a customer and Brad, who never gets nervous around anyone, was so nervous he dropped a piece of carrot cake on his own shoe. It was quite sweet actually. And they have been happily in love ever since.

Brad reaches out and grabs the end of one of my brown curls. He stretches it out straight and then lets it go. "*Boing!*" he says, then flashes me a smile as he disappears into the back room.

I just smirk and shake my head. I pretend that it's silly whenever Brad talks about finding me a boyfriend, that I don't even *want* one. But the truth is, yes, I do. It's just that not having something because you don't want it is far less pathetic than wanting something you can't have. I'm sixteen and in two months I'll be a junior, but all of my guy experiences up until this point, a grand total of three brief make-outs with three different people, have been with friends of whoever my best friend, Amanda, was dating at the time, and just kind of happened randomly. Just once I'd like to kiss a guy because we actually like each other, not because we've been left alone by our respective friends, who are messing around in the next room, and have run out of stuff to say and need something else to do with our mouths.

I look out over the counter. It's quiet in here, pretty average for an early Friday evening, before the nighttime rush. A dozen or so people are working on laptops or reading or talking quietly. A lanky guy with bright orange hair and an earring in each ear dumps his paper cup into the garbage and turns to wave as he walks out. Earl Grey, double tea bags, with extra milk. That's what he drinks when he comes in here, which is only about once a month. Why do I know this? It's the funny thing about working in a coffee bar, I guess. You get to know a tiny little bit about an awful lot of people. I don't know most of my customers' names or where they live or how old they are, but I know all the weird stuff they like to do to their caffeinated (or decaf) drinks.

Two girls approach the counter.

One is younger than I am, maybe fifteen or so. The other is older, probably around nineteen. The younger one has this big, bright, ecstatic grin on her face that is taking over all of her features. When you see a smile this genuine, it makes you realize just how many of the smiles you see during an average day aren't. Looking at her, I find it almost impossible not to smile back.

The older girl has the same expression on her face, like there is light pouring out of her. And she has the same eyes. And similar bone structure and . . . There's a weird tugging inside my chest as I realize something—they're sisters, these girls. Instantly I know everything about them. And I feel a little sick.

They haven't seen each other in a while. The older one was at college, or away on a long trip, and she's just returned home. When she was gone, it felt like she'd been gone forever, but now that she's back, it's like she never left. Growing up, they fought a lot, Younger was jealous of Older, resented her and all the stuff she got to do that Younger didn't. Older had always thought Younger was a pain, who would never leave her alone. But years have passed since then, and all that petty stuff that once seemed so important stopped mattering, the way it always does. Or the way it's supposed to, anyway. They realized they can be friends now, real friends. And it means so much to both of them because they know how much they went through to get there.

I take a deep breath and try to keep my face completely still, expressionless. I know it's not fair, but I suddenly hate them.

"Hi!" says Younger, perky behind long bangs. "We would like, um, some zucchini bread and . . . LaurLaur?" She looks up. "What else should we get?"

"Um, are the brownies good?" Older asks. And then smiles and lightly smacks herself in the forehead, "Why am I even asking, right? They're *brownies*. So yeah, a zucchini bread, and a brownie of course, and a croissant . . ."

Younger starts giggling, "And another croissant! An almond one!"

"And an iced latte," says Older. "And a cupcake and a smoothie and . . ."

The girls keep ordering, their smiles growing bigger and bigger, exchanging looks like coming here and ordering all this food is the culmination of a private joke. Probably something they'd been discussing for months while Older was gone, like, "When we're together again, we'll go to Mon Coeur . . . and order one of everything!"

I make their drinks and try to avoid eye contact. They're chatty in that way people are when they're just really happy, a little high on how happy they are.

"I just love this place," says Younger.

"I know, I really missed it," says Older. "I think, it's what I missed most while gone. Yup!" She opens her eyes really wide and Younger mock punches her in the arm. Older grabs Younger around the shoulder and kisses her on the cheek and Younger pretends to wipe it off. They both laugh.

All their food is lined up on the counter now. I stand there staring at them.

"Oooh, sorry!" Older says. She takes out a lime green leather wallet, pays for everything with crisp new bills. "Thank you so much!" she says.

"Yes! Thank you!" says Younger. "So much!" It's as though they're giving me credit for how happy they are, as though just by being there to witness it, I had something to do with it.

It takes them three trips to carry all their food over to the table. Normally, I would have offered to help. But I just stand there watching. Older puts money in the tip jar—two dollars. No one ever puts in more than one. I can barely muster a "Thank you."

Less than a minute later Brad is back, standing next to me. He watches me watching them, and puts one arm around my shoulder. "It's time for you to go," he says, and hands me a white paper bag. Inside are a dozen broken cookies iced in pink and green and white. "We can't sell these," Brad says. "I was going to give them to Thomas, but you should probably take them instead. Just make sure you remember to throw up after so you don't destroy your adorable figure!"

I stick my nose in the bag and take a sweet breath of almondy air. The tightness in my chest starts to loosen. I am, I decide, very lucky to have Brad in my life who, for all his ridiculousness, knows exactly when I might need a big bag of cookie pieces. And also knows exactly when I won't want to talk about why.

two

I'm outside. The air is cooler now and the sun is going down. My eyes adjust to the dimming light as I walk.

I pass a day spa, a design store, a gourmet shop. I keep walking. Mon Coeur, where I work, and Attic, where my best friend Amanda works, are in the middle of town in Edgebridge, Illinois, which is a suburb of Chicago. It's a fancy suburb for rich people, the Disneyland version of where people are supposed to live. There are beautiful new streetlights lighting up every corner and pink and orange flowers blooming in the tall wooden boxes that dot the sidewalk. In the fall this part of town is decorated with pumpkins and ears of dried corn, and in winter it's all glittering Christmas lights and jingle bells. The town is about a two-minute drive from Amanda's house, which is why we both got jobs here in the first place. There's nowhere to work in my neighborhood, except liquor stores and used-car dealerships. Besides, I practically live at her house anyway.

Amanda's waiting for me at the door to Attic. She kisses

me on the cheek. Then she stands back and motions to her outfit. "I'm trying something out here, what do you think?"

She's wearing a tiny navy-blue pair of kid's running shorts, and a tiny boy's ribbed white tank top. She has a pair of navy blue soccer socks pulled up to her knees.

"Well, if you're trying out being a prepubescent boy, you forgot about a couple of rather important, ahem"—I stare directly at her boobs—"things." We both laugh.

"I saw something like this in a magazine," Amanda says. "You don't think I can pull it off?"

"Oh, I think it would be very, very easy to pull off."

"Ha-ha." She adjusts her sock. "My parents are out tonight and so I'm thinking we should have a bunch of people over, including a lot of extremely hot guys we barely know. I'm sure *they'll* like my outfit even if you don't." She sticks out her tongue and smiles. I can't help but smile back. Amanda has a good life: Her parents love each other, she has two nice, funny brothers who she gets along with, and a giant house full of Jacuzzi tubs and flat-screen TVs, where everything looks beautiful and comfortable because someone has put effort into making it so, because they have the luxury of thinking about those things.

"What about Eric?" I ask. Eric is Amanda's not-quite-boyfriend whose not-quite-ness is due to the fact that he continues to date other girls.

"I'm done with Eric," Amanda says.

"Good," I say.

And we both know this isn't true, but we leave it at that.

"I already picked out some stuff for you," Amanda says. She grabs my hand and leads me toward the back room, where we always try on clothes. "Good thing Morgette is rich, right?" Amanda grins, as though somehow she doesn't realize her own family is pretty rich, too. Morgette, the owner of Attic, leaves early every Friday in the summer to go to her country house for the weekend, and she gives Amanda keys to the store so she can lock up. Basically this means that Amanda and I can pretty much borrow whatever we want from the store so long as we bring it back by Monday morning. The clothes are already used so it's not even like it's wrong or anything. All we're doing is using them, y'know, a little bit more.

As I get dressed I tell Amanda about all the interesting customers who came in today—the skim milk guy, the lady with the obviously fake British accent, the guy with the parrot on his shoulder, the girl who ordered while her boyfriend was nibbling on her ear. Amanda laughs at all the funny parts and rolls her eyes at all the eye-rolly parts. I don't mention anything about the sisters, though. Amanda's my best friend, but even with her there are limits to what I feel like I can say.

A few minutes later I'm standing barefoot in front of the mirror wearing a tiny boy's white button-up shirt (the sleeves reach just past my elbows), a wide gold belt, and a floaty white skirt with gold threads running through it that reaches just below my butt.

I stare at myself in the mirror.

Amanda is behind me. "Stop frowning," she says to my reflection. "As usual you look hot spelled with about five extra t's."

"Ha-ha," I say, and roll my eyes.

Truth is, no matter how much time I spend staring into the mirror, I don't really have any idea what I actually look like. Does anyone?

I'm not tall and I'm not short, and I'm on the thin side but I'm definitely not skinny. I have curly hair that reaches to the middle of my back, it's light brown but gets blonder in the summer. The guy who cuts it is always telling me that it's "gorgeous and luxurious" but then he tries to sell me a whole bunch of products to "tame and define," none of which I ever end up getting, which is okay since I usually just wear a ponytail most days, anyway. My face gets blotchy when I get nervous or embarrassed, but other than that, my skin is okay, I think. My eyes are big and green. My nose is kind of round. I have one dimple. Whenever I see pictures of myself, my smile looks crooked.

Amanda tosses me a pair of gold lace-up sandals that look like they could be part of a costume in a play about ancient Greece.

"Try these," she says.

I sit down and slip off my shoes. There's a cardboard box next to me on the floor with *Sunny Grove Citrus* printed on it in orange and green.

"What's in here?" I poke the box.

"Crap Day," Amanda says. "The third Friday of every month Morgette buys anything anyone wants to get rid of for twenty-five cents a pound."

"Anything?" I ask. "Like old bananas and expired vitamins?"

"I guess enough people accidentally sell her first editions of old books or pieces of antique silverware that it makes it worth it." Amanda shrugs.

I sit down on the floor and start digging through it — a bag of plastic spiders, three unopened jars of cloves, a glob of dried-up neon Play-Doh, and at the bottom of the box a copy of a book with the cover ripped off — *Encyclopedia of Abnormal Psychology.*

"Hey, Amanda," I say. I pick up the book and stand, "Do you think we'll find Eric's picture in here under . . . " but then I stop.

A rectangular piece of cardboard with slightly rounded edges, a little smaller than an index card, has fallen out of the book and fluttered to the floor. I reach out and grab it. As soon as my skin touches it, my heart starts pounding, and I feel dizzy, like I've been spinning and just stopped. The room tilts. Everything around me looks wrong all of a sudden, and

I think maybe I'm going to pass out. I sink to the floor; I'm vaguely aware of Amanda's voice calling my name, but I can't answer. She sounds far away and unfamiliar. Everything is unfamiliar, except for one thing. The piece of paper in my hand, covered in blue vines. I stare at them so hard they begin to swirl, like delicate navy thread snakes on a field of white. And in the center of these vines is a drawing of a girl: big round eyes, round face, round nose, crazy hair curling out in all directions, one dimple, a crooked smile. *I know this drawing.*

I've seen it since I was a little kid, on the backs of notebooks, on napkins, paper tablecloths, in an entire comic given to me once by someone whom I haven't seen in two years, whom I try not to think about because I have no idea where she is or what she's doing or if she's even still alive, whom I've tried to convince myself to forget about, whom I've almost completely given up on ever hearing from again, whom a teeny, tiny part of me still believes will reappear, will send me a sign at some time when I am least expecting it.

And this is the sign, and that time is now.

Because this drawing is of me.

I blink and turn toward Amanda, who is still standing there in her ridiculous outfit.

"Amanda," I whisper, "look . . ." And I hold the paper high up over my head so the light shines through and the drawing glows. "My sister."

three

For three nights after Nina vanished, I didn't sleep. I just lay in my bed, my head inches from the open window, the thick, humid late June air blowing against my skin like hot breath. Waiting.

When I would hear the sound of a car in the distance, approaching the house, my heart would start thumping so hard I could feel it throughout my entire body. I would imagine my sister inside this car, and that at any moment I would hear the sounds of her coming home: the faint click of a car door opening and the sudden rush of all the noises from the inside of the car coming out, laughing, whispering, the thump of music with a heavy bass line, loud for a split second before someone turns it down, a pause, car door slam, the quick *slap, slap, slap* of flip-flops against driveway, the crunch of a key in the front door, and the slow creak of the door opening. And then the almost soundless padding of my sister tiptoeing up the carpeted stairs. I would bite my lip and squeeze my hands into fists, hoping, hoping, hoping to hear this, but every single time the car would drive past without even slowing down, and I would feel the weight of disappointment, so heavy I'd almost stop breathing. The adrenalized high of hope, the crush of losing it, over and over thirty times a night. Exhausting, sure, but never enough to let me sleep.

During those three days, I wandered around in a haze. Time stopped meaning anything, faces all blurred together. I forgot words. A serious lack of sleep can feel a lot like a drug but a bad drug that no one would ever do on purpose.

Finally, on the fourth night, all that adrenaline was trumped by the feeling of wet cement coating my eyelids and filling the inside of my skull. As soon as I lay down, I was sucked through my bed into the center of the earth where my brain finally released the thoughts I could not allow it to have during the day. At first it seemed like I hadn't fallen asleep at all, because my dream started off with me awake in my bed. I got up, to use the bathroom, and saw a clump of Nina's hair, the bright ocean blue she'd dyed it a week before she vanished, wet and matted at the bottom of the tub. I felt a flood of relief so huge it almost knocked me over, because this meant Nina was here, had been here all along, and, silly me, I just hadn't noticed her. I laughed. And then leaned down, picked up the hair — it felt heavy, like wet rope in my hand. I held it up, but only then did I notice the ragged chunk of skin clinging to the end of it, like raw meat. And I didn't have to wonder, I knew exactly what this meant.

Then everything went black and I heard only a high-pitched animal scream until I woke up, the sound ringing in my ears, unsure whether it came from inside me or from outside.

FOur

Here are the facts, just the facts, everything I know, which is barely anything at all: Two years ago, on the afternoon of June 24, Nina Melissa Wrigley disappeared. She'd gone out in the late afternoon, and then, she just never came back.

When she was gone, she was *gone*. She didn't have a MySpace page or a Facebook account or a cell phone. All her stuff remained in her room exactly as it always had been—clothes in piles on the floor, tubes of hair dye on the nightstand, sketch pads and drawing pencils and pastels and pots of ink scattered everywhere. The only thing in her room that was in any way notable was the graduation gown hanging in her closet—Nina had graduated from high school a week before. She'd turned eighteen two months before that.

Nina was an amazing artist. That might sound like an opinion, but I think it's fair to say it's a fact because no one who saw her drawings ever disagreed. She could draw a photographic reproduction of absolutely anything. But real skill, her skill, wasn't in drawing things that were obviously there, but noticing and capturing things that weren't—the weird angle of the sunlight in late winter, the slightly scared expression on a person's face that even they're not aware of making.

Nina made everything into art. She inked elaborate landscapes onto the soles of her Converse, and covered her tank tops in portraits of the people she saw on the street. Every few weeks she'd dye her hair a different bright crayon color to match whatever was going on in her life at the time. Two weeks before she disappeared she'd decided to dye it blue, "graduation-hat blue," she'd called it. I remember sitting in the kitchen with her, watching from my seat at the table, as she squeezed the dye onto her head, swirling it around like someone squirting ketchup onto a plate of fries. "There's some left," she'd said when she finished. She'd held the bottle up and shook it around. "You want a streak, Belly?" And I'd nodded, thrilled to be included, even though my stomach was already filling with anxiety about what my mother would say when she saw it. Nina chose a chunk behind my left ear and coated it. I remember exactly how the dye felt on my head, cold and heavy. I'd put a paper towel on my shoulder to catch the drips. And then we just sat there, just the two of us while the dye did its thing, making jokes and laughing and dancing along with some song she put on the stereo. I remember thinking this was a sign that finally, finally, I was old enough for Nina and I to really be friends, not older-sister/younger-sister friends, but real friends who just so happened to be related and I was so happy. Nina hadn't been home much around then, and when she was it was like she was there and not there at the same time. But I remember thinking that day, as we sat there surrounded by the sweet smell of chemicals, that this was the start of something new, that everything would be different after this. And it was, just not in the ways I'd imagined.

Two weeks later, Nina was gone, a dye-stained towel left in a ball on her floor. I never did show my mother the streak in my hair, or anyone else for that matter. I wore my hair down until it faded away so Nina and I were the only two people who ever saw it.

Here's another thing about my sister: Nina did what she wanted. She wasn't reckless, but she didn't worry about things other people worried about—getting in trouble, getting laughed at, looking stupid. She pool hopped late at night and cut class and talked to strangers. She was the type of person who, if she saw a guy wearing a big cowboy hat that she liked, would say, "Hey, cowboy! Can I try on your hat?" And he'd probably end up letting her keep it.

When she was sixteen, she started sneaking out at night. She'd go to bed like regular, and I'd only know she snuck out because I'd hear her tiptoeing back up the stairs just before the sun came up, smelling like a mix of alcohol and smoke and her ginger orange perfume. What she was off doing, I don't really know. She was never barfing drunk, just at most a little giggly. And when I'd ask her where she'd been, her response would usually be a wink or a grin. Nina was an expert at dodging questions.

For a while my mother tried to stop her from sneaking out, but my dad had left us by that point and our mother was working nights most of the time and so there was not much she could do. Besides, Nina was always, always, always home by morning. Well, except until she wasn't.

I wish this next fact weren't true, but it is and there's nothing I can do about it now: The very last time I ever saw Nina, I yelled at her. She'd been about to eat one of the ice-cream sandwiches I'd asked our mom to get from the store. And I stopped her, shouted something about how it was my ice cream and if she wasn't going to be around then she wasn't allowed to eat it. It was incredibly petty, and terribly stupid. I was just hurt because she hadn't been around much, and I wanted her to be sorry about it. And I thought somehow yelling was the best way to make that happen. But she just looked up at me. "Okay, Belly," she said. "I'll go put it back, okay? I'll just go put it back." And I remember the exact expression on her face then, not angry, just a little confused and a little hurt, like she just couldn't figure out why I'd been so mad. For months after she was gone I would replay this scene over and over in my head, imagining a different version of this story in which I let her eat the ice-cream sandwich, in which I gave her the entire box of them, as though somehow that could have prevented what happened next.

Another unfortunate fact: When Nina first vanished, my mother barely seemed to notice. I guess when you spend all night working at the hospital and have seen some of the things she's seen, your worry bar is set a little higher than most people's. "Your sister's not missing" is all my mother had said. "She's just not here." And any argument on my part, that Nina would never just leave us like that, that Nina would never leave *me* like that, she barely seemed to register. I wanted my mother to be concerned, too, so I didn't have to carry this all on my own. But all I got was my mother's somber exhaustion. And what, I swear, seemed like the tiniest hint of relief. Certain lines in my mother's face seemed to soften, like she'd been clenching her jaw for eighteen years and only now could finally relax.

I gave up on the idea of my mother doing anything and took matters into my own hands. I printed *Have You Seen My Sister?* signs on Amanda's parents' fancy color printer and Amanda and I hung them up all over town. I called as many of her friends whose names I could remember. I even called our father (who left us when I was seven), who I had not spoken to in over two years. The connection was bad and I had to yell my name three times before he understood who I was. Finally, I called the police. But when they arrived at our house, my mother sent me out of the room. She talked with them in hushed tones in the kitchen over glasses of weak iced tea she'd made from a mix. They left about twenty minutes later looking rather unconcerned, while my mother rinsed their glasses out in the sink.

But then the phone calls came. First a few, and then a flood of them, all at once. I don't know if they were from one person or from many because my mother instructed me to stop answering the phone. I remember one night, it was very late and I was supposed to be in bed and the phone rang, the phone had been ringing all day. I went to my mother's doorway and watched her through the crack between the frame and the door. She was sitting on her bed in her bathrobe. I could only see her back. "Nina's not home," my mother was saying into the phone. Her voice sounded funny, like she was talking under water.

"No." Pause. "No, I haven't." Pause. "I don't know." Pause. "Nina's not the kind of girl who informs her mother of her whereabouts." Pause. "So stop calling here."

Then she hung up. And she just sat there for the longest time after that, phone cradled in her lap, head hanging down, shoulders shaking as she wiped her face over and over with her hands, barely making any sound at all.

Five

Sitting on the floor of Attic, I'm trying to remain completely still, which somehow feels necessary and important, although I'm not sure why. Maybe it's because I know how fragile things can be, and if I move, I'm afraid I'll pop the bubble of this moment and it will turn out that I've imagined the entire thing. I will look down and the doodles will be someone else's doodles, or gone entirely. I've had this happen before . . . thought something meant one thing when really it meant nothing at all. But I have waited too long for this to let go so easily.

I don't know how much time passes before Amanda says, "Oh shit." And I look up.

There are so many questions bouncing around inside my head, each trying to get turned into words first. But I make myself take a breath, as much as part of me wants to GO GO GO, part of me needs to slow this down, to hold onto this moment for just a second longer, because right now whatever's going to happen next hasn't happened yet, and moments of thinking *maybe* are so much better than stretches of knowing *no*. But I can't wait any longer so I take another breath and say, "Now what?"

I'm not even sure who I'm asking.

I look back down at Nina's drawing, at my own face. And then I flip the card over. On the other side, the little piece of cardboard has been printed to look like a credit-card—Bank of the USA at the top in blue letters next to a little blue and white symbol, *Your Name Goes Here* in a typewriter font under a fake card number at the bottom. I flip the card back again.

And then I gasp because all of a sudden, for the first time since my sister disappeared two years ago, *I know exactly what I'm supposed to do next.* Swirled in with the leaves and vines next to my face is a phone number. *303-555-6271.* I know the number must have been there all along and I just didn't notice it before, but part of me feels like the number didn't even appear until just now, like I willed it into existence by wanting it so badly.

"The phone," I say. "I need the phone."

Amanda takes the phone off Morgette's desk and hands it to me.

And somehow I manage to dial.

The phone is ringing.

Someone picks up. First there's loud music, a guitar, heavy drums, and a second later, "*He*llo." It's a guy. Southern maybe.

"Hi." My heart is pounding.

"Hey there." He's definitely Southern. He sounds amused.

"Hello." My mouth is suddenly frozen.

"Can I help you with something?"

I should have planned this out.

"Do you know a girl named Nina Wrigley?" The words tumble out fast. My heart squeezes when I say her name and I realize this is the first time in a very long time that I've even said it out loud.

There's a pause. "What's that now?" Someone has turned the music down in the background.

"Nina Wrigley."

He doesn't say anything. I close my eyes. "Do you know her?" I hold my breath. I don't want him to answer too fast. I want just half a second more of not knowing, of getting to hope.

"Am I supposed to?" The guy sounds suspicious, like he's being set up for something.

"She wrote your phone number down on a piece of paper, maybe a long time ago. So you at least met her at some point. You don't remember her?"

"Sorry, sugar." He snorts a laugh. "If I remembered every girl who has my phone number, I wouldn't have enough room left in my brain to remember to wipe my ass after I took a dump."

I feel my heart starting its slow descent toward the floor. "I'm sure you do meet a lot of people, but she's the type of girl people usually remember. She's really pretty, about five foot six, always had her hair dyed crazy colors . . ."

He doesn't say anything.

"She definitely got your number from you at some point."

"I told you I didn't know her." His tone is less friendly now. He pauses again. "Deb put you up to this, didn't she?"

"No," I say. "Who's Deb?"

"*Who's Deb?* Yeah, right." He curses under his breath. "Listen, sugar, I don't know *Nina* and I never gave my phone number to any girls, okay? So you can just go tell your little buddy Deb that she should leave me the hell alone. Tell Deb I broke up with her for a reason and that reason is that she's a crazy jealous stalker, and if she and all her friends don't quit calling me, I'm going to get a restraining order . . ." He stops talking and I hear a woman's voice in the background, "Who are you on the phone with?!" And then a quick whispered "I swear I'll fucking do it," and then he hangs up.

Amanda has crouched down next to me on the floor. "What happened?"

I have to turn away because I don't want to start crying. "Just some guy who has no idea who she is." I try to say this matter-of-factly, force a shrug. After two years of this you'd think I would be used to it—the thrill of getting to hope, the black pit of knowing there is no point in hoping. Maybe this is just not something people are designed to get used to.

Amanda nods and puts her arm around me, because she's heard this story about a thousand times before, because she's been here with me for all of this. Because she is the closest thing I have to a sister now.

I let my head rest against her shoulder, breathe in the smell of her expensive hair products.

"Oh, El," Amanda says. And we sit there like this for a moment and then I start lacing up those silly gold sandals because I'm just not sure what else to do. I crisscross the gold straps around my ankles and try to focus on the fact that I really have a pretty good tan already this year. It's nice to have a good tan. And it's nice to have a nice pair of shoes and these are the things I am going to think about right now. I turn to Amanda and force a smile, stick my foot out in front of me and shake it around.

"I mean, no matter what happens, at least my feet will look fashionable, right?"

Amanda smiles back, and I can tell she's relieved that I'm trying, that I'm not letting myself sink into that familiar pit. But then before she can say anything, I realize something. And I almost let out a laugh because it is so obvious. I get up and run.

*   *   *

"Seeing my day like this is such an eye-opener," Amanda says, grinning. It's a few minutes later, and Amanda and I are sitting in Morgette's office, watching the Attic surveillance tape on fast-forward. "Because I kinda thought I actually did some work during the day sometimes, but as it turns out . . . nope!"

I nod and smile, even though I'm not really listening. All my attention is focused on the tiny little people zipping around on the tiny little TV: There's Amanda putting on lipgloss, there's a girl walking in, there are three girls going through the clothes racks, there's a couple who seem to be fighting, there's a girl around our age popping a zit in the mirror when she thinks no one is looking. There's Amanda experimenting with many different hairstyles.

"It's kind of hypnotizing," Amanda says, shaking her head. "I should have stopped at the high pony, that one looked best."

A few people come to the counter with bags of stuff to drop off, but so far no one has appeared with the big white box. The big white box that contained the book that contained the drawing that just might somehow lead me to Nina. Some guy walks in carrying a big box. I inhale and hold my breath. But he puts it down near the door, tries on a belt, goes to the counter with the belt, discusses the belt with Morgette, picks up his box, and leaves.

Amanda takes a deep breath, she lets it out. "El, I'm not trying to be a bitch here, and you know that I would do anything that I could to help you, but what exactly do you think watching this is going to do? Even if we see someone dropping off a box full of what looks to be books and *maybe* one of them is the book that you found Nina's doodle in, then what? You're going to track him down how? Because unless he has his name and address tattooed on the top of his head, it's going to be pretty impossible . . ."

But I tune her out completely then because *there he is*.

Stop. Rewind. Play. He looks a few years older than us, wearing longish cargo shorts and a white T-shirt, pale blond hair, skinny arms covered in tattoos, holding a big white cardboard box up at the counter. I stop the tape and put my finger over the tiny guy on the screen, pressing so hard my finger turns white. I hit play and watch as he puts the box on the counter, says something, Morgette nods, he hands the box to Morgette, she takes it to the scale, weighs it, comes back to the counter, hands him some money. And then he starts walking toward the door and then, right past where Amanda is trying on hats, then turns back and . . . this is the perfect part—he goes over to this community bulletin board that Morgette has hanging near the door, takes something out of his pocket, and sticks it up on the board. And then he's gone.

I turn toward Amanda who is looking at me with her eyes wide. "Oh!" I say.

I run through Morgette's office, out into the main room, and stop in front of the bulletin board. Amanda is at my side.

"Ellie?" Her voice sounds strained. She puts her hand on my arm and when I turn toward her she's looking at me with such concern that for a second I think she's maybe about to cry. "We don't have any idea how her drawing got into that book, or when she drew it, or how the guy who brought the book here even got it, I mean he could have bought it at a garage sale or found it on the street or . . . something." She stops herself and shakes her head. But I don't let it hurt me. I know why Amanda is saying this. We've been down this road before.

When Nina first vanished, finding her was all I talked about and all I thought about. And there were at least a dozen times when I was sure I was *this close* to finding her. Like the time I saw a girl on the street with hair the exact blue color Nina's had been when she left and spent an hour following this girl so I could ask her questions, as though maybe she and Nina were part of some Girls With Blue Hair club and by locating one member I'd be led to the rest. (The girl turned out to be visiting from Russia and didn't speak a word of English.) Or the time I found a crumpled-up ad for an art supply store in the pocket of an old pair of Nina's jeans and spent three hours each way on the bus going to this store, only to find that they'd gone out of business. For each of these occasions and the dozens like it, Amanda was always right there with me, as supportive as a best friend could be. And each time when the "clues" led nowhere, as they inevitably did, and I was newly crushed as though Nina had just vanished all over again, Amanda was right there helping put me back together. As time went on, the possibility that one of these mazes might actually lead to my sister seemed smaller and smaller. And I guess eventually Amanda decided that helping me wasn't actually helping me at all anymore.

So I know what she's trying to say, but I'm also not going to listen.

I turn back to the bulletin board. I feel my face spreading into a smile.

"Ellie . . ."

I reach my hand out and take the flier off the wall. I'm not sinking anymore. I'm floating up, up, up, because *here it is.* Bright red paper covered in bold black handwriting. This is so obviously his. And I know there can be only one explanation for this — this is fate. So whatever happens next, it's going to work out, and it's going to be perfect. I've waited far too long for it not to be.

YOU HAVE HEREBY BEEN CORDIALLY INVITED TO A
HOUSEWRECKING PARTY
AT THE MOTHERSHIP (349 Belmont Ave)
Come help us tear this sucker down.

For 15 years we've been home to a rotating band of
musicians, artists, transients, travelers, angels, devils,
do-gooders, and ne'er-do-wells

But we've lost our lease, an era is ending,
the time has come to say goodbye.
Bring your hammers, your crowbars, your spray paint, and
your cameras,
because after tonight
your pictures and your memories will be all that's left.
Friday, June 27th, from dusk til dust

SIX

We can hear the party long before we see it. The *boom boom boom* of the music, the hum of hundreds of human voices blended together, it sounds like all parties do from far away, except for the occasional loud, crashing noise, followed by even louder cheers.

We're near the top of a giant hill, Amanda and I. It's lined on either side by a thick forest, trees curling over the road, threatening to topple over on the dozens of parked cars. This part of town is only ten miles from Amanda's house, but it feels like an entirely different world out here. The houses are huge and far apart, and they all look ancient, but perfectly preserved like this place exists outside of regular time. Behind us it's pitch-black, in front of us tiny points of light blink on and off like fireflies, only they're cell phone screens and the cherries of lit cigarettes.

"Are you sure that this is a good idea?" Amanda asks.

"There'll be lots of guys at the party I bet!" I say. I sound so pathetically earnest. I feel a stab of self-pity just hearing myself. And then I swallow that pity back down my throat, because stabs of self-pity are stupid. And incredibly unproductive.

"Just please, please, please, please," she says. "Please don't get your hopes up, okay?"

I look away. And then I look back and I give her this small half smile and she shakes her head slightly because we both know it's already far too late.

To our left, two girls get out of a dented green car. One of them has short white hair, and is taking sips from a Poland Spring bottle filled with purple liquid. She's wearing silver lamé boy shorts and a silver bikini top. Swirling silver dragon wings rise up out of her back and point toward the sky.

The other girl is leaning over, looking for something in the backseat, her face obscured by the mass of black hair that's piled on top of her head. She's wearing what looks like a black rubber tank top that stops right below her butt, a pair of fishnets, and giant black boots.

"Come on, Freshie," says the white-haired one. Her voice is clear and sweet. It's easy to imagine what she would sound like singing. "My psychic powers are telling me your boyfriend is this close"—she holds her thumb and first finger up, pressed together even though Freshie can't see her—"to hooking up with some other girl. If you don't hurry up, you're going to find someone else attached to the end of his tongue when we get there."

"Well, use your psychic powers to tell him he can attach

36

his tongue to whatever he wants!" Freshie laughs. "His tongue is his business. And my business is . . . THIS!" She stands up, a sledgehammer clutched in her right hand, its gnarled wooden handle is as thick as her skinny arm. "Smashing time, baby. Let's go!"

"Wait!" The white-haired one reaches down and fishes a tiny digital camera out of her boot. "Excuse me!" She's looking right at me. "Would you mind taking a picture of me and Freshie?" Her head is tipped to the side. Her bright green eyes are lined in black and silver. She's holding out her camera.

"Sure," I say. I take it. I can feel myself blushing in the dark, embarrassed to be caught staring. But they don't seem to mind.

Freshie comes over and they put their arms around each other.

"Smile," I say. Their smiles are dazzling. They're exactly the type of people Nina would have been friends with. The flash goes off. At the last second, Freshie opens her mouth wide and licks her friend's cheek. Her friend bursts out laughing.

I hand the white-haired girl back her camera.

My heart is pounding.

"Hey," I say. "Can I ask you guys something?"

I take the photograph out of my pocket, the one I always carry with me. It's this snapshot of Nina that I found in her room shortly after she disappeared. It might be my favorite picture of her. I don't know who took the photo, but the way she's looking at the camera, her green eyes twinkling, her enormous sunny smile taking over half her face, it's as though she's sharing a joke with whoever's behind it. Sometimes when I look at the picture, I pretend that person is me.

I hold the picture out to Freshie and her friend.

"Have you seen this girl here before? Maybe at another party or something?" Freshie looks at me, and takes the picture from my hand. She leans down so she can see it by the car's interior light. Her friend leans over her shoulder. They look at it for about five seconds, during which time I do not breathe. Then they stand back up.

"Sorry," Freshie says, shaking her head. "Never seen her."

Her friend shrugs. "Yeah, sorry," and then, "but I like her hair!" As though that's a consolation.

"Well thanks for looking," I say. I feel Amanda reach out and squeeze my arm.

"Thanks for taking our picture," Freshie says. And then Freshie slams the car door shut with her hip and the girls walk hand in hand down the hill.

We follow them silently, our eyes slowly adjusting to the light. The back of my neck starts tingling. I look around. It's so deserted out here.

"Hey," I say quietly. Amanda looks over at me, I can see her eyes shining in the dark.

"Yeah?"

"Thanks for coming," I say. She nods and links her arm through mine, and we walk, the sounds of the party getting louder with every step. A few minutes later, we round a corner, walk past a clump of bushes, and then, there we are.

Up ahead is an enormous, eerily beautiful mansion out of another era, the sort of place where there would be uniformed servants inside, silently serving tea cakes on expensive china to immaculately dressed people with perfect table manners. But what's actually in front of us is a futuristic art carnival on acid dressed up for Halloween, sprinkled in glitter. There are so many people spilling in every direction we don't even know where to begin looking. Right in the middle of the front lawn is a giant guy with a shaved head, standing behind a giant folding table, wearing an enormous set of headphones. The table in front of him is covered in laptops and various other pieces of electrical equipment, all the wires leading to a black van that's parked behind him. On top of the van is a row of a dozen giant speakers facing in every direction, blasting what sounds like traditional Indian music backed by heavy electronic drums, loud and fast. I can feel my heartbeat speeding up to match it.

Off to one side a few dozen people dressed up as an assortment of sea creatures—mermaids, mermen, giant glittering starfish—are dancing under a massive silver net.

Off to the other side a half-dozen girls with Bettie Page haircuts and little sailor suits and a half-dozen guys in vintage motorcycle helmets are jumping on a giant trampoline.

Up ahead a girl on stilts walks by wearing a flowing dark green wig, holding a long clear plastic tube that leads into a large green backpack. She stops in front of a cute guy who's dressed as a pirate and holds the tube up over him. He tips his head back and opens his mouth just in time to catch a gulp of gold-flecked drink.

And about twenty feet straight back two shirtless guys are emerging from the front door with a green velvet couch hoisted up on their shoulders on which two girls are sitting dressed in jewels and elaborate ball gowns. The guys lower the couch down in the middle of the grass and the girls step off, like princesses exiting a carriage.

Amanda and I just stand there, staring at all this. "I guess it's now or never," I say. And we walk toward the door just as the girls in the ball gowns rev up a pair of chain saws and start chipping away at the front of the house.

There's a boom, a crash, loud cheers, and then all around me, tiny bits of plaster detach themselves from the ceiling and flutter to the floor like snowflakes. The white plaster flakes are everywhere. I can feel them on my skin and in my hair. When I breathe, I can taste them.

The last three hours have been a series of tiny disappointments. Since we got here I've shown exactly sixty-four different people the photograph of Nina. And twenty-one of them said she was pretty and nineteen of them liked her hair, but sixty-three of the sixty-four people told me they had never seen her before. And the sixty-fourth couldn't answer because he was too busy puking an inch away from my shoe.

I know I shouldn't be surprised. It was a long shot anyway, finding someone who'd remember a girl they might not have seen for two entire years in a house full of probably six hundred people. I knew that coming into this. But there is still one person I really *need* to find, the guy from the video, and so far there's been no sign of him. I once heard if you're looking for someone in a big crowded place, the best way to find them is to stand still, because they're bound to pass you eventually. I'm not sure if this is true or not, but I figure this standing-still thing is worth a try, since moving around wasn't working out too well.

About twenty minutes ago Amanda went outside to talk on the phone to Eric. So here I am standing by myself against the wall while people swirl around me, part of a chaotic dance of big blinking eyes and wild arm gestures. Only there's one other person who is not moving. And he's been staring at me for the last five minutes. A guy, in loose jeans, a black T-shirt, and black skater shoes. His face is covered by a big rubber-person face mask. It's pretty damn realistic looking and I would have thought it was his regular face, except the features are just a little bit too big and the hair is plastic. The eye part of the mask has been cut out and his real eyes show through. They're dark gray, the color of wet slate. The crowd parts and joins together and parts and joins together and parts, but every time I catch a glimpse of him, his eyes are locked on me.

Under other circumstances this might have been mildly intriguing, but I have already determined by looking at his arms, which are not covered in tattoos, that he is not the guy from the video. Therefore, he is a distraction, taking attention away from my mission of watching people until I find the one I am looking for.

To my right is a girl with a perfect doll-like face, with choppy hot pink hair, dressed all in pink. She's speaking what sounds like Swedish crossed with Japanese to the guy next to her, who is nodding and smiling although I kind of get the feeling he has no idea what she's talking about. To my left is a tall thin girl wearing a dress that only a very tall thin person could wear—a stiff-looking piece of industrial-looking yellow fabric, secured to the body with pieces of twine. The back is totally opened with two pieces of what looks like twine crisscrossing in the back. She's standing with three friends.

"Yeah," says a guy with a slight British accent. "But with more synth and eighties backbeats!" And then he rolls his eyes; everyone cracks up laughing.

The crowd parts again and there's Rubber Head, still staring. This time he starts walking over.

"Finally!" he says. He stops right next to me. "You're here."

I stare at his eyes. They don't look familiar, and I don't think I recognize his voice. "Do I know you?"

He shakes his head. "Well . . . no. But you are here, aren't you?"

I raise my eyebrows. "It would seem that way."

"Well, this is just great news then, isn't it." His eyes crinkle in the corners. He's grinning. "So how'd you end up at this crazy place? I mean other than the fact it was fated that we should meet, written in the stars long before either of us was even born, of course."

I stare at him. I feel myself blushing. If he's hitting on me — and it's hard to tell if he is — at least he's original.

"Okaaaaay," he says. "I'll go first. So picture it this morning: The sun was shining and the birds were singing and I was at the gas station paying for gas. I was looking around in the little mini-mart, for an iced-coffee drink for me and a gift for you, of course, but didn't see anything I thought you'd like. So I paid for my coffee and I went back outside and what do you know! Someone had stuck a flier for this party on the windshield of my car. And I'd heard about this place, and had always kind of wanted to see it, but had never been here before tonight. But then I figured it would be my very last chance so . . . here I am! Clearly I was right in deciding to come, although now that I'm here talking to you I'm really wishing I'd gotten you that sixty-four ounce travel mug, or at the very least that classy lighter that was shaped like a pair of legs." I can hear him smiling again. "Sorry," he says. "I promise I'll make it up to you."

"Don't worry about it," I say. I feel myself grinning. There's something different about this guy, and I think I kinda like it. "Here's how I got here. Picture it, it was this afternoon and I'd just left work, I work at this place called Mon Coeur. And my best friend works at this store called Attic which is right down the street and I was visiting her after work and . . ." I pause, on instinct I start reaching for the photograph in my pocket. But then I stop myself as I realize something—if this guy has never been to the Mothership before, that means he couldn't have met Nina here and therefore I don't have to show him Nina's picture and explain that she's gone. And with this thought I feel just the tiniest hint of relief. I'm exhausted from telling this story all night, and I'm so glad to be talking to someone who doesn't need to hear it. And I'm pretty sure that he's flirting with me. And even though his face is ninety percent obscured by painted rubber, I have to admit I'm enjoying it.

"And we saw a flier for the party up on the bulletin board. And so we said well why not and now we're here."

I look back up, he's still staring.

"And what about your placement at this wall in particular?"

"I'm looking for someone."

"Who are you looking for?"

"I'm not exactly sure."

"Are you playing hide-and-seek?" He tips his head to the side. He's trying to be cute.

It's working.

"If you are, maybe I could offer you a few tips. You're never going to win just standing around like this . . ." He reaches out and takes my hand like he's going to shake it, but instead of shaking it, he just holds it. Like my hand is very precious and he doesn't want to break it, but also doesn't want to let it go. His hand is strong and warm, the heat of it stretches all the way up my arm. I look down. I can feel myself blushing. I look back up, our eyes meet again.

"I'm Sean," he says. He starts shaking my hand then, as if that's what he intended all along.

"I'm Ellie," I say.

"Well, Ellie, as a former hide-and-seek gold medal winner . . ."

But before either of us has a chance to say anything else, a guy walks out of a room off the hallway, kicking plaster chunks out of the way with a pair of black boots. His wiry arms are covered in ugly bright-yellow tattoos, and his blond hair is so light you can see the pink of his scalp through it. I breathe in sharply. It's him. He's the guy from Attic. He is the reason I am here. He is walking toward the stairs. He's getting away. I start chasing after him.

I hear Sean calling after me. "Ellie!" he says, "Wait!"

But I don't turn around. There's no time. The guy from the video is walking down the stairs, being swallowed up by the crowd. I will not let him get away.

"Hey!" I call out. But the guy doesn't hear me. He starts walking down the stairs. I reach my arm through the railing and I grab his shoulder. I can feel his bones through his shirt.

He turns toward me. The whites of his eyes are slightly yellow, and his skin is pale, blue-veined like blue cheese. He's holding a red Solo cup in each hand.

"Yeah?" he says. There's a crash, a pause, a cheer.

"Hi," I say.

He walks back up the stairs and stops when our heads are exactly level. He looks at me and raises his eyebrows. "What's up?"

"Ijustwanted to askyoua questionbecause you sold-abunchof stuff toAttic today." The words come out in a jumble. His eyebrow twitches but he doesn't say anything. "I was just wondering if I could ask you where you got it?" A couple of people push past us to get down the stairs, a guy and a girl. "The stuff you sold I mean." The guy whispers something and the girl grabs him by the neck and pulls his face to hers. They're right behind us, their fingers tangled in each other's hair, lips mashing against each other, breathing heavily. After a few seconds their lips part and they tumble down the rest of the stairs, their hands on each other's asses.

"I do not know what you're talking about," Blue Cheese says finally. He shakes his head, looks over his shoulder.

A girl walks by wearing nothing but bronze body paint. He stares.

"Attic?" I say. "That vintage store? You brought in a box of stuff and hung up a sign for this party."

"Why is everyone always accusing me of stuff," he says, and then, "You're mistaking me for someone else, hon, sorry." He turns and starts to walk off.

"Wait! Please!" I say, a little too loudly. "I kind of know that you did, is the thing. Sell that stuff. It's not like a bad thing or something. My friend works at the store," I say. "So I was just wondering if you could tell me where the stuff you brought in came from." I can feel my face getting hot, and I know I'm starting to sound desperate. "Please?"

Blue Cheese shrugs. His shoulders are tense, he takes a quick gulp of the beer in his left hand. "I was just looking through the basement for stuff to sell, and I found a bunch of old crap. And then I saw that Crap Day sign in the window of that store and I thought, well, what do you know?" He drains the left beer and drops the cup onto the floor. He lifts his second cup to his mouth and takes a gulp. "Why, are you looking for some crap? You didn't have to come all the way here for that, the entire world is full of it!" He lets out a phlegmy laugh, opening his mouth so wide I can see each of his tiny teeth.

"There was one specific thing you brought in, a psychology book and it had something inside of it, a little piece of cardboard that someone was using as a bookmark . . ."

From somewhere downstairs the music speeds up.

"And?" Blue Cheese yawns. A girl starts walking down the stairs next to him in a skintight rose-colored dress. He watches her ass.

"And there were these drawings all over it, and my sister did those drawings."

"So?"

"Well, she's missing," I say. This is easily the thirtieth time I've told this story tonight, but it never gets any less weird to hear myself tell.

"And what does that mean?" Blue Cheese's expression changes slightly, the way people's expressions always do when I start to tell them. His Adam's apple bobs as he swallows.

"It means I don't know where she is and my mom doesn't know where she is." It still feels fresh. It always does. "Two years ago my sister Nina went out and that night she was supposed to come home." He's looking at me like he doesn't know if I'm lying or not. I wish so much, *so much*, that I was. "And she didn't. And then she never came home after that, either."

Blue Cheese is nodding. "Intense," he says. His expression has changed again but I can't understand what the new one is supposed to mean.

"That's why I came here," I say, "to find you and ask you about this and see if maybe you knew her. I bet she was here at some point. Her name's Nina Wrigley . . ."

"Listen," Blue Cheese holds out his hand, cutting me off. "*Everyone* has been here at some point, okay? That was like the whole point of this place. So unless she was the girl I was with last night, I'm not going to remember her," he grins, "and even then it's questionable."

"But I have her picture," I say. My voice comes out in a slight whine. I take her picture out of my pocket and show it to him. He leers at her disgustingly, licks his lips and then shakes his head.

"Nope," he says. "Never seen that one."

"Well what about the place where you found the book that her drawing was in? Maybe there's something else there, another clue or something?"

He breathes in and then nods, like he's just decided something. "Follow me then, I guess." He looks me up and down and then shows me his gums again. "I think I have just what you need." And with that my stomach starts fizzling and he grabs my hand. "Come on."

We walk down one flight of stairs; he's crushing my hand. His skin is clammy. I wiggle my fingers. He holds on tighter. My brain is overflowing with questions and they bubble out my mouth, "Where are we going? How much more stuff is there? How long has it been there?" But he ignores all of them. He's speeding along now, and I have to jog a little to keep up. We make our way through the living room where a girl is sitting on a swing that's attached to the ceiling, swinging back and forth, kicking the wall with a giant pair of platform shoes each time she gets close, through the kitchen where ten people are gathered around the table drinking from a giant fish tank with super long straws, through a room where a dozen people are spray painting the walls.

Blue Cheese keeps going and I follow. We go down a long hallway, through a wooden door and down a very, very long flight of stairs in the dark with no railing. I'm grateful for his clammy hand now, glad just to have something to hold on to. When we get to the bottom, he reaches his arm up and a second later the basement is illuminated by the faint glow of a single bare lightbulb dangling from the ceiling. We are the only people down here. It's bizarrely quiet. The air is cool and damp.

"You could start down here," he says. I look around at the cement walls and exposed pipes. The floor is littered with cigarette butts and old beer cans and empty Pepsi bottles. There's a sagging beige couch in one corner with a pillow and blanket on it, the blanket is covered in dark spots, mold maybe.

I realize he's still holding my hand. He tugs it. "No, down *here*," he says. I look up. The wiry muscles in his arm twitch. His lips are wet, like he's been drooling. He looks down at his crotch, and then back up at me.

He tries to reach for my other hand and I back away. "What are you doing?" I say.

"You're lonely." He's walking forward. "And I get it. But you're not finding what you need because you don't even know what you're really looking for." He reaches out and puts one hand on my waist. "Maybe I can help you figure it out."

"*This* is why you brought me down here?" He steps in closer.

"There's nothing else down here," I say. "Is there." But this isn't really a question.

And he just shrugs. "That stuff I sold to Attic was all there was." And then he smiles a bizarrely sweet smile. "Sorry." Then he reaches his hand out and puts it on my ass and for a second I'm overcome with such sadness that I don't even stop him.

But that second passes, and my brain catches up with my body. And I think I'm about to be sick. What am I doing down here? What am I supposed to do now? What the *hell* am I supposed to do now? I don't know, so I just do what I always do when I have no idea what to do next: I close my eyes and I picture my sister, who was never scared of anything or anyone. And I think, what would Nina do in this situation? And it's easy to figure this one out.

I bring my knee up as hard as I can between Blue Cheese's legs.

He opens his mouth into an O and for a second he is too shocked to make any noise at all. And then his eyes fill up with tears and he just starts screaming his head off.

"Thanks for your help," I say calmly. I run up the stairs then and I don't look back.

seven

I'm back upstairs, part of the party now, and my heart is pounding. I take my phone out of my pocket, call Amanda. Voice mail. I hang up. Now what?

I walk back the way I came, through the spray paint room, through the kitchen, through the room with the girl on her swing.

I feel someone watching me. For a disgusting second I think maybe Blue Cheese is following me and I tighten my hands into fists in preparation, but when I turn around he's not there. I hear the crashing sound of another wall falling. More cheers. I walk through people, bumping into elbows and arms. I don't try and get out of the way. I climb the stairs and then up another flight and I'm in a hallway I haven't been in before. My eyes burn. It's hard to breathe up here.

Two shirtless guys in painter's overalls are walking toward me, each with a giant canvas bag over his shoulder. "Geeet your hammers here people, hammers, bowling balls, chunks of scrap metal. Geeeet your hammers!" When they get closer I can see that one of the guys has *demolition crew* written in paint on the front of his overalls. Demolition Crew stops right in front of me. "And for you, m'lady," he says. He hands me a giant sledgehammer. I stare at it in my hand. "See?" says the other guy. "It fits you perfectly." I tighten my fist around the handle. This feels good. "No matter what's wrong," he says, "smashing will fix it." The hammer guy looks me straight in the eye. "It's just human nature to want to smash things." And then they both walk away.

I squeeze the handle so hard my knuckles turn white. I push my way down the hallway. I'm standing in a giant room, staring at a silver wall covered in an enormous black outline of a spaceship. I'm numb now. There's nothing in my head. I swing the hammer up toward the ceiling, feeling the weight of it tugging against my shoulders. When the hammer is up at the top of the arc, it feels, just for a second, like time has frozen. And then, it swings back down. The head of the hammer connects with the wall, and there's just the slightest bit of resistance before it passes right through with a delicate crunch like eggshells breaking. A cloud of plaster dust swirls away from the new hole like smoke. That was a piece of solid wall that had been there for who knows how many years, witness to who knows how many things, but with one swift motion it has been transformed into an empty space and a pile of rubble. And I did that. I stand there, looking at the empty space, the ragged edges, and I feel a strange sense of relief.

But it only lasts for a second, because then the screaming starts — a girl's voice calling the same thing over and over and over, one word, but I can't make out what it is. And then a flood of people start running past me, one giant writhing unit of arms and legs and heads. A girl trips on her spike heels, and a guy reaches down and pulls her up under one of his arms, dragging her with him, her skinny little legs dangling a few inches above the floor.

And then comes the smoke, heavy and thick, an impossible amount of it all at once. I start to cough. Inside my head I am screaming, but my whole body is frozen. Hours pass, days pass, years pass, all of time passes in that one second before I hear a voice next to my head shouting, "RUN!" It's like I've woken up. "RUN!" And this time I do.

The air is opaque with smoke. I don't even know what direction to go in, but I see a girl's back, tumbling forward, and I tumble after her. I take a breath but there's no relief in it, the air doesn't seem to be doing its job. I'm choking, still running forward, my eyes burning. I hear voices but all I can see is white, everywhere. My arms are out in front of me and the smoke is so thick I can't even see my hands. I keep going, keep going, keep going.

Finally I burst out onto the front lawn, gasping for breath, the air sweeter than any air I've ever breathed before in my life. The music has stopped. And hundreds of people are outside now. The pirates, the mermaids, the stilt walkers, the girl in the bronze body paint, a group of guys who look like they're from the future, a bunch of girls dressed as sexy robots, Freshie and her friend. They're all out here with the same slightly dazed expression on their faces, *did that really just happen?*

I stand there panting. But where the hell is Amanda? I turn to the left and to the right. I don't have to worry long because my phone starts ringing. It's her. "HOLY SHIT, ELLIE!"

She's talking fast, and even though I know I'm outside and that I'm safe now, the panic in her voice scares me. Amanda never panics. "I was up at the car talking on the phone to Eric and I smelled the smoke and saw the fire and I ran back down and oh my God!" I tell her where I am. She says she's coming to find me. And then I just stand and watch the flames.

Have you ever seen a house burning down? If you landed here from another planet and didn't know what fire meant, you'd think it was beautiful, gentle even — delicate orange and gold and red and yellow flames, licking the house into nothingness.

A couple minutes later I feel Amanda wrapping her arms around me. We hug tightly. I can hear the sirens in the distance.

"Ellie," Amanda says. "It's time to go home now."

We start walking up the hill, the smell of smoke behind us. By the time we reach the top, the music is back on, mixing with the sound of sirens. I can just imagine everyone back at the party, dancing outside while the house burns all the way to the ground.

eIGht

"Glitter kitten," Brad says, "say *helloooo, Braddypoo!*" It's the next day, Saturday, and I am standing behind the counter at Mon Coeur making a latte. I turn toward the camera and raise one eyebrow just before the flash goes off.

"You didn't say it." Brad frowns.

"Sorry," I say. "Hello, Braddypoo."

Brad looks at the camera's display screen and then comes over and shakes his head slowly. "This is just about the saddest picture I have ever seen! Good thing I am a Photoshop master and will have no problem replacing your frowning mouth with a smiling one . . . or a cupcake!"

I try and smile, but my face refuses. Less than twenty-four hours ago I was on my way to that party. The night was full of possibilities and promise and it had seemed like something magical was going to happen. And I'd felt so sure of it, *so sure of it.*

And now here I am, back at work, as though nothing at all has changed, which makes sense, since it hasn't.

"What's wrong, honeykins? Tell Braddy."

If only it were so simple. I would love to talk about it, I am, in fact, dying to. But the thing is, talking about my sister doesn't help. Watching the pity spread over other people's faces just makes me feel worse, makes me feel more lonely. So while one script plays in my head, another one has to come out of my mouth. And it's so tiring, it's all so very tiring.

"Sorry, Braddy," I say. "Not now, okay?"

"Okay, well when you want to talk about what's making your face look like that, and have someone listen and nod while making a variety of incredibly genuine and sympathetic facial expressions, I'm your . . ."

The bell on the door jingles and Amanda is walking in, all smiles. "Mandy!" Brad calls out. "What is wrong with our dear Ellie? Haven't you been taking good care of her?" He shakes his finger at Amanda, mock scolding.

"I've been trying," Amanda says, and leans over and kisses Brad on the cheek.

"So," Amanda says, turning toward me. "My parents are going out again tonight and I talked to Eric who talked to some other guys from the football team at Adams and they definitely want to come over to hot-tub. So, that'll be good, right? We can raid my parents' wine cellar and make sangriiiiiaaaaa!"

I imagine myself standing in Amanda's backyard, surrounded by people I barely know, unable to get enough out of my own head to say anything at all except perhaps occasionally an awkward ha-ha, just so no one asks me what's wrong.

"Will there be cute guys there? Maybe someone who will help cheer Ellie up?" Brad puts his arm around my waist and leans his head on my shoulder.

"Eric has a lot of cute friends," Amanda says. "But I doubt Ellie's going to stop frowning anytime soon."

I feel my jaw clenching. Amanda puts on a slightly different personality when she's around Brad. She acts bitchier, as though that's how she thinks you're supposed to act around a gay guy.

"What's that supposed to mean?" I say.

"Nothing." Amanda sighs. "Just that I think you're kind of wallowing a little."

"I'm not *wallowing*." I'm suddenly annoyed. "I think I have an actual reason to be upset."

"I didn't say you don't," Amanda says. She looks toward Brad and then quickly looks away.

"The word wallowing kinda implies it."

"Well, that's not what I meant." Amanda puts her hands on her hips.

"Whatever," I say. My voice comes out sounding meaner than I intended. Regardless of what word Amanda used, I do sort of know what she meant. But I'm frustrated. And I am taking it out on her a little bit.

Amanda sighs. "Look, I think you have plenty of real things to be upset about, like how some asshole tried to take advantage of you in the basement last night or how we almost both died in a fire but . . ."

"Whoa," says Brad. He backs up. "Hold on there. Wait, what happened? Are you *okay*, Ellie? What happened?"

I turn toward Brad. "I'm okay," I say. "It wasn't that big a deal."

Amanda continues, "I guess I just think instead of thinking about what I know you're thinking about, you should just try and do other stuff, have fun . . ."

I look down and breathe out hard through my nose. I glance back up. Brad is staring at me, fiddling with his camera uncomfortably. He holds it up to his face.

"Smile!" he says. We both ignore him.

"You can't keep doing this to yourself," Amanda says. And then she just gives me this look, this horrible look like she feels sorry for me, not sorry *with* me, but *for* me. Like we're totally separate, unconnected people. And I'm all on my own.

"I'm not doing anything to myself," I say. "I didn't choose for things to be like this." My stomach is starting to hurt. I wish someone would come in and pluck me out of this conversation and deposit me in a different one. Or maybe tuck me back in my bed with my fan blowing on my face and my comforter pulled all the way up to my nose.

"You didn't. But you can choose to get over it."

I am hit by a sudden wave of loneliness, so intense it's like my insides are hollowed out. "No, I can't," I say. I look at Amanda's face; suddenly she looks like a stranger. "And you know that."

We stop then. We're all silent.

Amanda's phone buzzes and she takes it out of her giant bag. She flips her phone open with her thumb and reads her text. "I'm supposed to go meet Liz now so . . . I guess I'm going to go." She snaps her phone shut and looks at me. "Do you still need me to come and pick you up later?"

I feel an ache in my chest. It's that word "need" that gets me. And the way Amanda says it, with just the littlest hint of exasperation in her voice, like I'm a chore she has to take care of.

"Nah," I say. "That's alright." I turn around and do something totally unnecessary with the milk jug so Amanda won't see my face.

"You're not coming to my house later?" Does she sound confused or relieved?

I shake my head. "I think I just want to go home tonight." And a cold heaviness fills the pit of my stomach. I'm not even really sure why I said this, I don't want to go to my house at all. And besides, I think of Amanda's house as home more than I do my own. But it's too late now because Amanda is saying, "Okay then," and, "Well, I guess I'll just talk to you later then." And she's kissing Brad on the cheek and walking out the door.

I stand there and I watch her go.

I feel a tightening in my chest, so intense I gasp. I miss

Nina all the time, but it is in moments like these, when I feel like I am totally alone in this world, that I miss her the most.

"Ellie?" Brad says again. I just nod, still staring at the door and then I squeeze my eyes shut and will Nina to materialize. It is dangerous and childish, I know, to let myself wish like this, to pour my whole self into wanting something that I can't have that I don't even know how to go about trying to get. But I can't stop. I keep my eyes closed and I hold my breath as a tear works its way down my cheek. And I just stay like that, wishing, wishing, wishing, until I hear Brad making a high-pitched beeping noise. I open my eyes.

"I don't mean to interrupt your unhappiness, Ellie, or seem like I'm not taking it seriously, but my hot-guy-who-could-be-Ellie's-next-boyfriend-dar" — Brad motions with his chin toward the door where a guy has just walked in — "has just gone off like *cah-razy*! *Beep-beep-beeeeep.*"

I shake my head. It's sweet of Brad to try to distract me, but I'm not in the mood for this right now. I am so not in the mood for this.

I look at this guy who's walking toward the counter with his hands in his pockets. He *is* undeniably hot. He has a swimmer's body and he walks like a skateboarder, leaning back slightly like he's in no kind of hurry. He's staring at me, like he knows me. Our eyes meet and I feel something inside me flash.

Brad is squeezing my arm and whispering in my ear, "*beep beep beeeeeeep.*"

The guy is up at the counter now, the corners of his mouth curling up into a slow, sweet smile. Up close, he's even hotter—wide-spaced eyes the color of wet slate, amazing eyelashes, dark brown hair flopping over one eye. I feel a sudden craving for something, like I'm hungry or thirsty, except not either of those things. He's still watching me.

"Hey, Ellie," he says.

Do I know this person? I stare back at him. Feel another flash. No, definitely not. I would not forget this face.

"You don't remember me," he says. He blinks. His eyes! I know those eyes!

I feel myself smiling.

"You're Sean! From the party," I say. I think back to that moment, at the top of the stairs, that brief and strange moment with the rubber-face guy. This is what his rubber mask was hiding.

Brad lets go of my arm. I hear his sharp intake of breath.

"Hey, buddy." Sean smiles at Brad, tips his head back slightly, then reaches up and scratches the back of his neck. "What's up?"

Brad lets out a quick, "Hey."

I'm back in that moment when we shook hands at the party, when Sean just held my hand there, like it was something so precious. I feel my face get hot.

"Anyway." Sean looks back at me. "I never got to tell you."

"Tell me what?

"How to play. Hide-and-seek. Remember? See, you almost got it, but you were missing a key element. Here's how it goes . . ." He grins. "Okay. First you have to close your eyes and count to ten while the people hide. Then you open your eyes and then, and this is key"—he holds up one finger—"then you *seek* them. See? That's the step you were missing, I think." He smiles again. "The seeking one. You had the opening eyes part down perfectly, though, so no need to feel bad." He's nodding, all serious now. "It takes practice."

I wish I weren't blushing. "Well, thanks." I can't help but smile. "For the help . . . with that." I reach up and touch my face. We just stand there, the three of us, staring at one another. I am wholly confused by what's going on. But at least I'm not quite as sad anymore.

The silence, however, is getting awkward.

"Do you want something?" I say suddenly. "Like . . . um . . . a muffin? We have these muffins here. They're not really that great, but they're huge. So if you're into eating a lot of something . . ."

Sean laughs. "No, thanks," he says. "But I'd love an iced coffee if you don't mind. Or you could just give me a regular coffee and some ice and I'll just mix them together in my mouth."

I smile again and go to the big refrigerator to get the iced coffee pitcher. I can see Sean's reflection in the glass, watching me. I pour the coffee, then turn back and hand him the plastic cup, already covered in beads of sweat. He reaches out to take it. Our fingers touch. An electric shock shoots up my arm. And we just stand there like that, holding the cup together, our fingers touching, until I realize it's time for me to let go.

Brad clears his throat. "Ellie?" he says loudly. He's using his fake voice, the one that's an octave higher than his regular one. Oh no. This can't be good. "Since your shift ends in ten minutes, anyway"—Brad looks at his watch—"if you want to head out a little bit early, that's fine with me."

I look at my watch. It's only three-fifty, I'm not actually supposed to be done with work until seven. I look at Brad. He just stares at me and nods slowly, his eyes open wide. He is trying very, very hard to keep a straight face.

"Okaaaaaay," I say, slowly nodding back. Alright, so far not too embarrassing.

Brad turns toward Sean. "Hey, do you have a car?"
Oh God.

"Yeah." Sean tips his head.

"Great," says Brad. "Can you give your friend Ellie here a ride home? Her ride cancelled on her and the bus, well, that's just not safe."

My face is burning. I look down.

"Sure," Sean says. "I'd be glad to. Hey, good timing on my part, right?" He's grinning. If what Brad said sounds as fake to him as it does to me, he's doing an admirable job pretending not to notice.

"Thank you," I say to Sean. And I'm suddenly very nervous, although I'm not really sure why.

"Bye, El." Brad leans over, kisses me on the cheek, and whispers, "You owe me a latte." Which is what he always says when he does something especially nice for me.

"Ready?" Sean says. His hair is flopping into his face, he pushes it out of the way and looks me straight in the eye. And there's that flash again.

He smiles.

My stomach twists. "Okay," I say.

nine

Outside the sky is weirdly dark and the air thick and humid, the way it gets before a storm. Sean leads me over to a navy blue Volvo. "Ta-da!" he says. The paint is scratched and the back bumper is covered in the remnants of bumper stickers that someone tried to tear off, but eventually gave up on—a piece of light blue with a lacy-looking white shape in the corner, a dark green sticker with everything torn off except for a white *UR*. Sean unlocks the passenger side and opens the door, then walks around to the driver's side and gets in. I get in, too.

There are four different plastic cups in the cupholder, and cups scattered all over the floor. On the backseat there's a black leather messenger bag closed with a shiny brass lock. The car smells like pine trees.

"Sorry about all the cups, you can just kick them out of the way," Sean says. "Iced coffee is my crack."

"What a coincidence," I say. "Crack is my iced coffee."

Sean laughs. "I knew there was a reason I liked you," he

says. He shakes his head a little bit. He starts his car. "So where am I taking you?"

"I'm in the Sunrise Village condo complex," I say, "behind the A&P on Grays Avenue."

Sean starts his car, starts driving, neither of us says anything for a while. I watch his hands as he turns the steering wheel. I cannot recall ever having any sort of opinion about a guy's hands before, but his are beautiful.

"So . . . I have to confess something." Sean reaches up with one of his beautiful hands and pushes his hair out of his face. "I didn't really come here to tell you the rules of hide-and-seek." He pauses. "The truth is, Ellie, it's really not that hard of a game. And besides, you could just look it up online."

"The Internet is good like that," I say. My heart is starting to race. "Then why are you here?"

"The truth? I looked for you after the party and when I didn't see you I got worried. I thought maybe the fire ate you up. The fire department said everyone got out okay, but you just never know, I guess." He glances at me and then looks back at the road. "I remembered you said you worked at the coffee place, so I figured I'd just come by and make sure you were alright. I hope that doesn't seem stalkery or weird seeing as we only talked for like thirty seconds . . ."

"No, it's nice of you," I say. "I'm okay, thanks for checking."

"You don't look that okay actually . . . When I came in to Mon Coeur, you looked really sad. And at the party, too." Sean pauses. I don't say anything. "So did you ever find him?"

"Who?" I feel myself blushing.

"Whoever you were looking for at the party. Was it that guy with the bad tattoos?"

"Oh," I say. "Yeah. Sort of. I mean I thought so, only it turned out no."

"He isn't like your boyfriend or something, is he?"

"Ha!" I say. "Definitely not."

"Okay, good. I didn't think so. I mean, he didn't look like the kind of dude I'd imagine you usually date. He looked kind of like a loser."

And I'm oddly flattered by this comment, as it implies that I have actually ever dated anyone before. Which, of course, I haven't.

"So, tattoo dude didn't deliver?"

"He delivered his hand to my ass," I say. "So I delivered my knee to his balls. And that was it."

"Good for you," Sean says. "But why were you looking for him?"

I take a deep breath. And as I breathe in, I realize something, that I'm going to have to tell him the truth. It's not that I've somehow decided this is a good idea or anything, it's just what I'm going to do.

"I was looking for my sister," I say. "I haven't seen her in over two years." There's no going back now. We're stopped at a stoplight. I glance at Sean again. He turns toward me, nodding ever so slightly. I hope telling him isn't a mistake. "I didn't think *she'd* be there at the party exactly, I just thought . . ." I get the story over with as quickly as I can, just spit it out so it's out and I don't have to have the words in my mouth anymore. "So I showed her picture to tons of people but no one knew her but I thought if I found the guy who brought in the box, he might know something about where she was, or that someone at the party might." I look over at Sean but he's watching the road again. "But I was wrong." I feel my eyes filling with tears, but I blink them back. "So I guess that's why I looked sad."

"That's a pretty understandable reason," he says.

"My best friend Amanda thinks I need to get on with my life now. Stop focusing on my sister so much and just act, I don't know, like she never existed or something. It's been two years since she disappeared and nothing has changed." I inhale and exhale slowly. "I don't know, Amanda might be right, it *might* be time to give up now." I look down at my hands. "But I just don't know how to."

Sean is silent. And we both stare straight ahead at the rain pounding down.

"I think I know why I met you now," Sean says finally. And then I feel Sean place his hand gently over mine on the seat between us. "There are some things a person just never gets over, that the phrase 'get over' doesn't really apply to," he says. "And when one of those things happens in your life, it doesn't matter how much time has passed, or if you're sitting alone in your room or at a party surrounded by a hundred people, and it doesn't even matter if you're actually thinking about it or not because no matter where you are or what you're doing, it's still there. It's not just something that happened. It's become a part of you."

And then he shuts his mouth and keeps driving. This is it so exactly. And no one else I've ever talked to has ever really gotten it before.

He turns toward me, our eyes meet, and I'm just sitting there blinking. He grins, shrugs his shoulders, and tips his head to the side, all casual now. "Or, y'know, whatever." And I burst out laughing and it's a real hiccuping, doubled-over laugh, the kind of laugh I haven't had in a long time. And he laughs with me. Things are the funniest when they are a mix of sad and absurd and true.

"So you know what I'm talking about, then," I say.

"Something like that," Sean says.

"How do you know all of that?" I ask. "I mean, what happened to you?"

But as soon as the words are out, I wish I could take them back. The last thing I want him to think is that I'm mining him for his tragedies, the way I've felt so many others do to me. "Sorry," I say. "You don't need to answer that."

We are pulling into the apartment complex where I live

now, the streetlights lighting up the inside of the car. Lighting up Sean's face.

"Seventeen-ten," I say. "Up there on the right." And Sean pulls up in the empty parking spot in front of my front door.

"Well," I say. "Thanks for the ride." I look out the window, there's so much rain pounding down it's like the whole world is underwater. It's like here, in this car with Sean, is the only safe place left on earth.

"No problem," he says.

I reach down and unfasten my seat belt. "So . . . um." I know I'm supposed to get out now, but I am struck with the sudden intensity of *how much I do not want to.* "Well . . . thanks again." I cringe, hearing myself. This is ridiculous. I have to go.

I start to reach for the door handle and glance over at him one last time. Our eyes meet and there's that flash again.

Sean takes a deep breath.

"I had a brother once," he says. His hair flops over one eye and he pushes it away. "But he died."

My breath catches in my throat. The rain starts pounding harder now, and there is thunder in the distance.

"What?" I blink.

I watch his mouth.

"My brother died," he says again. "So that's how I know about that stuff I said."

I raise my hand up to my mouth. "Oh God."

He smiles this sad half smile. "It was a long time ago." He looks down, looks back up, his face is flushed. "If there was even the slightest chance that I could see him again, that there was something I could do to make that possible, I would never stop trying. Ever. This is fate, Ellie, me meeting you, I think. Because I don't have a chance to get my brother back. Nothing I do can change the fact that he's gone. But maybe what I'm supposed to do now is help you." Sean pauses. "Do you think that sounds crazy?"

I shake my head. I feel something inside me warming up.

"So should I come in, then?" he says. "Maybe see the drawing?"

I hesitate for only the tiniest shred of a second, enough time for me to look through all that rain at the front windows of our building and remember that my mother is working the night shift tonight, which means she is gone now and won't be home until early in the morning.

"Yeah," I say quietly. "That would be great."

ten

I realize, as we walk into my room, that this is the first time a guy has ever been up here.

I try and imagine how it must look to Sean, messy unmade bed, a dresser, a nightstand, a desk, a few items of clothing tossed around on the floor. It probably looks like no one spends much time in here, which is true since I'm almost always at Amanda's.

I sit on my bed and Sean sits in my desk chair and I continue explaining Nina's drawing. "So then I called the number on there but the guy didn't know anything, didn't even remember her. And the guy at the Mothership says he just found the book in the basement and it was practically empty when I was down there, and even if there were any more clues there, they're all burned up now."

Sean reaches out his hand and I give him the drawing. My fingertips brush against his, just for a moment. I am very aware of it. Sean holds the drawing close to his face and stares. He doesn't move, he doesn't blink, it doesn't even look like he's breathing. And I'm wondering if he's beginning to regret offering to help me since he is probably quickly realizing how futile this is.

"No pressure," I say. "I mean, or . . ." And then I stop because Sean's mouth has just dropped open, and then this huge grin spreads over his face. "Ellie," he says slowly. His eyes are shining. "Did you notice *this*?" He jumps off the chair and lands next to me on the bed. He flips the drawing over so I can see the fake credit card printed on the back.

"What about it?" My heart is pounding.

"This is a cardboard credit card." He taps it with his finger.

I nod, blinking. "Right."

"And do you know where people get these? With credit card offers in the mail . . ." Sean is nodding at me, trying to lead me to his conclusion. "So . . ."

I shake my head slowly. "So . . ."

"So, your sister turned eighteen only a couple months before she left, right? Credit card companies have this list, of all the people in America who are about to turn eighteen. So they can start sending them credit card offers right around their birthday and sucker them in."

"I'm not sure what you're saying."

"Chances are your sister got a ton of credit card offers in the mail before she disappeared, right? So what if she actually applied for one?" He turns the card over and points to the bank's name on the back. "Say from Bank of the USA? I bet we could sign into her account no problem since you're her sister. All we'd need is her Social Security number, and then we'd probably just have to answer a bunch of random security questions and the answers would be things like your mom's maiden name and other stuff you'd already know."

"Oh," I say. I try and force a smile.

"What's wrong?"

"It's a nice idea! And thanks for thinking of it!" I frown.

"You're frowning," he says.

"I just don't think it'll work."

"Why not?"

"It's too easy."

"But that," Sean looks me straight in the eye, his mouth curled into a mischievous little smile, "is exactly why it's going to."

Three minutes later we're in the spare bedroom, which I think of as Nina's room even though Mom uses it for storage and we moved here after Nina was already gone. One of the only jokes I can remember my mother making in the last few years is one she made right after we moved in. She said, "Ellie, you know you've really made it when you're so rich you have an entire room for just your shoes," and then she opened the door and tossed in a pair of discount black flats that she said pinched her feet but the store wouldn't take back because she'd already worn them. She meant this, of course, ironically. So now this is just where we keep all the stuff that has nowhere else to go — old tax returns and report cards and a lamp that was my grandmother's that's too nice to throw out but too depressing to display.

"So apparently I was a top-notch user of scissors in first grade," I say, holding up a report card. I'm crouched down on the floor behind a big, green plastic box. "But occasionally I ate the paste." I put the card back in the box, and keep digging. Sean is crouched down next to me looking over my shoulder.

"And you've had all your immunizations," he says, nodding, "which is important." He reaches down into the box. He picks up what looks like a small blue notebook. A passport. He opens it.

I look over his shoulder. It's Nina's. In the photo Nina's about the same age that I am now. Her hair is pale pink hanging just above her jawline. She's smirking, like she has a secret. I've never seen this picture before.

"I guess my mom must have tossed that in there when we moved from our old house," I say. "Nina was already gone then."

Sean is staring at it, then looks up at me and then back down at it. He's shaking his head slowly, his face is flushed. "You look so much alike it's insane. You could be twins."

I look at the picture again. "You think?"

I don't believe him, but I'm flattered, anyway.

"You ever think about dyeing your hair like that?" He taps Nina's picture.

"Not really," I say.

"It'd look good I bet." Sean shrugs and hands me the passport. "You should keep this with you." I slip it in my back pocket. "You never know when you'll need to make a last-minute international getaway."

I laugh and then look back down into the box I was searching through. A little dog is staring up at me, with a curly mustache under his nose and a giant beret on top of his head. "Bijoux!" I say, and I feel myself start to smile at the memory. I pick up Nina's drawing. I haven't thought about Bijoux in a very long time.

"What's that?"

"A picture of our old dog," I say. "Bijoux."

Sean is looking over my shoulder, grinning. "Bijoux must have had incredible balance to keep such a big hat situated so perfectly on top of his head. Most dogs can't do that."

"Yes," I say. "Well, most real dogs can't, but a few imaginary ones can."

Sean cocks his head to the side.

"We didn't have an *actual* dog," I say. "We were never allowed to get one. But we got the very best imaginary dog ever one summer." I pause. "Nina got him for us."

And Sean nods as though of course this makes perfect sense. He glances back down at the stack of papers in his hands and then before I can continue he's shouting "Yes!" and holding out a piece of paper so I can see. "Ellie, look!"

It's a photocopy of an insurance claim form. Sean begins to read it out loud. "On October twenty-third, two thousand-four, Nina Wrigley had a regular cleaning at the dentist, a check-up, and a set of X-rays . . ." Sean flips the form over and points to a spot right near the top where her Social Security number is written out neatly in my mother's serious-looking handwriting. "There it is," he says.

I stand up, suddenly breathless. "The computer's downstairs."

A minute later Sean and I are sitting side by side on the couch in my living room, waiting for my mother's ancient 45-pound laptop to boot up.

"Looking at porn on this thing must be a bitch," Sean says.

"Hello, Ellie."

I turn around. My mother is standing in the doorway between the kitchen and the living room, in her bathrobe, drinking juice.

Oh shit.

"Mom," I say. I can feel the blood rushing to my face.

She rubs her eyes, half smiles at me. I can't tell if she's smiling because she didn't hear Sean's porn comment, or because she did. My mom is a mystery sometimes. "I haven't seen you in days." She glances at Sean and raises one eyebrow. Sometimes she's not a mystery at all.

"I've been sleeping at Amanda's," I say.

"Oh," she says. "You're sure they don't mind you over there all the time?"

"They don't."

"Okay." She nods, as though we haven't had this conversation dozens of times before.

And then my mom just stands there, not even acknowledging the fact that there is another person beside me on the couch. She's not being intentionally rude, she just doesn't understand things like this sometimes. Like how people act. How people are supposed to act.

Sean stands up finally. "Hi," he says. "I'm Sean." He sticks out his hand.

My mother just stares at it. She looks him up and down. Then over to me on the couch. Then back to Sean. "Hello," she says, awkwardly. "I'm Ellie's mother."

I put my hand in my pocket and touch the drawing, but I know I can't show it to her. I wish I could.

"I thought you were working tonight," I say.

"My schedule changed. I did an overnight last night instead. Got home an hour ago."

"How were the babies?" I ask. I turn toward Sean. "My mom works at the neonatal ICU at the hospital."

"Wow," Sean says. "That must be crazy."

"Preemie twins tonight," she says. "Sixteen weeks early. They're stable for now. But it's hard to say what might happen later." My mother shakes her head. There is a special kind of exhaustion my mother always carries around. It radiates off her. When I haven't seen her for a few days, it's all the more obvious. Being around it, I catch it, like a flu. It makes me feel like someone is sitting on my chest. It makes me want to go outside, somewhere light and loud with lots of other people.

"That's awful," I say.

"That's life, I guess," my mom says. And she shrugs and lets out a sigh.

When I was younger I would always beg her to take me to work, imagining all the cute little babies I'd get to play with, but she would never let me come with her. Once, when I was nine years old, Nina showed me a picture on the Internet of a tiny preemie, seventeen weeks early. "Mom worked with this baby," Nina had told me. Its head reminded me of an apricot — small and covered in downy little hairs, and soft looking. Its tiny arms and legs as thick as my pointer finger. The baby's skin was so translucent I could see each vein swirling underneath. According to the article that the picture was attached to, the baby only survived for three hours. Looking at this picture and knowing this filled me with an almost unbearable sadness that I didn't understand at the time. I was sad not just for the baby, but for everyone in the entire world. This baby reminded me of something that we are all born knowing, but that if we're lucky, we forget — the world doesn't make sense, things just happen, often without any reason, and life isn't fair, it was never supposed to be. I understood my mom in a different way after that.

"I guess I'm going to go back upstairs now," she says. I watch her walk away in her bathrobe, clutching her mug.

"Hey, Mom?" I call out. For a second, one brief second, even though I know better, I consider telling her what's really going on.

"Yeah, Ellie?" My mom turns back. Her shoulders are sagging slightly.

But I can't tell her. I'm not going to. And I'm not sure if it's for her sake, or for my own.

"Good night, Mom," I say.

"Good night, Ellie," my mom says. And then she's gone.

"Your mom's pretty cool," Sean says. "Didn't even mind that you have some random dude sitting here on the couch?"

"I'm not sure if 'cool' is the word I'd use exactly," I say. "But thanks."

"Better than my mom," Sean says. He's smirking. "Who is insane."

I look down. The laptop's finally booted up. Only when I hear the door to my mom's room creak shut upstairs do I start typing.

I do a search and go to the bank's website. It loads slowly, a picture of a man and a woman, sitting at a computer, each with a cup of coffee, smiling. My heart is pounding.

I click on customer login. There's a tiny link under it.

Having trouble logging in? Forgot your username or password?

I click and am taken to another screen. *Please answer these questions to access your account:*

Account Holder's Name? I type in N-I-N-A W-R-I-G-L-E-Y and press return. And then I suck in my breath, my heart pounding as the webpage reloads.

"If she doesn't have an account, it'll tell us, right?" I ask. But Sean doesn't answer; we're both staring at the screen.

A new screen has appeared, *Primary Cardholder's SSN?*

"Does this mean she has an account? I think this must, right?" My voice sounds higher than normal, which is what happens when I'm freaking the fuck out.

"I think so," Sean whispers.

I type in the number.

Date of birth? My hands are literally shaking.

Please answer the following four security questions.

"Almost in," Sean whispers.

Mother's maiden name?

R-A-I-N-E-R.

Name of first pet? When Nina was six, she got a hamster. I was too young to remember, but I remember hearing the story about how my dad took it back to the pet shop because it wouldn't stop squeaking. His name was Squeekers spelled with two *e*'s and no *a* because she didn't know how to spell squeak. I type in S-Q-U-E-E-K-E-R-S.

I hit return again. I feel like I'm about to vomit.

Name of elementary school?

E-A-S-T O-R-C-H-A-R-D E-L-E-M-E-N-T-A-R-Y.

The last question pops up.

Favorite song?

I start to smile. Nina's favorite song is *Happy Birthday*.

I type it in. Hit return.

The screen goes white and a tiny globe spins in the upper right corner of the screen, and then a new message appears.

Welcome, Nina Wrigley.

"Holy fuck," Sean says.

I click on billing history archive. There are only two charges.

One for $855 at Edge Sports in Edgebridge, Illinois, three weeks before she disappeared. And one for $11.90 at a place called Sweetie's Diner in Pointview, Nebraska, a week after she was gone.

"Nebraska," I say. "What the hell was she doing there?"

"I don't know," he says. "Maybe we should go and find out."

I turn toward Sean.

Is he serious? He cocks his head toward the door.

I raise my eyebrows.

He grins.

Holy shit, I think he's actually serious.

But can I really do this?

I stare down at the computer. Sean is almost a complete stranger. But somehow I feel like I already know him. And he really seems to want to help me. And right now he's the only person in my life who does. And I need to find Nina. And this might be my only chance . . .

I look at Sean again. He's staring at me, smiling, nodding slightly.

I take a deep breath.

I nod back.

And that's how it's decided.

eLeven

The summer I was twelve my mother sent Nina and me to stay with our Great-aunt Cynthia at her beach house. Our mother had insisted it would be good for us to have a change of scenery, to get out in the sea air, and spend time with our aunt. "But what she really means," Nina had told me, the night before we left, as she stuffed her old blue duffel bag with handfuls of tank tops, "is that it will be good for her to have us gone."

"Seriously," I had said, and rolled my eyes in agreement.

But secretly, I was thrilled about the trip. I loved my aunt's weird house and the warm Dr. Peppers she kept in the pantry and the lemony soap in the bathroom and the fact that her house was so close to the beach that sand blew in under the door and one time we found a sand crab walking around the living room like he owned the place. But what I was most excited about was the promise of an entire summer of just me and Nina.

Nina complained a lot leading up to the trip, but everything changed after we boarded the train for our aunt's house. We walked through the train car until we found two empty seats. Without speaking, Nina stopped, stood on her tiptoes, and pushed both our bags up into the racks. Then she turned toward me, gave me her crazy-looking Nina-grin and said, "Looks like it's just you and me now, buddy," and flopped down into her seat.

Suddenly she was back to her regular self. And when the ticket taker came by and said "tickets, please," Nina turned toward me and winked like "check *this* out" and said to the ticket taker, in a flawless French accent, "Oh, but ov course, here arr our teeckets." And the ticket taker, a nice-looking older gentleman, took the tickets and smiled, not the humoring smile of an adult who was on to her joke, but the smile of a man who thinks it's charming that two French sisters were traveling together on his train.

And when the ticket taker walked away, Nina turned toward me and smiled. "Oh, I forgot to tell you, El, this summer we are from France."

And I just nodded and grinned right back, because this was turning out even better than I could have hoped. I remember leaning back with my knees against the back of the seat in front of me, looking out the window at the power lines and trees whizzing by, sucking the last bits of Sprite off the ice cubes in my plastic cup, giddy with anticipation of what was ahead. I felt like I'd won a fabulous prize in a contest I hadn't even known I'd entered—without Nina's friends around, I had been promoted to the number one spot. I wasn't just her little sister anymore, I was half of Team Nina, which was just about the best thing a person could ever hope for.

The first four days were perfect. In the mornings we went to the beach, with a bag of books and Nina's iPod, and lay out on our towels and talked in our accents and discussed the details of our made-up French lives: We were the daughters of French aristocrats and we lived in a French mansion and had a pet dog named Bijoux. Every so often, while we were walking on the beach Nina would just call out, "Bijoux? Come heeeere Bijoux? Where are you, *mon cherie*!?!" as though Bijoux was missing and we were out looking for her. At some point every day we'd go swimming and at some point after that we'd eat lunch and take a walk on the boardwalk and then maybe play Skee-Ball or something, then eat dinner. Our aunt let us do pretty much whatever we wanted, so long as we stayed together and were home by nine. Every day felt so magical and amazing and unreal in its preciousness. I must have somehow known it couldn't really last.

On the fifth day Nina met Nick. I knew from the first moment he came up to us, tall and lanky in low-hanging surf shorts, bearing two "lemonade Popsicles," that he was going to ruin the rest of my summer. I wanted him to go away. I wanted to tell him that really lemonade was our least favorite flavor of Popsicle. And if he knew anything, he would have known that most reasonable people like cherry the best and then grape and then orange, in that order. I also wanted to mention that, by the way, when lemonade is made into a Popsicle, you're just supposed to call it a *lemon* Popsicle, you don't need to say the "ade" part. But Nina just accepted the Popsicles with a flirty smirk and a coy *merci*. And in that moment something shifted. Up until then I'd thought the accents were about me and Nina having a joke together, but as it turned out, I was very wrong. I was welcome to participate in the joke, but it was her joke. Not mine. And watching Nina "ex-Q-zeh mwa see voo play" with Nick gave me that sudden sickening feeling that comes along with the dawning of some obvious but unfortunate realization — my sister was a person even when I wasn't with her. And most of what she did in the world had nothing to do with me.

After that, Nina and I had a new routine: We'd get up, pack our bag, and go to the beach, and then I'd spend the rest of the day all by myself under the umbrella, with the books and her iPod, while she went off with Nick and his group of surfer friends. I was always invited along, but I never went. They were only asking because they felt obligated, which made sense since they were all sixteen, seventeen, and eighteen and I was only twelve.

At night Nina and I would lie in our beds in the room we were sharing, with the window opened and the warm salt air blowing in past the blue and white striped curtains. "Isn't it wonderful here?" she'd say. "Don't you just want to stay here forever?" But she was talking to herself then, not to me.

And that is how the summer passed.

The night before we were set to leave, we packed our stuff and went to bed. Sometime in the middle of the night I awoke to the sound of Nina sneaking out. I still remember what she looked like climbing through the bedroom window in a white sundress, running across the lawn, her sun-bleached hair flying behind her as she went. I got up then, stood there at the window waving, but she never looked back to see.

She returned sometime before dawn that morning, and cried quietly into her pillow. Somehow I knew I was supposed to pretend to be asleep.

twelve

It's an hour later, and we're in the car, zooming west. I turn toward Sean, I still can't quite believe we're really doing this. "And you're *sure*?" I say. "I mean, you're *sure* you don't mind doing all this driving and everything?"

Sean shakes his head. "Ellie, I once drove to Canada for pancakes in the middle of the night because I didn't like the syrup they gave me at IHOP. I love driving. It's like playing the world's most realistic driving video game! Besides," he turns toward me and grins. "After this you'll owe me." I blush and grin back.

I guess if there's one thing I have learned about the world, it's this: Things can always, always, always change, and those big changes often come a lot faster than you think. No matter how many times I learn this lesson, it feels like a new one. Less than three hours ago I was standing behind the counter at Mon Coeur, about to cry, and now I'm in a car on my way to Nebraska with a cute guy that I barely know.

There's a chirping sound, like a bunch of birds singing at once. Sean reaches behind him on the seat where his phone has fallen out of his pocket. "What's that say?" Sean asks. "I have a phone call?" He flips his phone open and holds it to his ear. Through the back of the phone I can hear a guy's voice calling out, "Hello? Hello? Hello?" Sean doesn't say anything, just takes the phone away from his ear and snaps it shut. "Wrong number."

"How did you know it was a wrong number if you didn't say hello?"

"I get them all the time. I'm pretty sure there's some girl out there who gives my number out as her fake, like for when she's getting hit on by a guy who wears too much gel or has sores on his face and she doesn't want to hurt his feelings."

I smile. But before I can even respond, my phone starts buzzing.

"I guess she gave out your number, too?"

I check the caller ID. "It's my friend," I say. "The one who thinks I should give up."

"So pick it up and tell her to fuck off," Sean shrugs.

I laugh, even though I would never, ever do that to Amanda. I hit *Ignore*. Truth is, I'm worried that even hearing her voice will somehow break the spell that has made this all possible. Amanda has a way of bringing me back to earth, whether I want her to or not. The phone starts buzzing again. "It's Amanda again," I say. I bet she's just going to keep calling over and over until I pick up. I can't avoid her forever.

I flip open my phone.

"Heeelleeeeeew," Amanda says. I can already tell she's drunk. It's only seven-fifteen.

"Hey," I say. There's loud dance music pumping in the background.

"Ellieeeeeeee? Sorry, honey, I can't hear you, hold on one second," and then she yells to someone in the background, "Can you turn it down please. Adam . . . can you? TURN IT DOWN A LITTLE PUH-LEASE!" and then into the phone, "Hey, babe! What are you doing?!!" And then she turns away from the phone for a second, "I'M TALKING TO ELLIE, MY BESTEST BESTEST BESTEST!" And then into the phone again, "Adam wants to know why you're not here."

"Who's Adam?" I hear a loud "woo-hoo" in the background.

"Adam is this total *asshole*." Amanda's laughing. "Eric never showed up but I DON'T EVEN CARE!"

And then I hear a shuffling noise and a guy says into the phone "Hey, Ellie," and in the background I hear Amanda yelling, "GIVE THE PHONE BACK!!!" and then her hysterical laughter, like having her phone taken away is the funniest thing that's ever happened to her.

"Hello," I say.

"What are you up to, how come you're not over here?" the guy says.

And then more shuffling. "Sorry." Amanda's back. "He is *such* an asshole." More laughter. And then Amanda yells into the background, "YES! OF COURSE SHE'S HOT!" And then back to me, "How'd you get home from Mon Coeur?"

"Got a ride."

"From Brad?" She sounds confused, like she can't imagine anyone else other than her being willing to drive me home. "Brad's Thomas?" This is annoying.

"Sean drove me." She's waiting for me to explain. "No one you know," I say.

"Oh," she says. "Sorry, can you hold on a sec?" I hear more laughing in the background and a splash. There's a shuffling sound and then I hear Amanda yell, "PUT ME DOWN, YOU BEHEEEEEEEEMOTH!!!" She's laughing, and then she's back. "Well, where are you now?"

"In a car," I say.

"Where are you *going?*"

"To Nebraska." I glance at Sean. Our eyes meet and he grins and waggles his eyebrows.

The music in the background gets suddenly louder. "WHAT DID YOU SAY?"

"I SAID I'M GOING TO NEBRASKA," I yell.

"GUYS, TURN IT DOWN I'M ON THE PHO-WOAH-N," Amanda yells. The noise in the background fades. "Hello? What did you say, Ellie?"

"I'm on my way to Nebraska," I say.

"Ellie, what are you even talking about?" Amanda sounds annoyed. "Nebraska isn't even a real place."

"I think it probably is, actually," I say. "I saw it on a map once."

"Well, not a real place anyone actually *goes* to," Amanda says.

"I'm going there," I say. "Right now."

"Okay, fine," Amanda says. "You're on your way to Nebraska, yeah, sure. Whatever, Ellie. I would have thought you'd stopped being weird by now, but I guess I was wrong."

"I'm not kidding," I say flatly.

"You're not kidding," Amanda says. She suddenly sounds very serious, in a drunk sort of way. "*Why?*"

"Just because."

"*With who?*"

"Sean."

"Sean *who?*"

I turn toward Sean. "Sean, what's your last name?"

"You're going to *Nebraska* with a guy whose last name you don't even know?"

"Lerner," Sean says.

"Lerner," I say.

"Where does he go to school?"

"My friend Amanda wants to know where you go to school, Sean."

"Beacon Prep," Sean says. "Boarding school in Lake Forest for preppie rich kids."

I turn toward Sean and raise my eyebrows.

"Beacon Prep," I say into the phone. "Boarding school in Lake Forest for preppie rich kids."

"I know that place," Amanda says. "Mom's friend Helen's nephew goes there. Where do you know him from?"

"Sean, where do I know you from?"

"The future," Sean says.

"What?" says Amanda. "I couldn't hear you."

"I met him at the Mothership," I say into the phone.

"You met a guy *there*? You didn't even tell me." I think I hear the tiniest hint of jealousy in her voice, but I might be imagining it.

"I guess I forgot," I say. And then neither of us says anything for a while.

"Alright," Amanda says. "Weeell . . . I guess I'll let you go then." I can tell she's pissed.

That makes two of us.

"Okay," I say.

"I hope you know what you're doing, Ellie," Amanda says. "Bye."

"Bye," I say. I lean back against my seat and watch the trees zip by.

"Well, that sounded fun," Sean says.

"She didn't seem to understand the concept of Nebraska."

The sun is going down now, and we are both quiet. I feel Sean looking at the side of my face. I glance over and he looks away quickly, back at the road. Then he turns toward me and grins this crazy grin. His eyes are sparkling. He rolls down the window and sticks his head out. "FUCK YEAH, NEBRASKA!" He looks at me, "Try it," he says.

I roll down the window and the wind rushes in, whipping my hair in my face.

"HOORAY, NEBRASKA!"

"GO, GO, NEBRASKA!"

"YAHOO, NEBRASKA!"

"WORD TO YOUR MOTHER, NEBRASKA!"

The mood in the car has shifted, just like that.

thir-
teen

The rumble of the road beneath us becomes the soundtrack for a very long movie about cars on a long flat highway under a giant sky. I am lulled into a trance watching it.

Except for the road sounds, the car is silent, no music, no talking, but it's the kind of comfortable silence that only occurs between two people who are secure in the fact that they have plenty to say to each other. Which is funny because Sean and I have barely spent two hours in each other's presence.

Time passes strangely in the car, marked mainly by the changing color of the sky, from blue to deep blue and finally to black. And there is nothing but tiny car lights up ahead, and giant stretches of flat land on either side of us. Each time a car or a truck passes, I feel a little poke in my chest, like we are all part of some special club of people who are up late doing secret things, and I can't help but feel like some-how all of them must be looking for my sister, too.

Around one o'clock in the morning, I spot a sign on the side of the highway showing a big slice of cherry pie with

Sweetie's Diner, All-American Roadside Favorite Open Round The Clock Since 1953. World's Best Pancakes. Next Exit written below. I look at Sean and he looks at me and we both break into huge, giant, ridiculous grins. I cannot quite believe that we've really just done this.

Sean gets off at the exit and circles around and then there, in the dark Nebraska night, is an enormous pink and silver diner with SWEETIE's written in orange neon lights at the top, the brightest thing for miles around. Sean pulls into the large parking lot, there are two other cars, three eighteen-wheelers with *Interstate Heavy Hauling* printed on the back, and one large bus with *MidAmerican Busline* written on the side and a big white 257 sign behind glass up above the windshield.

Sean parks. We get out.

The air feels cool and clear out here, and when I look up at the star filled sky I remind myself that those tiny pinpoints of light are larger than I can ever even imagine, and that all that menacing blackness is actually nothing at all.

We walk toward the door, and push through.

Sweetie's Diner feels instantly familiar the way all good diners do: It's all big giant booths and scratched chrome stools up at the counter and whirring fake-wood ceiling fans blowing the smoky scent of bacon, slightly burnt coffee, and warm pie all around the room. We stand there blinking under the bright lights like two people who have just been born.

She was here once, I think. Nina. My sister was in this

very room. I breathe in deep, as though some part of her is still here, and if I can catch it with my breath I'll know all the answers I've been looking for. But all I get is the smell of food. My stomach grumbles and I am suddenly very aware of the fact that Sean and I drove straight through dinner.

A woman with gray hair pulled back into a bun walks by with two plates balanced on each arm. "Wherever you like, kids," she says and motions toward the back of the diner with her chin, like a woman who is used to having her hands full.

Sean starts walking toward a booth in the back, slowly, looking around as he goes. Up at the wooden fans on the ceiling, down at the flecked linoleum tile floor. We pass a woman in her late twenties with a toddler in a Chicago Bears T-shirt sleeping in her arms, an older couple sitting next to each other, sipping cups of tea, a man in his early thirties, slumped ever so slightly in his seat, his hand poised on his fork, his eyes closed, as though he's taking a nap but doesn't want anyone to know about it. Sean sits down in a booth and I slide in across from him. He opens his menu but stares out at nothing. "Sean?" I say.

Sean shakes his head and looks at me. "Sorry." He smiles again.

A waitress approaches. She's big and mushy-looking, in a friendly and comforting way, like she'd be nice to hug. *Rosie* is printed on her name tag. "Hi there, what can I get for you, honeys?" Rosie says.

And I want to answer, "My missing sister, please!" but instead I just reach in my pocket for her photograph. I am suddenly nervous. Sean is staring right at me with his beautiful slate-colored eyes, and when his eyes meet mine, I feel that same flash, now familiar, but still surprising in its intensity and the knot in my stomach loosens. Just a little.

I look up at Rosie. I hesitate for one more second, resting in this moment before I know what she is about to tell me, in this moment where anything is still possible, and then I open my mouth. "I was just wondering if you or anyone who works here might have ever seen this girl." I put the photograph on the table. Rosie looks down. "I'm trying to find my sister," I say. "And so I was wondering if you'd ever seen her before. She was here at least once, two years ago."

As soon as I hear myself say the words, I feel a squeezing in my chest. I got caught up in the excitement of the moment, in the thrill of finding a piece of new information in the credit card statement, in finding someone willing to help me. Coming here, putting all that effort in, really made me feel like we were *doing* something and therefore were guaranteed to find the next clue. But just because you have sat in the car for hours and hours does not mean you're going to find anything if there isn't anything to find. We're at a diner in the middle of Nebraska where Nina once came two entire years ago. What did I *think* we'd find? Before Rosie even opens her mouth, I know what the answer is going to be.

"I wish I could help you, hon." She has taken her glasses from a chain around her neck and put them up on the tip of her nose. She stares down at Nina's picture, then back up at me. And I feel something inside me sinking. "I can't say that I remember her. We don't attract much of a regular customer base out here on the highway. Back when this place first opened, the head waitress was dating one of the bus drivers, so he'd stop in to see her whenever he was passing through, and then it just became tradition for the bus company that does this route to use us as their rest stop. I dare say the only repeat customers we get are the bus drivers and the truckers." Rosie looks at Nina's picture one last time and hands it back to me, shaking her head. "It's a shame. Real pretty girl. Your sister's missing or something?" She asks this like someone who won't be surprised at the answer.

"Yeah," I say. "For two years."

"Aw, I'm sorry, hon," Rosie nods. "You two really look alike, you know? If I didn't know you were looking for her and I saw this picture, I might think this was you. You don't know where she was headed or anything?"

I shake my head.

"Yeah," Rosie says. "Guess not or she wouldn't be missing."

I look down at the beige Formica tabletop, at the white and green paper Sweetie's place mat, and I feel my insides squeeze again.

"Is there someone else we could talk to?" Sean asks. "Someone else who might have seen her?"

"Don't think so," Rosie says. "Most of the other girls just started. People don't usually last too long here."

I nod.

"Can I get you kids anything?"

"Three large iced coffees," Sean says. "And a grilled cheese." He closes the menu.

"For you, hon?" I shake my head.

"You sure?" Sean says. "You must be hungry by now." His voice is soft and sweet, as though my hunger is his concern. He reaches out and takes my hand.

"I'll have a grilled cheese, too, I guess," I say. Rosie nods and then walks away.

Sean leaves his hand on top of mine, squeezing rhythmically like a beating heart.

A minute later the three iced coffees arrive and a few minutes after that, our food.

Sean's phone starts vibrating on the table in front of us. He looks down at it. "Leave us alone!" he says. And he smiles at me. I try and smile back, but I can't. It's late at night and we're so far from home. And our mission has failed. And now we are just two people sitting in a diner in the middle of

Nebraska for, as it turns out, no reason at all. I just want to get back so I can pretend like none of this ever happened.

"Attention passengers on bus two fifty-seven." A short man in a navy blue uniform is standing up at the front of the diner. "We'll be leaving in five minutes. Five minutes! Anyone not on the bus will get left behind so I suggest if you haven't already settled up your checks that you do that right now." Everyone starts moving.

We continue eating in silence. Or rather, Sean eats and I just stare at my plate. The place is emptying out. I look up at Sean and ask what is at once the most pointless and obvious question of all: "Now what?"

"Now we pay, and then we go find somewhere to crash for the night. And in the morning we figure out the next step." And Sean looks so determined and so hopeful, that all I can do is nod even though I'm thinking that there *is* no next step. The next step is we go back home and I try and forget that I ever found Nina's drawing in the first place. "We're going to find her, Ellie," Sean says. He looks me straight in the eye. "There's going to be another clue, okay? There just will be. I know it. But if you give up now, you might not be able to see it even if it's right in front of you."

I look down at my plate. I am suddenly very, very tired. I could fall asleep right here with my grilled cheese sandwich as a pillow. Sean takes the last sip of his second iced coffee and puts the cup back down. He points to the third one. "There are ideas in there. Brilliant ideas that are going to blow your mind, I just have to drink it and then I will tell you what they are."

I try and smile. This trip was a failure and we both know it. It's sweet that he's being so positive but that doesn't change the facts. I feel like I'm about to cry.

"I'll be right back," I say. I get up. "I'm going to the bathroom."

I can feel Sean watching me as I walk toward the back. I push against the wooden door. Every bit of the bathroom is covered in graffiti—the walls, the sinks, the floor, the ceiling, the toilets, the paper towel dispenser, the trash can, the windows. *Jack loves Sarah* is written on the outside of one of the stalls in thick black marker. And there's *AJ and CJ forever* in pink right near my foot. There's *Lindsay and Jeanine* next to a picture of two sets of lips, kissing on one side of the garbage can. And on the other side of the garbage can there's *SP would never toss TM in the trash!*

A woman comes out of one of the stalls, sniffling, her eyes red and puffy. "Don't believe any of it," she says. I turn around.

"Excuse me?"

She blows her nose loudly on a piece of toilet paper.

"All that crap people on those busses say about that first bus driver and the first diner waitress when this place first opened and their special love and blah-blah-blah and how because of them this bathroom is all magical and shit, and how people love each other forever after they write their names together on the wall? Don't believe any of it." She bends down and points to a spot on the floor, which reads *Desmond loves Annie.* "It's all bullshit." She reaches into her back pocket and produces a dark-purple Sharpie. She crosses out the *loves Annie* and replaces it with *has a skinny penis.* She looks up at me. "It's true, you know. Like a Twizzler." Then she puts the cap back on and walks out.

I am alone again, staring at the wall. I pee. And then while I'm washing my hands, I look at the mirror, which is entirely covered in scribbles.

And right there in the center of the mirror above one of the sinks is a simple line drawing of a guy's face — strong jaw, wide mouth, big eyes — and right underneath it in Nina's graceful curved script, *Cakey ❤'s J.*

I reach out and touch the mirror. The glass is cool, but the letters feel hot under my skin, like they're alive.

I race back to our table where Sean is draining the last sip of coffee number three.

"I found something."

And I grab Sean's hand and drag him toward the bathroom.

I go inside first and bend down to make sure no one is in any of the stalls. I motion for Sean to follow me in.

"Nina did this," I say and point to the spot on the mirror. "So I guess I know why she left." My voice is shaking a little.

Sean is just staring, not saying anything. My sister had an entire life I knew nothing about, apparently. An entire life and an entirely different name to go along with it. So that's it. She left to be with some guy. Now I know.

"People in love do crazy things sometimes, I guess," Sean says quietly.

I shake my head. "That's not an excuse."

Just then I hear the slow screech of the bathroom door creaking open. "Shit," Sean says. He grabs my arm and in one swift motion pulls me into one of the stalls and shuts the stall door behind us. I can smell him, the warm scent of his skin, the slight saltiness of the grease on his lips. I look up, I can't remember the last time I've seen someone's face from this close. I stare at his dark lower eyelashes, at the smooth curve of his cheekbones. His body is radiating heat. I can feel his heart pumping against mine. I start to laugh for no reason at all. Sean clamps his hand over my mouth.

We hear the *click-click-click* of a woman's shoes tapping against the tile floor. The rush of water from the faucet and then the creak of the door opening. "You don't have to hide, you know," the voice calls on the way out. "You think you're the first two people to come in here together?" And then the door creaks shut.

Sean looks down at me, and I can feel myself blushing. We leave the stall, go back to the sink. My mouth is still warm where his hand was. I look at Nina's mark on the mirror one last time, reach out the tip of my finger and trace the lines, following the path she must have followed with her pen. And I notice something that I hadn't noticed before, there next to the mirror, drawn on as though it is driving up the side, is a tiny little bus, dark deep red, drawn by Nina, with three tiny numbers written on the front: *257.*

I hold onto Sean's arm. I point, suddenly breathless with my own realization. Our eyes meet. And then I am grabbing Sean's hand, or maybe he is grabbing mine, and we are running back through the dining room, which is almost completely empty now. Through the front window we can see bus 257 starting to pull away. Sean takes out his wallet, tosses a couple twenties onto our table and together we tumble out into the night.

Fourteen

We run, our feet slapping against the pavement, and fling ourselves into the car. Sean peels out of the parking lot and we hold our breath until we catch up to the bus right before it pulls out onto the highway. It is only once we are safely situated behind its giant chrome bumper, that Sean turns to me and shakes his finger, saying, "Well, see? I told you so! There'd be a clue! A clue for which I have now decided to give myself full credit."

And I grin. "Thank you," I say. I lean back against the seat. I'm not tired anymore. It's not an I've-gone-to-sleep-and-woken-up kind of awake, it's an all-this-adrenaline-has-shifted-me-over-to-a-slightly-different-reality kind of awake. I sit back up. "But really, thank you for everything, for all of this."

"Eh, don't mention it. I have ulterior motives."

I feel my face getting hot. "Oh?"

"Yeah," he says. "Because there's nothing I can do to find my brother. So going with you on this trip makes me feel like, I don't know, like I'm *doing* something."

Oh.

"For siblings everywhere!" He punches the air, smiling, like he's trying to make things light, but his smile doesn't reach up to his eyes.

My stomach tightens. I'm an idiot. Both for somehow thinking he was flirting with me just now, and for somehow forgetting how hard all this must be for him. Going on a hunt for someone's sister can't be easy when a hunt for your brother would only lead you underground.

"I'm so sorry," I say. "I'm sorry that . . ."

"Don't." Sean turns toward me. He reaches out and puts his hand on my arm. "It's nice that you want to, but you don't need to." My skin feels hot where he's touching it. "We're the same, you and me." Something is happening in the car, the energy is changing in here. I hold my breath. We sit there like that, his hand still on my arm, his fingers moving ever so slightly. And then suddenly he takes his hand away.

He clears his throat. "So she was full of surprises, huh?"

I miss his hand. I want him to put his hand back. I shift in my seat. I put my own hand on my arm where his hand was.

"Your sister I mean. She was *surprising*." There's an edge to his voice and just for a second I feel protective of Nina, which is, of course, ridiculous. Sean doesn't know anything about Nina other than what I've told him. And what I've told him certainly doesn't make her sound like a rock of reliability.

Sean is staring straight ahead at the bus in front of us. The taillights are making his face glow red. I lean back against the seat and close my eyes. The images flash through my brain — the red ink on the mirror, the guy's face, the heart, at once comforting and terrible. Comforting because she was okay, she was happy. She was in love. Terrible because she left us all for a guy and she never looked back. "Yeah," I say. "I guess she was."

Maybe there was a sign and I missed it.

A month or so before Nina disappeared, I had gone into her room to look for a pencil, or that is what I told myself I was doing to have an excuse to snoop without feeling bad about it. The few months prior, Nina hadn't been around much and I missed her. The house felt different when she wasn't there, like no matter how many lights I'd turn on, it was always too dark.

I remember pushing her door open, the smell of oranges and ginger curling out to greet me. Her room looked the way it always did, jeans and tank tops tossed on the floor and the bed, a few bottles of hair dye on the desk, and drawings everywhere: on the walls, on the desk, on the floor, on the dresser, on her bed, torn up, crumpled, folded, in varying degrees of doneness. I remember looking at a row of faces, wondering who the people in the pictures were supposed to be. Were they all from inside Nina's head? Or was Nina's life populated by a whole world of people who I'd never even seen before?

There were the pencils in a can on the desk. I grabbed one and let myself look around her room one more time. There on the floor was a half crumpled piece of paper covered in tiny handwriting. I poked it with my toe, hoping to "accidentally" get it to uncurl so I could read it. I dropped my pencil and bent down to pick it up. I looked at the paper again, *I love you* was written on it over and over and over in blue ballpoint pen. The marks were extra dark, whoever had written the letter had pushed so hard with their pen that it had torn the paper in a few places, because that's how much they meant it. I stared at that paper, and tried to imagine what it would feel like to be Nina, to be so loved by everyone, that one individual person's love could mean so little to you. That you could just toss it on the floor. I felt a stab of something then, similar to jealousy, but not jealousy exactly, mixed with a little twinge of pity for whoever had written the letter. I remember having an urge to pick that letter up, to smooth it out and take it to my room, to pretend it had been written just for me.

For the next six hours, the view out the front window doesn't change — six red circles, four enormous wheels, a big chrome bumper. I might think we hadn't moved at all, except for the fact that when we started driving, it was dark, and now the sun has risen, turning the sky the cool light blue of morning. And the bus has finally stopped, on a side-street bus depot. And now here we are in Denver, Colorado.

Denver is what a city looks like when it's not afraid of running out of room. The buildings are far apart and the streets are wide. There's a giant dome of open sky over us, reminding us that the city is not all there is.

The bus door opens and a line of dazed and sleepy-looking passengers emerge. A girl just a couple years older than I am comes off the bus and claims her sagging red duffel bag from the pile of luggage on the sidewalk. Two years ago, this could have been Nina. The girl turns around, she looks like she's looking for someone, like she's worried they might not be here. I can't stop staring at her. I feel like I'm watching a movie about the past and the part of Nina is being played by this girl. I catch her eye and she smiles and I feel weirdly relieved, as though if this girl is okay, it means Nina was, too. This makes no sense.

I think *I am very, very tired*. I think *maybe it is time to lie down now*. I turn toward Sean who is leaning back against the seat, his eyes half closed, his hand resting against his stomach. An image flashes through my brain, the two of us together in a bed, my face resting against his chest.

I force myself to look away and concentrate on what's in front of me. What I see now is what my sister saw two years ago—this wide street, tall gray stone buildings, lush green trees. I step out of the car. What was in her head when she walked down the stairs of the bus onto this concrete sidewalk? Joy? Relief? Excitement? Sadness? I breathe in the clear morning air and try to imagine what it would feel like to be Nina arriving in this very spot. I reach up and touch my hair, imagine it ocean blue. I stand up straight and tip my head slightly back the way Nina always did. I close my eyes. When I open them, I notice there's a slightly crumbling community bulletin board in a grassy clearing about fifteen feet away, perfectly placed as to be directly in the line of vision of anyone getting off the bus. I walk toward it. It's covered in colored fliers: ads for a cheap motel, for restaurants and coffee houses, for rooms for rent and people looking for roommates. And up at the very top of the bulletin board are a few permanent ads behind glass. *Rocky Mountain Tours— See Denver With the People Who Know It Best. Keep Denver Beautiful—Get a Tattoo at Bijoux Ink. 2740 Colfax Avenue.* Bijoux. I stop, reach my hand out, and touch the thick glass.

Bijoux. As in "Bijoux wheere aaaaare yooou?" And I know it seems crazy, but I suddenly have this flash and I feel like I can picture perfectly how it must have gone: Nina standing here, new to this city, fresh off a fifteen-hour bus ride, and she reached out and she touched this sign, just like I'm doing now, in a city of unfamiliar people and unfamiliar things, this comforted her, she saw this and she thought *yes*. I can feel this yes coursing through my body as if it were coming from inside me. Maybe I think this because of some special connection I still have to my sister. Maybe after all this time the strength of our bond can cross space and time and I can understand one thought she might have had, even though I cannot understand them all.

Or maybe I just think this because I'm tired, and slightly delusional because of how badly I want this to be true.

I guess there's only one way to find out.

FIF-teen

But first, we need sleep.

Sean and I drive to the closest motel, a run-down place that rents rooms by the hour. And now the woman behind the counter stands in front of us, the room key dangling from her skinny index finger. "And you're sure you kids are over eighteen, right?" She raises one heavily penciled eyebrow and nods slowly.

"Of course," Sean says, nodding back.

"Okay, good." She hands him a key on a white plastic Travel Route Inn key chain. "Checkout is tomorrow morning at ten. Continental breakfast is served until nine." She looks at Sean, then at me, then back at Sean. "If you're up by then." And then she smirks like she knows something about why we're here and what we're up to. And even though what she thinks she knows is wrong, I blush.

We walk back outside, up a small set of concrete stairs and into the room. It smells like mold in here, and someone's bad breath. There are two twin beds covered in sad floral comforters and in between them there's a small chipped nightstand and above the small nightstand is a framed picture of what I think is supposed to be a pineapple made by someone who has obviously never seen one.

"Honey, we're home," Sean says. He pulls back the covers on one of the beds and crawls in, still wearing all his clothes. Before I've even taken off my shoes, I can hear the slow rhythmic breathing of sleep. I look over at him. His lips are parted and his face is relaxed. His eyelashes brush against his cheeks. My heart squeezes. He looks different to me now, just ever so slightly different than he did yesterday. I cannot explain this and I don't understand. All I know is I suddenly feel like I could sit here and watch him all day. But instead I change into some of the clothes I tossed in the bag with me last night and force myself to get in bed. Within minutes, I am sleeping, too.

six-teen

I have that dream again, the one I used to have all the time after Nina first disappeared. In the dream I go into the third bedroom in our apartment and there's a girl in there, sitting at a desk. I ask her who she is. How did she get in here? What does she want? But the girl doesn't answer, she just laughs like I'm making a joke. And she thinks this joke is very funny. And I feel so weirdly proud at making this strange girl laugh that I don't even bother to tell her that my questions were serious.

We stand there for a moment, this girl and I, and then she says, "Oh, Belly," and I realize the girl is Nina. She has a different haircut than when she vanished; her hair is made of thin strands of real gold and I decide that's probably why I didn't recognize her at first. But where has she been the last two years? I ask. She just shakes her head like I am crazy. Why, she's been here, of course! And I am confused, so confused, but Nina just shrugs and smiles. She asks me if I want to look through her clothes and help her pick out which ones would look best with her new haircut, and I say okay and she opens this door in her bedroom that I hadn't noticed before, which opens into a giant warehouse, filled up to the ceiling with beautiful things. Right near the door is a giant bunch of gold Mylar balloons on extra long strings. She tells me she's been selling them to make extra money, which is how she could afford all the new clothes. Normally she charges two hundred and fifty-seven dollars for each balloon. But I can have as many as I want, all for free, because I'm her sister. She starts walking around the enormous closet, gathering up the balloons for me. Once she has about six, the balloons start to lift her up off the floor and each time she adds to her collection she rises a little higher. She doesn't seem to notice, or if she does, she doesn't care. I look up at the ceiling and now it's nothing but sky. And she is still gathering those balloons, going up and up and up. And I realize something is going very, very wrong here. I start yelling, "Nina, stop!" and "Nina, let go!" but she isn't listening. "Nina, stop! Nina, stop!" I yell louder and louder. And this is usually how the dream ends, with me screaming and her rising higher and higher and higher until I can't see her anymore. Only this time, it's different. This time, right when she is about to pass between where the room ends and where the sky begins, she looks down and then, at the very last second, she lets go and starts to fall. Faster and faster, she hurtles toward the ground. And I gasp because I do not know if I will be able to catch her.

*　　*　　*

I wake up just after one-thirty in the afternoon, staring at Sean's dimly lit naked back. He's standing by the sink in the corner, wet from a shower, a thin motel towel wrapped around his waist. He looks so beautiful I can barely stand it. I can see his reflection in the mirror—his smooth chest, the faint line of hair leading down his stomach. I know I should look away, but I can't. He raises a smaller towel up to his head and starts rubbing his hair, the muscles in his shoulders and back flex as he moves the towel back and forth. And in the mirror I can see his biceps flexing and releasing, flexing and releasing. There's something on the inside of his upper arm, a smattering of white jagged lines. Scars. From an accident maybe? I wonder. I want to reach out and touch them.

When he starts to take his towel off, I finally force myself to squeeze my eyes shut, and behind my eyelids I picture what I'm not seeing. I breathe, in and out, trying to lie perfectly still.

"Ellie, wake uuuuuuupp."

"Mmmpph?" I make a noise which I hope makes it clear that I was not awake until this very second and certainly wasn't watching him get dressed only moments ago. I open my eyes. Sean is standing there in front of me, barefoot, fully clothed, his hair flopping over his face, his cheeks flushed from the steam of the shower, the damp towel around his neck. He's staring at my face and when our eyes meet, he smiles and I feel my heart in my chest.

"You sleep cute." Sean says. And then he flips on the light. I sit up in bed, swing my feet out onto the hard, scratchy carpet.

The moment my feet hit the floor I hear my phone vibrating on the nightstand. Without even thinking, I pick it up.

"Oh my God, what is going *on*? I've called you like a hundred times in a row!" It's Amanda.

"Huh?" I'm too groggy from sleep to deal with this right now.

"That guy? Sean? Are you still with him?"

"Hi, Amanda," I say.

"I've been calling you," she says. "Why didn't you call me back?"

Sean sits down at the end of the bed.

"I was busy," I say. And I glance at Sean, who is leaning over putting on his socks.

"Ellie. Helen was over here this morning picking my mom up for Pilates and she called her nephew Eddie from our house, you know, the one who goes to Beacon, and Eddie said one of his friends used to room with Sean and that Sean's a total freak."

I glance at Sean. He is leaning over and picking up his shoe.

"I'm not sure anyone in Helen's family is really in a place to make that kind of judgment," I say. Helen is Amanda's mom's friend, a woman who gets a new nose put on her face every other year at Christmastime. An actual new nose. Like from surgery.

"I'm serious. Eddie says he doesn't have any friends at school and just sits around by himself, like staring at things. And also I think he has a girlfriend."

"What?!" The word pops out. My insides start to twist.

"Yeah, Eddie said Sean keeps a picture of some girl in a frame next to his bed and he, like, makes out with it every night before he goes to sleep. And he's always writing letters late at night with a flashlight, like love letters to her or something."

"I don't know what you expect me to say to that. I mean, I doubt that's even true, and . . ." I pause. "What do you expect me to say to that?"

"That you're ditching the freak with the girlfriend and coming back home immediately."

"But I'm not going to do that."

"I don't get it, what are you even *doing* in Nebraska?"

"We're not there anymore."

"Then where are you?"

"Denver."

"*Denver?* Why would you be in Denver?"

"Why wouldn't I be in Denver?"

"Ellie, you don't just meet some guy at a party, decide he's cute, and then take off to *Denver*. That is so not like you. Have you been kidnapped or something? If you've been kidnapped, cough twice." I roll my eyes. If she were genuinely worried, I might feel bad, but she doesn't sound worried at all. Actually, she sounds kind of jealous. I can just imagine what she must be thinking, that *she's* the one who's always dating someone, *she's* the one who should be going on a romantic last-minute road trip with a cute guy who picked her up at a party.

"I'm not even going to humor that with a response," I say. "And I'm not really even sure why you called, actually."

"You're not *sure* why I called? Um, hi, I'm your friend and I'm worried about you. Why don't you come home now, Ellie. I'm seeing this new guy now, Adam, and he has a friend, Cody, and I think he'd be perfect for you, Ellie. Just come home."

She says this like it's a command. Like she has the right to make such commands. I shake my head.

Sean has both shoes on now, and he stands up and walks back to the bathroom.

"I have to go now," I say.

"But Ellie listen . . ." Amanda says. But before she finishes her sentence, I've already hung up.

seven- teen

It's hot out now and there's this manic energy in the air, like we're bubbles in a liquid that's just about to boil. Sean is walking fast and I'm right behind him, heading down Colfax Avenue, toward where we hope we'll find Bijoux Ink.

The street is full and we're dodging people as we go. Two girls are walking toward us. They're wearing these flimsy little sundresses and the sun is behind them. I can see the outlines of their legs, their small waists. And when they get closer, it's obvious that neither of them is wearing a bra. The one on the left is eating a red Popsicle, like something out of a men's magazine photo shoot. The Popsicle one whispers something to her friend and then points her Popsicle at Sean. She looks down at her Popsicle and then back at Sean and wiggles her eyebrows. Both girls start laughing. I feel the blood rushing to my face. I stare at the back of Sean's head to see if he's noticed them but I can't tell.

"Hey, Sean?" He doesn't turn around. My phone starts vibrating in my pocket and I glance at it—Amanda. I hit

Ignore. Sean has stopped walking now. A couple feet away a guy is leaning against a storefront smoking a cigarette. Black sleeveless shirt, jeans, shaved head, downy-looking goatee, both arms covered shoulder to wrist in black and gray tattoos.

"I think this is it," Sean says, pausing now, looking back.

We push through the door. No one looks up. It's loud inside, punk music and the whirring of an air conditioner. There's a giant gold-and-crystal chandelier hanging from the ceiling, the kind of thing you'd see in a fancy hotel lobby or at the opera. To the right two black leather couches are packed with people flipping through black binders. To the left is a huge glass case filled with jewelry—thick steel barbells, swirling ebony ear spacers, delicate gold hoops with captured rubies. There's a dark gray curtain against the back wall, and a woman walks through it. She has choppy black hair and a fierce shark underbite. There's a thick green snake inked all the way around her neck, its head resting on her collarbone, a bright red apple in its mouth.

Shark looks down at the clipboard next to the cash register.

"Sandrine Miller," she calls out. Her voice is slightly hoarse like she probably spends a lot of time yelling.

A tiny blonde girl rises from one of the couches, makes an exaggerated "I'm-so-nervous" face to her tiny blonde friend and then disappears behind the curtain. Sean and I walk up to the front. Up close I can see that Shark's shirt is covered in tiny white bows, it looks like she's wearing someone else's shirt, like she scared the original owner right out of it.

"Yeah?" She's staring at me, one eyebrow raised.

"Hi," I say. Over her shoulder I can see into the other room. Sandrine Miller is leaning back on what looks like a dentist's chair with her shirt pulled up, a guy with a blond crew cut is getting ready to pierce her nipple. A few feet away, a girl with bleached blonde dreadlocks tied in a knot on top of her head is applying a tattoo transfer onto the giant arm of a biker dude. The big biker dude's eyes are squeezed shut and he's biting his lower lip like he's about to cry. Shark catches me looking and shoots me a nasty glare.

A guy pops his head out from behind the curtain. "Eden?" He reaches up and scratches his thick dark hair. "Did the fourteen-gauge needles come in with the last shipment?" He sounds scared.

"Should be in the back if Cedar put the order in."

"I'll just keep looking."

"If she forgot to order them . . ." Shark aka Eden, shakes her head. "That girl's time has just about run out."

"We were really busy all week while you were away," the guy says. He looks at Shark/Eden, who raises one eyebrow and you can practically see him shrink. "I should have reminded her."

"Ron, just because she screwed you once doesn't mean you have to take the blame for her. Stop being such a sucker. When you're done with that client, you're going to watch the front. I'm going to have to head over to Utopia to pick them up."

He winces slightly, then disappears behind the curtain. She's looking at us again.

"Hi." I smile, but she doesn't smile back.

"Are you eighteen?"

"I'm not here for a tattoo," I say.

"Oh." She crosses her arms like, "Well, why the hell are you here then?"

"I'm looking for my sister," I say. "Her name is Nina Wrigley and I was wondering if she had ever come in here. It would have been a while ago, two years maybe, but maybe if I showed you a picture of her, you'd recognize her?"

Shark/Eden's expression is completely unchanged, almost like she hasn't heard me. She glances at Sean, then back at me.

"So," I say. "Can I show you her picture? Maybe see if you remember her?"

A muscle twitches in her jaw, but she still doesn't say anything. I take Nina's photo out of my pocket, open it. I hold it out in front of Eden. "This is her."

I watch Shark/Eden's face. There are deep lines around her mouth and creases between her eyebrows, like she's so sure that something is about to make her mad that she's making the appropriate angry face in advance. But when her eyes focus on Nina's picture, her face softens, just for a second. And then she quickly shakes her head. "Don't know her,"

Eden says. She shakes her head again. "Sorry." She shrugs, she turns around and starts walking away, then she stops, turns back. "Please don't stand here at the counter, this space is for customers." And then she disappears behind the curtain.

"Fuck," Sean whispers under his breath.

He starts walking toward the door, shaking his head. I just stand there frozen.

I look back at Shark/Eden and she's watching us. Sean comes back, grabs my arm. "Let's go," he whispers. This doesn't seem right. Something just isn't right here.

Back out in the bright sunlight, I turn toward Sean.

"I think she's lying," I say.

Sean stops, his lips part slightly. He cocks his head.

"About her not knowing Nina, I mean." As I hear myself say it, I become more sure. "I think she does."

"Reeeeeally." The word oozes slowly from Sean's mouth, and by the time he's done, he's grinning. "What makes you say that?"

"This is going to sound crazy," I say.

"All the best ideas do."

"It was the expression that was on her face when she looked at Nina's picture. Her face got softer, or something, and she smiled the tiniest bit just for a second, like she was a little bit amazed and a little bit amused and she wanted to take care of her . . . She was looking at the picture of Nina the way people always looked at Nina, the person. Which makes me think she actually *knew* her. Maybe even knew her well. But, then, why would she lie?"

I look up at Sean, but he's not looking at me anymore.

"Was she trying to protect Nina from someone or something?" I bite my bottom lip. "That's the only thing that . . ."

"So where do you want to get lunch then?" Sean says loudly. He puts his arm around my waist and pulls me close. Eden is passing right by us going fast up the hill. Sean keeps his arm around me until she's gone.

"Maybe she's just one of those people who likes to be in control," Sean says softly. "Wants to be the one with all the power."

"Fuck that," I say. "I'm going back in there." I turn around and start walking.

"To do what?" Sean calls out behind me.

"I don't know." I'm walking, faster and faster. "Just look around I guess. I'll figure it out when I get there."

I push back through the door. The girl who just had her nipple pierced is standing in front of the couch talking to her friend. "No, seriously," she's saying, she has her pointer finger looped inside the neckline of her clingy tank top and is holding it out away from her body. "It was just like a little pinch. I'm sure Mike's bit it harder a billion times! You should do it. We'll be nipple-twins!" She leans forward a little bit and her friend looks down her shirt. "Look how cute."

Her friend leans and looks down her shirt. "Awww," she says, in that voice people use when they're looking at a baby or a bunny rabbit. "*So* cute!"

I walk up to the register. The dark-haired guy, Ron, is standing at the front counter. He's leaning against it, reading a magazine called *Terminal Ink*. On the front cover is a picture of a girl covered in tattoos and wearing a black forties-style bathing suit. He is nodding at the magazine, like it's suggesting something to him that he agrees with.

Behind him the curtain is opened ever so slightly. I need to get back there.

"I'm interested in a tattoo," I blurt out.

He looks up. "Weren't you *just* in here? Talking to Eden?"

"I was," I say. "I was going to get one but I got scared." I bite my bottom lip, an exaggerated expression of coy embarrassment. "Y'know, needles, ack!" I hold up my hands and wave them around. "But I *really* want one." I'm making this up as I go along, but it seems right somehow.

"First one?" he asks. I nod. "You have a design in mind?"

"Um . . . nope." I shrug. "I'll just figure it out when I'm back there."

Ron looks at me suspiciously.

"I'm crazy like that!" I say.

"We like crazy here," he says and he starts to smile. "But,

Crazy, here's a question, are you eighteen?" He puts his hands on his hips. He's flirting with me. Guys like him *never* flirt with me, they barely even see me.

"Oh, yeah," I say. And then I roll my eyes although I'm not exactly sure what I mean by that.

"Do you have ID?"

My heart is pounding. I reach into my back pocket and take out Nina's passport. Before I even have time to think about it, I've opened it up and slapped it onto the counter. Ron picks it up, looks at it, then back at me, then at the picture again. I try to make my most Nina-esque face, flirty and warm, and at the same time edgy and unconcerned. I think I end up looking cross-eyed, but it doesn't even matter apparently, because Ron is nodding.

"Okay. Nina." Ron nods. He hands me back her passport. "I liked your hair better the other way," he says. He's talking about Nina's hair—in the picture it's pink. I feel a rush of something like triumph.

"Me, too," I say. A weird part of me is kind of enjoying this. "I had to dye it back to normal when I got my job."

"Oh?" Ron asks. "What's that?"

"I'm a bartender," I say.

"Where?"

"Um . . . New York!" I'm digging myself deeper. I don't even know why. Do bartenders in New York even *need* normal hair?"

"Cool," Ron says. "My buddy owns a rock-and-roll bar there, on the Lower East Side. Lipsynch."

"Oh of cooourse," I say, nodding. "Lipsynch."

I turn back and look at Sean who's standing a few feet behind me. He winks, and the Nina in me winks right back.

Ron leads me behind the curtain. "Nina, meet Petra." He motions to a girl with long black hair held off her face by a thick red headband.

"Petra, Nina." Petra is skinny in a cigarettes-and-too-much-coffee kind of way. She's wearing a paper-thin white tank top and a million heavy bracelets on each wrist. Both arms are covered in tattoos. We smile at each other.

"Petra's the best," Ron says. "We just stole her a month ago from the biggest tattoo shop in Nashville. She'll help you pick something out." He looks up at Petra. "Nina here is a virgin." He turns toward me and smiles. And then he walks back out into the front.

"So." Petra's grinning. "First one, huh?"

"Yup." I nod. "I just decided what the hell, y'know?"

"Oh, do I!" Her grin widens. "Five years ago I looked just like you and then one day I was bored and I'd just broken up with someone and was thinking about how I'm always either in love with someone or missing someone so I got this." She taps the outline of a red heart on her bicep. There's a dashed red line in the middle and underneath in tiny script letters is written *your name goes here*. "But be careful, they're addictive!" She holds out her arms, which are covered in red and black.

And even though, to be honest, I am not entirely sure *what* I think about all this, I just say, "fuck yeah!" because it seems like something Nina would do.

Petra nods and smiles at me like we're buddies, like we understand each other.

"I'll go get the books," Petra says. "And maybe you'll get inspired." Petra walks away and I'm left sitting in the leather tattoo chair. Off to the side the blonde-dreadlock girl is still tattooing the Harley Davidson man who is now actually whimpering out loud as the needle deposits ink into his skin. I look around the room, at the shelves full of equipment— latex gloves, disposable needles, antibiotic cream. I stand up to get a closer look at one of the framed photographs on the wall. It's of a group of guys in black T-shirts and jeans. The one in the middle has a cowboy hat on, and right next to him Petra is standing, looking proud. Suddenly Petra's standing behind me. "They're *Saddle Up Susie*, big in Nashville," she says. "I know, no one up here's ever heard of them . . . but they were passing through town two weeks ago. I absolutely love them."

"Cool," I say.

Petra hands me a thick black binder. "Take a look at this one, I'm just going to go get the others." She disappears down a small staircase. I get up and slowly continue wandering. Hung up on the walls, filling every available space, are more framed photos of Bijoux Tattoo's clients with their tattoo artists, proudly displaying their newly modified body parts. I vaguely recognize some of the people in the pictures: a guy from an indie-band that Eric pretends to like because he thinks it's cool, a giant-eyed model that Amanda thinks looks like a lizard, a performance artist I once read an article about when Amanda and I were flipping through magazines at the bookstore. I stop in front of one photo in the corner and freeze, staring at it, my heart thumping in my chest.

There in the photo is my sister, staring right back at me.

I raise my hand up to my mouth. Her hair is a very faded blue, the color of jeans that have been washed too many times. She's standing with three guys in their early twenties. Two of the guys have red hair and red goatees and they're pointing at a third dark-haired guy whose pants are pulled partway down to reveal a giant tattoo on his lower stomach right below his belly button. The tattoo is a stylized picture of the faces of the other two guys in the band, surrounded by musical notes. Nina did this. The tattooed guy has one arm around her shoulders. Her mouth is curved into the shape of a smile. She looks very far away, not how I'd pictured her when I saw the drawing on the mirror. At the bottom of the photo is a scrawly signature, but it's impossible to make out what it says. I turn around, the dreadlock girl is hunched over Harley Davidson's arm. His eyes are squeezed shut. I reach up and grab the framed photo off the wall. I flip it over, there are three little metal pieces on the back holding a piece of cardboard in place. I pry them up with my nail, my heart is pounding. I shake the cardboard out and grab the photograph. I lift the front of my T-shirt, push the edge of the photograph down my cutoffs, and pull my T-shirt down over it. I drop the now empty frame behind a black metal cart just as Petra walks back into the room, holding a big stack of black photo albums. She holds them out toward me expectantly.

"I think I changed my mind again," I say. "I'm sorry, I don't think I want a tattoo after all."

"Really?" she says. She looks at me with her eyebrows raised. I shake my head. "Poops!" She sticks her lower lip out in a jokey frown.

"Sorry," I say. And then I remind myself that I'm Nina. "I can be a little impulsive sometimes, I guess." I shrug and give her this big radiant smile. And because I am smiling Nina's smile, Petra can't resist it. No one ever could. Petra smiles back, and then I turn and walk back into the main room.

Sean is standing by the door looking nervous. I grab his arm and drag him outside.

"What happened?"

"Just keep walking." I lead us outside and up the hill, and only when we're three full blocks away do I stop and turn toward Sean. His eyes are sparkly, open wide. He's already nodding in anticipation of whatever it is I'm about to say.

I take the photo out from under my shirt.

"She actually *worked* there." I hand the photo to Sean. "Look."

"Whoa! Who are the dudes?" Sean is holding the picture up to his face.

"I don't know. I'm guessing they're at least kind of famous since the photo was up on display. I'm figuring they're in a band. So now we just need to figure out who they are."

Sean is nodding. "You know who knows an awful lot of stuff about guys in bands?"

"Girls who want to do it with guys in bands?"

"Well, yeah," Sean grins. "But also, guys who work in alty music stores who think they're going to get to do it with the girls who want to do it with the guys in the bands by knowing about them . . . Guys who work in places like *that*." Sean points diagonally across the street to a store with posters and band memorabilia covering the windows and BOTTOM FORTY printed on the black and green awning.

"Shall we?" Sean puts out his arm for me to grab onto. I take it and we cross the street.

Bottom Forty is another little pocket of anytime in the middle of this sunny summer day. The windows are covered entirely in band posters so the bright summer sun is blocked out. It smells sweet in here, like incense mixed with something else. A woman rapping in French plays loudly over the sound system.

The guy standing behind the counter is about our age

wearing a white T-shirt with *ASK ME ABOUT MY DUCK* written on it in black sharpie. His face is covered in giant painful-looking zits and there's a silver zit-shaped piercing protruding from the middle of his chin.

Sean takes the photo up to the front. The guy looks at Sean and nods the way people do when they think they've spotted one of their own.

"Hey, man," Sean says. "Can you help me out here? I'm trying to figure out who the band in this picture is." He slides the photo across the counter. The guy looks at it and nods.

"Of course, this is Monster Hands." He looks up at Sean. "You seriously didn't know?"

"I'm not from around here," Sean says.

"Yeah, I guess not." The guy shrugs, then hands the picture back to Sean. "They're really fucking good. They're Irish but they got their start here in Denver, then got signed a couple years ago by Paragon Records and have been touring pretty much solid for the last two years or so. You should check them out. Their old release is over in the *M* section. Well, obviously." The guy points. "But they have a new album coming out in two and a half months."

The guy glances at me, as if to see if I'm impressed by how much he knows. I'm flattered that he'd care.

Sean nods. "Cool," he says. "Thanks."

Sean starts walking toward the back. There's a guy and a girl standing in front of the *M*s, both about the same height, with straight, shiny, copper-colored hair. They both have pale clear skin, piggy looking upturned noses, and giant eyes. Like they're from another planet where this is just how people look. The girl has her hand in the guy's back pocket. Sean starts to reach for the *M*.

"Looking for Monster Hands?" The guy half of the couple is watching us, well, watching me, actually. But he's talking to Sean.

"Yeah," I say.

"Sorry, honeys!" the girl says. She's holding up a gray CD case with a black-and-white photo of a big monster hand holding a coffee cup on the front. "We got the last *wuh-uhn!*"

"Can we see the CD just for a second?" I say. The guy is still staring, at my boobs now.

"Sorry, I know that trick!" The girl is shaking her head. "We let you see it for a second and then you run off with it. Nice try, though. People get very snatchy-snatchy when it comes to Monster Hands CDs. That's why we have to get this replacement. Because a friend, well, an *ex*-friend, of ours stole our last one." The girl frowns. "Awww, you look so disappointed. Awww. Seriously. I can relate. Me and boyfi *loooove* Monster Hands, don't we, babes?"

Her boyfriend nods at my boobs. "We love them."

"Me and my smoochy-face here cannot *wait* until their new album comes out. We're going to camp out in line like a week before. We already bought the tent."

Then the four of us just stand there for a second, until the girl lets out a high-pitched animal scream.

"NO WAY!" She drops the CD, and snatches the Monster Hands photo from Sean. "Oh my God. I'm shitting in my pants. I'm shitting in my pants right now! They got the Bijoux picture of Ian's tattoo! Can you believe it?!?" She waves the picture in her boyfriend's face.

"How the fuck did you get this?" he says. "That lady who works in there is a *beast*! She could snap your leg in half with that jaw of hers."

I shrug.

"Rock and roll," the guy says. He holds his hand out, his pinky and pointer finger in the air. The girl gives me a nasty look, then links her arm through his and pulls him close to her. Then she goes back to staring at the picture.

"But seriously though, the people on the forum will pee their pants over this. Every single one of them in unison the second they see this." She shakes the photo around a little. She has green ink caked around each fingernail. "Okay. How much do you want for it?" She looks up and brushes her bangs to the side with her hand. She's wearing so much eyeliner.

"I'm not selling it," I say.

"Okay. I see what you're getting at. I can respect that." The girl nods. She takes a deep breath and then forces her mouth into a fake-looking smile. "I'm Jamie," she says. "And this is my boyfriend, Jamie. I know, Jamie and Jamie, so adorable, right? And what are your names?"

"I'm Ellie," I say.

"I'm Sean," he says.

"Well, Ellie and Sean, I understand why something like that might not be for sale, however, you might be open to a trade, right? Any reasonable person would be." Jamie-girl reaches into Jamie-boy's back pocket and takes out a homemade-looking duct tape wallet. She opens his wallet and removes a folded piece of paper. She leans in toward me. "Okay, like just the fact that I am even showing you this is a big deal and seriously there are people who would probably pay serious cash just for a tiny peek at this but . . ." She unfolds the paper, glances to her left and her right. "There. There it is. This is the drawing that's going to be on the cover of their new album." She holds it out in front of her with a proud smirk on her face.

I raise my hand up to my mouth, inhale sharply. My heartbeat starts playing in fast-forward.

There in the center of the paper is a photocopy of a drawing—a girl with her hands on her head, her feet spread apart, her head tipped back, screaming.

"Oh, shit," I whisper. A Nina Wrigley original. I can feel Sean pressed against my arm. His heart is pounding, too. "Where'd you get this?"

"We're just really well-connected," Jamie-girl says. And then she shrugs as though she doesn't think this is a huge

deal, but clearly we're supposed to. "This is just a copy of course, we keep the real one locked up. But if you'll give me that photo, I'll let you have this."

I stare at the drawing, I can barely even process what she's saying as my mind opens up to hold all this new information. Nina wasn't just some girl who tattooed them. She was probably someone they knew. Might still know. They might even know where she is.

"I need to meet them," I say. I look up. Jamie-guy is still staring at me, his tongue protruding ever so slightly from between his chapped lips.

Jamie-girl lets out a snorty little laugh. "Well, unless you have a way to get to Phoenix by tomorrow night, that's not gonna happen, girly. That's the last show of their American tour before they go to Europe for two months." She takes the drawing and folds it back up and puts it back in Jamie-boy's wallet, which she then puts back into his pocket. "If you're such big Monsties, how come you don't already know all this?" I'm about to explain that really we're just looking for my sister, but before I can say anything, Sean starts talking.

"We just heard them for the first time the other day," he says. "But right away it was like one of those things where you just connect to the music. You know how it is." Sean turns toward me and winks. "So, what about this Phoenix show tomorrow night? Where exactly is it?"

"This underground place that doesn't technically have a name," Jamie-boy says. "But everyone calls it Spit Pavilion, because it's really dusty out there in the desert and the dust makes everyone have to spit all the time. It's intense."

"You've been there?" Sean asks.

"Well . . . no, but we read all about it on this Monster Hands online forum," Jamie-girl says. "And it's not just a regular forum anyone can join, you have to be *invited*. Anyway, good luck getting in at this point without a ticket or some *serious* connections." She makes a little noise in the back of her throat. "Oh, and you'd also need a car because this place is basically in the middle of nowhere." She crosses her arms and smirks.

"Well, what if we have one," Sean says. "A car, I mean. And what if we were willing to drive out there . . ."

Jamie-girl leans forward. "Well then, maybe we could work something out . . ." She's trying to sound calm but under all her eyeliner her left eyelid starts to twitch. "Because we just so happen to have those very special connections one would need to get in last minute. We were planning on going but then smoochy-face's car broke down. But if you give us a ride there and throw in the picture of course, we might be . . ." She's starting to smile, she takes a deep breath and forces the corners of her mouth down. "Well, we might be *willing* to come with you to Phoenix and help you get in and help you get backstage. We'd have to leave, like, now though."

"And we'd have to stay overnight somewhere," Jamie-boy says. "Y'know, all together." He grins, still staring at me.

"You guys in?" He sticks his hand out to shake. He has bits of green ink on his fingers, too. Jamie-girl glances at him and opens her mouth slightly.

"We're in," Sean says. But as he starts to stick his hand out, Jamie-girl steps forward and wedges herself in between Sean and her boyfriend. "Wait! Before we agree to anything"—she glances at me and for a second almost looks embarrassed—"you guys *are* a couple, right? I mean, because otherwise, this could get . . ."—she glances at her boyfriend, who is still staring at me—". . . awkward."

"No, we're not a couple," Sean says slowly, shaking his head. "Where did you get that idea? We're brother and sister!" And then without missing a beat, Sean reaches up and puts his hand on the back of my neck. He turns so he's facing me and then starts gently pulling me toward him. I see his face coming closer, closer, his lips are starting to part. I can't breathe. And then, his lips are touching mine, his mouth slightly open. I close my eyes. I'm floating in space and the only parts of my body I can feel are the ones he's touching. He holds me against him for one more moment and then let's me go long before I'm ready. Jamie and Jamie stand there with their mouths wide open.

"Kidding!" Sean puts his arm around my waist and gives me a little squeeze. "Ellie's my girl. Right, El?"

And all I can do is nod because I'm too shocked to do anything else.

eigh-teen

Sean and I are sitting in the car pulled up in front of the Jamies' apartment building, acting like nothing happened. Or rather, Sean is acting like nothing happened, while I am silently freaking out.

"Riding for twelve hours with the Jamies is definitely going to be funny," Sean says. He pauses. "Question is will it be the kind of funny that makes a person laugh? Or the kind that makes a person barf a little?" Sean grins. I try and laugh too but it comes out sounding like a cough. I know it didn't mean anything, Sean was being resourceful, just doing what he needed to do to get the Jamies to come with us, but I can't stop thinking about the kiss. Lip against lip, the heat from the inside of his mouth entering my own. I know it was just for show, and I know I don't have much experience to judge it against, but I swear, I *swear*, that kiss felt real.

Sean's phone starts vibrating. He takes it out, looks at it, presses a button to make it stop. I glance at him, half expecting him to say who it was, but he doesn't, just shoves the phone back in his pocket.

"Oh!" I say loudly, awkwardly. "I should call Brad. At work. I'm supposed to go in tomorrow."

"Uh-huh," Sean says. "Go for it."

And as I dial Mon Coeur, I hear a buzzing coming from Sean's pocket. His phone is vibrating again. He reaches into his pocket and makes it stop without even looking at who it was. A thought I don't want in my head pops in and won't leave. What if Amanda was right? What if all those "wrong numbers" he's been getting are actually some poor girl calling to see where her boyfriend is, and all the while he's off in another state with me, ignoring her calls? I shake my head. I am thinking Amanda's thoughts here. Not my own. I press *Talk* and hold the phone to my ear.

Brad answers on the second ring with a singsongy, "Bonjooooour, Mon Cooooouer."

"Hi, Braddy," I say.

"Ellie-face! Hello! So is he your boyfriend yet? Are you preggo? Are you naming the baby after me?!?"

I laugh. "Um . . ." I feel myself blushing. I glance at Sean. He's staring out the window, his expression blank.

"Don't you 'um' me, missy. So how was the ride home? Did you invite him up? Did you smooooooch him?"

"It was good," I say.

"What was good? The ride *or the smooch*?!"

I don't say anything.

"Ellie . . ." Brad says slowly. "You are not answering with

the candor to which I am accustomed . . . *Are you with him right now?*"

"*Yeeeesss,*" I say. "I am."

"No way! What are you guys doing?"

"We're in Denver. And we're on our way to Phoenix."

Brad pauses. "Hold on," he says. "I have to go put my head back together because *you just made my brain explode.* Are you serious?" Brad sounds thrilled.

"Yup," I say.

"What are you doing there? *Is this your honeymoon?*"

I bite my bottom lip. I really don't like lying to Brad, but I know he kinda shares Amanda's view that there's not much I can do about Nina being gone. And he sounds so excited about the idea of me dating Sean, I don't want to burst his bubble. Then again, omitting some details is not really the same thing as lying, is it? "We're going to see a band play," I say. "This band called Monster Hands. Which is part of why I'm calling you, actually. Would it be okay if I didn't come in to work tomorrow?"

"You're calling me to say you suddenly, out of nowhere, hopped in a car with a hot stranger and now he's driving you to Phoenix to see a band and *you want to know if you can have off work?*"

"Um . . . yeah?"

Brad lets out a loud *WHOOOP.* "Well, of course you can! Hold on!" And then I hear him repeating what I just told him to a guy in the background. Thomas probably. The guy lets out a cheer, too. "You just have to promise me one thing, Ellie-bean."

"What's that?"

"When you and hot skater are sexin' it up, you'll video-tape the entire thing."

I laugh. "Okay, I will."

"No, seriously," Brad says. "I swear it won't even be weird or anything if I watch a video of you and Sean doing it because I won't even *glance* at you I *promise*! I've been learning this new video-editing program, we can just blur you out!"

I hear a scuffling sound in the background.

"Hi, Ellie." It's Thomas. "Please excuse my el-pervo boyfriend. What he meant to say is that he is so excited for you, and I cannot wait to meet this hot stud-cake you're with and get back safe."

More scuffling.

Brad again. "And take a video!"

I'm laughing. "Bye, guys," I say. "See you when I get back."

"HAVE FUN!" they call into the phone together. And then they hang up.

"Everything cool?" Sean asks. He turns toward me and there's the slightest hint of a smirk on his face, and immediately I start blushing until I realize that he's not smirking at me, but what's behind me: Jamie-girl and Jamie-boy emerging from the front door of their building, red-faced, each hauling one end of an enormous blue duffel bag, like the kind of bag you might have if you were going on a three-month-long sea voyage for which you also needed to pack your own food. Sean leans toward me. "Which do you think is most likely to be in that bag, a month's worth of clothes? Or the chopped-up bodies of the last two people they hitched a ride with?" But before I can answer, grunting Jamies-boy-and-girl are shoving their bag into Sean's open trunk and piling themselves into the car.

"Seriously," Jamie-girl says, as she shuts the door behind them. "You guys are soooooooooooo lucky you met us. A Jamie-Jamie road trip is a special and unique thing. No one who goes on one ever forgets it."

"Well, that"— Sean turns to me and grins—"That I do not doubt for a second."

nine-teen

Six hours into the trip and the Jamies are in the backseat doing something that sounds an awful lot like sex although I'm not planning on turning around so I cannot say for sure.

All I know is that there's a rhythmic thumping against the back door; and it's growing faster. And for some reason that I do not even care to think about, the car is starting to smell like yogurt.

Sean cracks the window and turns the music up. I stare straight ahead.

Truth is, even this might be preferable to what they were doing for the first five and a half hours of the trip, namely singing along loudly (and badly) with the Monster Hands CD, telling us a very, very, very long story about how they met, followed by them fighting about: 1) the details of their meeting (they disagreed on what Jamie-girl was wearing that night), and 2) a joke Jamie-boy made about Jamie-girl being controlling (which, while possibly true, was mean and not very funny).

I glance over at Sean again. He turns the stereo up. The Monster Hands song, "Some Things I'd Rather Not Discuss (About My Face)" is playing:

Stop looking, stop stop looking at this, stop looking at this thing on my faaaaace. On my faaaaaa . . .

Monster Hands is just about to hit the chorus when the music stops. Just stops, completely.

And then, quite suddenly, a new noise emerges from the backseat, a little *yip yip yip* like a tiny dog yelping in pain.

Yip yip yip. Yip yip yiiiiip.

I feel a laugh starting to bubble up from deep in my stomach.

Yip yip yyyiiippp. And then I realize something. These sounds are not coming from Jamie-girl, but from Jamie-boy, which makes the whole thing even funnier

Yip yip yip yip.

I hold my breath and press my lips together, ball my hands into fists, squeeze my nails into my palms, but the *yip-yip-yipping* is faster now, higher pitched.

Yipyipyipyipyipyip.

I turn toward Sean, his face a mirror of my own, lips pressed together, cheeks puffed out, eyes starting to water. My chin starts trembling with pent-up laughs and then . . .

"*Woof,*" Sean whispers. And then it's all over. A laughter bomb explodes in the car. The more I hear Sean laughing, the more I laugh, and the more I laugh, the more he laughs, and really at this point it's completely out of my control. If someone waved a thousand-dollar bill in front of my face and said I could have it if I stopped laughing that second, I wouldn't be able to. My stomach hurts, and there are tears trickling down my cheeks.

It's a full minute and a half before our laughter subsides, both of us gasping for hiccuppy breaths.

And then, finally, the car is quiet except for a soft shuffling and the sound of a zipper being zipped. I turn toward Sean again, and he shrugs and I shrug and then Jamie-girl says, loudly, "We've been in the car for like six hours now, and it's like twelve-thirty, don't you think it's about time we stopped for the night?"

And Sean says, "There's a little place about ten miles from here in New Mexico that I've been to before, we'll stop there."

And then Jamie-boy says, "Good. I could really use some sleep, I'm exhausted."

And then I look at Sean and he looks at me, and it turns out we weren't done laughing after all.

twenty

Twenty minutes later we drive up in front of a fancy stone building. At first I think we're just turning around because this couldn't possibly be the "little place" Sean was talking about. This is the kind of hotel people stay at when they have so much money that they just never have to think about the fact that money even exists. Even Amanda's family doesn't stay in hotels like this one.

But Sean pulls all the way up to the front and stops the car where the valets are. A guy in a navy-blue uniform opens the door and Sean gets out, and meanwhile more people in identical blue suits are opening the Jamies' doors and my door, too, and I am so confused as to what exactly is going on here that at first I just stare at the guy who just opened my door. He's this guy in his twenties with blond hair who looks kind of amused at what I'm assuming is the rather shocked look on my face. He holds out his hand, and I finally get the hint and take his hand and get out of the car.

Sean gives the valet his keys and the valet gives him a ticket. And then the valet says he'll get someone to come out and take our bags for us and then Sean says thank you and smiles and gives the valet a bill that he has somehow magically procured from his wallet without ever opening his wallet and the valet is all "very good, sir" and "thank you, sir" and none of them seem to think it's odd that he's calling Sean "sir" even though Sean's younger than he is. Then we stand there for a second, the four of us, and Sean reaches up in the air and stretches his arms over his head.

"I think this place might be a little bit out of our price range," says Jamie-girl.

"Don't worry about it," Sean says. "My treat." Then he raises his arms over his head one last time before he starts walking toward the building.

"So, what, is your boyfriend like some trust-fund baby or something?" Jamie-girl puts her hands on her hips and gives me this weird, almost *accusatory* look, but then instead of waiting for me to answer, she whips her head around and follows Sean toward the tall oak doors. Good thing, because I'm just about as confused by this as she is.

The four of us walk through the doors together, and the moment we're inside, three of our jaws drop. This is, without question, the fanciest room I have ever been in in my life: There are pure white marble floors flecked with gold, floor-to-ceiling windows draped in yards and yards of cream colored silk, an arched ceiling rising four stories overhead, and what must be the world's largest crystal chandelier dangling in the center of the room like a glittering planet.

"And you're paying for this for real? Like with money?" Jamie-boy asks slowly. "We're not going to have to jump out the windows in the morning or sneak out in the laundry hamper or some shit?"

Sean laughs and shakes his head. "Don't worry about it, dude," he says. "Seriously. I'm paying. With money." And with that Sean walks up to the counter and starts talking to the receptionist. A minute later, I walk up behind him just as she is saying, "And so the rate for each room will be four hundred fifty for the night, plus tax." I hear her voice catch for a second when she says the price. I wonder how many of these rooms she rents to teenagers in T-shirts and jeans. I feel my heart pounding. Maybe Sean didn't realize it was going to cost this much when he offered to pay for all of it. I mean, obviously he didn't because that is insane, right? I try and calculate how many days of working at Mon Coeur it takes me to earn this much money, how many days it probably takes my own mother working at her job to earn this. The total for the two rooms is about what my mom pays in rent every month for our entire condo.

But Sean just nods casually and hands her a black and gold credit card and a moment later, she hands him the two sets of swipe-card room keys. Two bellhops come to lead the four of us up to our rooms. Jamie and Jamie are completely silent in the elevator, they just keep exchanging these glances like they think they've just won the lottery.

"See you guys tomorrow," Sean says. A second later we walk into the room and Sean gives the bellhop a couple folded bills. And then a second after that the bellhop's shutting the door behind him with the faintest of clicks.

twenty-one

And then we're alone.

"I hope you're not too disappointed that I put our Jamies in a separate room," Sean says. "I just thought perhaps they needed some private time." Sean grins.

And I grin back. "I think they already had their *private* time in the car," I say.

"Well, maybe *we* needed some private time," Sean says. He's joking but I can feel my face getting hot.

I look around the room, which is at least as big as the entire top floor of our condo, and probably bigger. It's decorated in chocolate browns, crisp whites, and deep reds. There's a seating area off to one side, a wood-and-glass coffee table surrounded by an enormous brown leather couch. In the center of the table is a thick glass bowl filled with perfect-looking dark red apples. There's a giant flat screen mounted on one wall, and across from it is an enormous king-size bed covered in a pristine-looking white duvet and about fifty dark red and chocolate brown pillows. The air smells faintly of honey.

"Since it was so last minute, they didn't have any rooms with two beds. Sorry about that. I'll crash on the couch."

And I just nod. An image of Sean and I in that bed together tries to work itself into my brain but I do not let it. There's a little basket on top of each nightstand filled with beautiful things—a silk eye pillow, lavender-scented pillow spray, a little vial of something, a little jar of something else, and on top of it a card on thick card stock. *With our compliments.* I pick up the eye pillow.

"This place is amazing," I say. I hold the eye pillow up against my cheek. The fabric is cool and smooth.

Sean turns toward me and taps his bottom lip. And then he grins. "Yeah, it's nice. Sometimes these places can be a little ridiculous." He reaches into the bowl and takes out an apple, wipes it off on his shirt, and takes a bite.

"We didn't have to stay somewhere like this, though."

"I know," Sean says. "But it's fun, right? I mean, I love me a shit-box as much as the next guy, but sometimes you just need to go deluxe."

"But it's crazy expensive . . ."

"Oh." Sean waves his hand in front of his face. "*That* you don't need to worry about. Like at all. My family is . . . comfortable." He looks up at me and shrugs.

"How comfortable exactly?" I clamp my hand over my mouth. "Sorry, I take it back. That was rude."

Sean laughs. "You can ask me anything you want."

"Okay, then I take back my taking back. How rich are we talking here?"

"Let's just say I once stayed in a hotel like this for six weeks straight, and I doubt my father ever even noticed when he got the bill."

"Damn," I say.

"Yeah," Sean says. "It's not even my dad's money. It's my mom's money, but she's not around, so I feel it's like my duty to spend it before the stepbitch does."

"Your mom is . . ." I stop. I feel a pain in my chest, an actual pain.

"Not dead," Sean says. Shaking his head quickly. "Just not around."

"Where is she?"

Sean shrugs. "She lives in a 'therapeutic living community' which is basically the rich-person's version of a mental hospital."

"Why is she in there?"

"Because she enjoys their healthful 'spa cuisine.'" He grins. "Well, that and she's batshit crazy."

"Do you miss her?"

"I miss the *idea* of her," Sean says. "Y'know, the idea of a mom. But I don't remember her well enough to miss the actual her. She went there for a 'break' when I was about six, and then never came back. Less than a year after, my stepmom and my stepbrother moved in. My stepbrother is the one who . . . y'know. Anyway, even though he's remarried now, my father still has power of attorney over her because she's been deemed 'unfit,' which basically means he can spend as much of her money as he wants."

"That's crazy," I say.

"Yeah," Sean says. "All I need is an evil identical twin to come and toss me down a well and my family could star on daytime TV." He walks over to the shiny mahogany desk. "But what are you gonna do? It's why I don't feel bad spending the money."

"Do you ever see her?"

"Not really," Sean says. "I went to visit her once when I was seven, the Thanksgiving after she left. It was just too weird, though. She didn't recognize me at first because they had her on so many drugs." He finishes the apple and tosses the core across the room into a black wood trash bin where it lands with a *thunk*.

"That's horrible."

"It is what it is, I guess." Sean shakes his head and smiles. "Sorry, I don't mean to be a downer. I don't usually talk about this stuff, to anyone, I just feel like I can with you, I guess, which is kind of a relief."

"You can," I say. And I feel a squeezing in my chest. It's strange to be the listener for once, to be able to be there for someone else. "You can talk about anything."

Sean sits down on the leather couch and looks up at me, "Well, let's talk about room service then. I don't know about you but spending a bunch of hours in the car listening to strangers have sex always puts me in the mood for cheeseburgers and champagne."

"Funny," I say. "I was just thinking the exact same thing."

A few minutes later a bellhop comes in pushing a rolling silver cart bearing two cheeseburgers, an oversized bottle of champagne in a silver bucket, and a giant slice of chocolate cake. The waiter stops pushing the cart near the couch, opens the champagne, and pours two glasses. He looks at Sean's black Converse and his floppy skater hair, at my cutoff shorts and black tank top. He shakes his head slightly, to no one. Sean signs the bill. He leaves a minute later and Sean and I are alone again.

He sits down on one end of the leather couch, and I sit on the other. Sean hands me a glass. I've only had champagne once before, at Amanda's house, when her parents had a party and Eric stole a bottle for us. Eric and Amanda drank most of it and I only had a little sip.

"To being understood," Sean says. We clink and I feel a little fluttering in my stomach. The champagne is very cold. I feel like I'm impersonating a much older and more sophisticated person by drinking it. A second later, my glass is empty.

Sean's is, too. He leans back on the couch and picks up the bottle. "Glasses are for pussies," he says. He lifts it to his lips and takes a long swig. He's staring at me, smiling a little, like he's challenging me. He passes the bottle back, never breaking eye contact.

"To not being pussies," I say. And I raise the bottle up like I'm toasting and Sean gives a fist bump. I take a gulp and pass it back to him. And we just do this for a while; pass the bottle back and forth and back and forth until finally, all the champagne is almost gone. Sean leans back against the couch and stares at me, *really stares*.

"What?" I say. I raise my hands up to my face.

Sean reaches out and gently pulls my hand away. "I'm just looking at you," he says. And he smiles so sweetly that I don't even blush this time. I just close my eyes for a second and just think how even though there are hard things and scary things in the world, there are also really nice things, like drinking expensive champagne in a fancy hotel room with a guy you're developing a huge crush on. A guy who maybe, just maybe, could have a crush on you, too.

But then suddenly, I remember something and pop my eyes open. And the champagne has dissolved my filter, so I just open my mouth and say it.

"Do you have a girlfriend?"

He puts the bottle down and stares at me. "What made you ask that?" I'm instantly sorry I did. "Oh, wait, because of what Amanda was talking about on the phone?" He pauses. "Yeah, I wondered when you were going to bring that up."

"You heard that?" I say. "Oh God."

"Your speaker volume is up really high," Sean says, smiling.

"I'm so sorry," I say. "Amanda's just . . ."

"Don't even worry about it," Sean says, waving his hand. "Stories tend to get screwed up when they get passed from person to person, and I don't give a shit what those people think, anyway, but the short version is that there was a girl and I loved her and I knew she loved me." He looks down. "But things were really complicated and we couldn't be together, and I tried to fix it so that we could be. But it didn't work." Sean frowns for a second, just for a second. Then he looks away. "I think when you find someone you really love, you have to do everything you can to make it work. Because all that shit people say about how love is really the only thing that's important, it's cheesy but it's also true. Only sometimes love makes people do crazy things. And sometimes, no matter what you do, a relationship can't work. Especially when one of the people in it isn't even trying."

Sean gets this really sad look on his face then, and on instinct, I just reach out and put my hand on his knee.

"Whoever that girl was, she made a mistake."

"You're a sweetie," he says. And our eyes meet and I feel my face getting hot, so I take my hand off his knee and grab a fork off the table in front of us and stick it in the slice of cake.

I hear a low hum coming from across the room and I realize that my phone is vibrating again. *Oh no.* The phone. My conversation with Brad.

"Does that mean you can hear *everything* that someone on the other end of the phone is saying?" My arm is out in front of me, a bite of cake balanced on top of the silver tines.

"Yup," Sean says. And then he waggles his eyebrows and winks.

Sean heard Brad making those jokes about the two of us together and he heard me totally going along with them. Oh God.

"I was just trying to be nice to him!" I say frantically. "I didn't want Brad to have to worry about me and . . ." But before I can say anything more Sean just says, "Sssshhhh," and starts leaning toward me. He reaches up and closes his hand over mine. I'm still holding the fork. He's leaning forward, his arm resting on the back of the couch behind me. His mouth is getting closer. His lips look moist. Is he going to kiss me? *He's going to kiss me!*

I tip my head to the side. I open my mouth the tiniest bit and I wait.

And wait.

And wait.

"Dude," Sean says. I open my eyes. He's nodding his head and pointing to his mouth. "Now *that* is some good fucking cake."

I look over at my fork. It's empty.

He wasn't going in for the kiss, he was going in for the cake.

"Your face is red," Sean says. "Are you okay?"

My champagne buzz is completely gone.

"Oh, did you think I was about to . . ." Sean says. He points back and forth between our mouths.

I shake my head. I am suddenly dying of embarrassment. I'm going to go into the bathroom now. I'm going to go into the bathroom and hide and not come out until Sean is asleep. I start to stand. But Sean has wrapped his fingers around my wrist again. And he's pulling me in slow motion toward him. "Ellie, don't go," he says. And I do not have any cake on my fork this time. I close my eyes.

twenty-two

I wake up and the events of last night come back in flashes, the way dreams do:

Lip against lip, mouths opening. Time slowing down, speeding up, slowing down. We are on the couch. We are on the bed. We are on the floor. We are magnets. We are melting. We are drunk. We are ordering more champagne. We are drinking from each other's mouths. We are drinking from each other's skin. We are breathing heavy. We are *yip yip yipping*. We are cracking up. We are playing strip poker with fries as cards. We are winning. We are losing. We are naked. We are covered in sweat. We are licking it off. We are pressed together. We are going faster. We aren't stopping. *We are going too fast.* We are slowing down. We are curling ourselves together into a ball. We are comparing our scars: white lines on my shin from slipping on wet rocks, tiny white circle of an ancient chicken pockmark on my hip, scratches on his arms from a lifetime of dogs, scraped up knees from falling off a bike, that tangle of jagged white lines on the inside of his arm for reasons he can't say. We are breathing together. We are heartbeating together. We are starting all over again. We are not sure where his body stops and mine begins. We are drifting off into something like sleep.

I lie here now, on this beautiful bed in this beautiful hotel room. Silk eye pillow wrapped around my wrist like a bracelet. One sock on, one sock off. My head pressed against the pillow, my face stuck in a smile. I reach out for Sean. But the bed is empty. I'm alone.

Alone.

Alone?

I sit up. There's a glass of water next to the bed. I don't know how it got there. I pick it up and drain it. My head aches, like my skull is slightly too small to hold my brain. My tongue feels fuzzy. My lips are sore. I get out of bed. I am naked except for the sock, and suddenly embarrassed. I pull the sheet off the bed and wrap it around myself.

"Hello?" I say. My voice isn't working right. "Sean?" He's not here. My whole body feels fragile, like I'm made of glass. I walk around the room, the sheet dragging behind me. Every bit of evidence from the night before has been cleared away. No champagne bottles, no room service cart. Even the balled-up napkins we used in the napkin war have magically disappeared.

My cell phone is on the table. It's flashing. I have two text messages: *stop ignoring me*, from Amanda, and also *I'm worried about you.* And four missed calls. All from her. But nothing from Sean. And I realize I can't even call him. Because, ha-ha, I do not know his phone number.

I walk to the enormous bathroom. The door's halfway open. No Sean.

I lean against the wall.

My heart is suddenly pounding. I squeeze my eyes shut.

What if I imagined everything that happened last night? Or I changed it all around in my head to make it what I wanted it to be?

A new picture starts to present itself. Me, drunk, falling all over the place. Talking too much. Laughing too loud. Spilling my whole soul to poor Sean who just wanted to eat some dinner and go to sleep.

I go into the bathroom and look at myself in the giant mirror over the sink. There are bags under my eyes and my hair is sticking out in all directions, there are pillow creases on my face and dried drool on my cheek. I turn the shower on steaming hot. I get in and let the water run over me. There's a basket in the shower, containing tiny bottles of fifteen different types of shampoo, conditioner, and bath gel. I close my eyes and tip my head back. I wash my hair with basil mint shampoo. Brush my teeth, hard. Floss. I remind myself that what happened last night doesn't even matter. This trip isn't about Sean. I was just drunk. I thought we had a connection. I was wrong. This is about Nina. This is about finding Nina. But what if he's gone now? Then what will I do?

I'm out of the shower. I dry off with a thick white towel, wrap myself in it.

I open the bathroom door and watch the steam escape. I pad out into the bedroom, I smell something. It smells salty and familiar and before I even realize what it is, my stomach starts grumbling.

"Greasy bacon, egg, and cheese?" Sean's back, standing in front of the couch, a grease-stained brown paper bag clutched in his hand. My heart thumps painfully in my chest. I'm suddenly very aware that I'm in my towel.

"When you're hungover, you need grease," he says, staring into the bag. "Scientists, they've done studies." He pulls out a tinfoil-wrapped sandwich. "I found a diner a couple miles away. The Jamies are still sleeping, I think." He tosses the sandwich toward me, barely glancing in my direction. I reach out awkwardly with one hand. The egg and cheese falls to the floor at my feet. Sean goes over to the couch, sits down, and starts unwrapping his sandwich. "We should hurry up," he says. "Get on the road as soon as possible." He takes a bite of his egg sandwich, staring straight ahead. "It's already past noon and we have about six hours more driving to do."

"I'm just going to get dressed," I say, pointing to the bathroom. "Then I'll be ready to go."

Sean doesn't even look up, just nods to his sandwich.

I'm standing here in a towel and he's staring at a sandwich.

This is worse than I thought.

twenty-three

The four of us are in the car again.

"Do you want me to turn the air down?" Sean asks. He's not looking at me.

"That's okay," I say.

"What?"

"This is fine."

"Okay," Sean says.

"Okay," I say. "Thanks for asking."

"No problem," says Sean. This is how it's been since he came back with the sandwiches: horrible, awkward, weird. Like we have no idea how to talk to each other.

"Look how polite they are!" Jamie-girl says. "That's so sweeeeeet. He treats her like she's this *lady*? Why don't *you* ever treat me like a lady?"

"Well, maybe I'll treat you like a lady when you start acting like one," Jamie-boy says. In the rearview mirror I see him grab her boob. She squeals and starts giggling.

More images from last night pop into my head—I shut my eyes. Sean stroking my hair. Sean kissing my neck. Sean's hands on my . . . I turn toward him, he's watching the road. He doesn't turn toward me and smirk, or make a funny face, or roll his eyes about the Jamies. I feel my heart squeezing and a wave of loneliness sucking at my insides. How are we the same two people that did all that stuff together just last night? It feels like it happened a hundred years ago or that maybe I imagined the entire thing. I think back to Saturday afternoon when he showed up at the store, and Friday when he was staring at me at the party. We feel more like strangers now than we did the very first time we met. My eyes ache with tears trying to get out. I swallow hard, try and remind myself that I'm just here to find Nina, that things with Sean don't really matter.

But I can't help feeling like they do.

I bet Nina never had a morning after like this. She never seemed to feel awkward, always felt comfortable, no matter who she was with or what the situation. It's probably one of the things that made her so attractive to people, her constant ease. I want to say *Why can't we just be normal to each other?* I want to say *Don't you like me anymore?* But instead all I do is force a cough, because this is the most appropriate conversation starter I can think of.

"You okay?" Sean says.

"Yeah, I just had a tickle in my throat."

Pause.

"I hate that," he says.

Pause.

"Me, too," I say.

Then silence again. If we actually do find Nina, I'll definitely need to ask her what the hell a person is supposed to say in a situation like this. But for now, all I can think to do is lean my head against the window and stare out.

twenty-four

It's like another planet out here: giant green tubes topped with spiky red and yellow balls sit next to cabbage-size flowers with inch-thick petals and delicate ten-foot stalks curve their graceful limbs up toward the sky. The sun is setting now, all brilliant pinks and oranges, somehow different than any sunset I've ever seen. The colors are brighter maybe, or the light is different somehow. I don't know. But my brain has decided we're no longer on earth, a fact it supports with the strange plants, the hair-dryer hot air, and the red mountains off in the distance. This is, I guess, why people travel in the first place. Surrounded by all this, I am having trouble holding on to my own sadness. It no longer seems to make sense. Nothing does.

It is hours later now and we are in the desert in Arizona.

"Two more miles on this road," Jamie-boy says, reading from a computer printout. "And then one more left and then it should be right there on our right." We keep driving and a few minutes later, we see a long line of people standing on the side of the road, next to a long line of cars pulled off on the shoulder.

"Looks like this must be it," Sean says.

Jamie-girl claps her hands together. "Yeee!"

Sean parks his car at the end of the row and then we all get out, the Jamies dragging their giant duffel bag behind them.

"You can just leave that in the car," Sean says. "I mean, you don't want to carry it around for the whole show do you?"

"Ah," Jamie-boy says. "But we do!" He puts the bag down on the dusty ground, bends over, and unzips it halfway. He removes two black T-shirts, hands one to Jamie-girl. They put them on, then turn around. *Monster Hands Monstrosity Tour Staff* is silk-screened in green on the back.

"Okay, so they're not the most *professional* T-shirts, but they get the job done," Jamie-girl says, winking. "We make them ourselves, you know!"

Jamie-boy hoists the bag back up onto his shoulder and pats it like it's his pet.

"Thanks for the ride, guys," Jamie-girl says. She gets next to the bag, unzips a side pocket, and removes a piece of fabric, which she unfolds and pins to the side of the duffel bag. *Official Monster Hands Merch* is silk-screened on it in the same green ink. "And for the hotel room and everything."

"But wait!" I say. I hear the franticness rising in my voice. Reality is suddenly catching up with me, and it does not look good. "What about the concert and you helping us get in and everything? What about us meeting the band?"

"Oh, yeah, that," Jamie-girl says. She frowns for a second. "Well, I mean, you'll be fine. Just buy a ticket. I'm sure there's some left, they have a cult following but they hardly ever sell out a show. The ticket line's right there." She motions with her head. "As for meeting the band, well, you're on your own with that one, sweetie. We've been trying to meet the band for years and the closest we've ever gotten is the time their manager kicked us out of their show for selling unofficial merchandise." Then she grins. "Anyway, we gotta run, this bag o' Monsty isn't going to sell itself! Oh, and don't worry about us getting back, we'll figure it out. As you might have noticed, we're really quite resourceful!" Jamie-boy gives me a final up-down look and then the two of them walk off, calling "Official Monster Hands T-shirts, twenty-five dollars! Official posters of the new Monster Hands album cover, fifteen dollars! Monster Hands monster hands, twenty dollars! Official bottles of Monster Hands monster water, five dollars."

And Sean and I are both left standing there in the warm Arizona sunset staring at their backs, watching them go.

"Whoa," Sean says. "What just happened there?" But he's more talking to himself than to me. "I think we've just been Jamie'd."

We stand at the end of the line, behind a girl in black flip-flops, a denim miniskirt, and a gray T-shirt with the neck cutout that keeps drifting down exposing one smooth tan shoulder. She has a pair of large gray rubber hands strapped over her real ones like gloves.

"I have no idea," I say. "I really have no idea." The girl in front of us turns around, she's beautiful—heart-shaped face, perfectly arched eyebrows, long dark hair. When she sees Sean, she smiles a big gorgeous grin. "You know those guys?" She motions with her monster hands to where Jamie and Jamie are working their way down the line.

"Not really," Sean says. "Although we did just spend the last like thirty-six hours with them."

"Oh my, my, my," the girl glances at me, then back at Sean, then glances at me again. She's trying to figure out if I'm his girlfriend. "Ah yes, the Creepy-Jamies infamous in the Monsty scene for being total scammers and also . . . being rather, um, *open* about their private activities. Did you happen to notice that during your thirty-six hours of Jamie?"

Sean nods. "We've been treated to some triple-X live Jamie-on-Jamie action."

The girl reaches out her monster hands and puts her hand on his shoulder. "Oh, you poor dears," she says. But she's looking only at him.

I feel a hot prickle of jealousy creeping up the back of my neck. A warm wind blows and ruffles her silky hair.

"So where are you guys from?" the girl asks.

"Awfully far away," Sean says.

They keep talking as we work our way up to the front of the line. They're chatting it up like long-lost best friends and I feel completely invisible, which I don't mind at the moment, because I sort of wish I were. Fifteen minutes pass and we're only a few feet away from the doorway now. The girl in front of us flashes her ID and heads inside. And that's when I spot a big sign *21+ for entry. No IDs, No Entry, No exceptions!* I nudge Sean, who takes something out of his wallet and shows it to the bouncer. A fake ID. I'm standing at the front counter, paralyzed. "Come on, Nina," Sean says, standing just past me inside the doorway. I look at him. Of course. I have her passport. I take it out and hand it to the very hairy guy who's sitting on top of a tiny wooden chair. He barely glances at it before stamping the inside of my wrist with the face of a tiny monster and ushering me inside.

Spit Pavilion is one giant room with scuffed wood floors and super high industrial-looking ceilings. There's a stage straight back and a bar off to the left with dozens of people crowded in front of it and hung up behind it is a giant white-horned animal skull, the kind of thing you'd see tied to the front of a truck. The place smells like a mix of beer and wood smoke. I glance at Sean. His hands are in his pockets and he's looking around, maybe trying to find the monster hands girl? I force myself to turn away and remind myself why I'm here.

An opening band is playing: two guys on drums and a girl in lederhosen and combat boots singing:

Nein nein nein! No no no! Nein nein nein I shoot you with crossbow.

And then, finally, the lederhosen girl stops singing, and a guy in a bright red suit comes onstage and takes the mic.

"That was Lady Bratvoorst direct from Germantown, Maryland. Give it up for Lady Bratvoorst everyone!" The crowd lets out a weak cheer. "And now, The Spit Pavilion could not be more fucking thrilled to bring back one of our very favorite bands of all time. We love them. You love them. *Your momma loved them last night.* Put your gray rubber hands together foooooor Monster Hands!" The crowd goes insane, cheering, screaming, making loud growly monster noises while two guys run out onstage and a third cartwheels out behind them. A moment later the music starts and the bar explodes in even louder cheers. All around me, people start dancing. I feel something inside me beginning to lift.

And then I feel something cold and wet splashing on my leg.

"Oh shit! I'm sorry!" I turn to my right, there's a great big guy about one-and-a-half times the size of a regular person, with curly blond hair and giant rubber monster hands, standing there grinning apologetically. "Gravity!" he calls out. "It's particularly strong over here I think!" I look down, there's an empty beer glass tipped over on its side, pouring out around my flip-flops.

"It's okay," I call back.

"No one likes beer-feet! Let me get something to dry you off at least." The guy takes one of my hands in his monster hand and drags me toward the bar. I turn back to look at Sean, but the spot he was standing in just seconds ago is now empty.

"Hey, Eddie! Big clumsy idiot over here spilled all over this girl! Hook me up with some napkins!"

The bartender smirks as he pours two different bottles simultaneously into a glass. "Spilling on a girl so you get to mop her? Oldest trick in the book!" He turns toward me. "Watch out for Danny over here!"

The bartender hands Danny a big stack of napkins which Danny promptly hands to me. "Lest you think I am not a gentleman, I will not attempt to dry you."

I bend over and dry myself off, and when I stand back up, Danny is still there smiling.

"I swear I didn't spill on you on purpose just so I'd get to talk to you," Danny says. "But if I'd seen you before I spilled . . . I might have!"

"Thanks?" I say. "I think?" Danny's smiling a big goofy grin, more funny than flirty. I crane my neck looking for Sean again. Where *is* he?

"Shall we dance?" Danny says. He sticks out his hand.

I keep looking around. No Sean. I feel a stab of disappointment. But then remind myself of that thing I seem to keep having occasion to need to remember—I'm not here for Sean, I'm here for Nina. He's not my boyfriend, he's just a friend, and we were drunk, and it didn't mean anything, so if Sean wants to go off and do whatever else with whoever else, well that is not my concern, *that's his business* . . . now if only I could really believe this.

For the next hour, Danny and I dance like crazy. We do the Shopping Cart, the Roger Rabbit, the Moonwalk, the Lawnmower, and then a bunch of dances we make up—the Time Keeper, the Tooth Brusher, the Hair Comber, the Sandwich Eater. As we dance I can feel myself sweating out the hangover sadness. Whenever I start to think about Sean, about last night, or about the weirdness today, I just dance harder, dance sillier. And by the time Monster Hands plays the final chord of their encore, "Cupcake Battle Dome," I am feeling kind of okay.

"Thanks for the dancing," I say to Danny. And then I excuse myself. It's time to do what I came here for.

"I'll never forget you, beer-shoe girl!" Danny calls out behind me. "I'm going to get these dirty napkins framed!" I turn back and he smiles, and I wave. And that's it. There's a shiny black door next to the stage blocked by a giant guy with waist-length curly hair and a giant brown leather jacket.

I watch as two girls in tiny matching gray dresses approach the door. They're saying something to the guy. He's shaking his head. They're pouting. He crosses his arms. One of the girls pulls down the front of her dress and shakes her boobs at him. He's barely even looking. Finally the girls give up, give the guy the finger, and walk away.

I take a deep breath. And as I walk forward, I try and channel my inner Nina. I close my eyes and I suddenly remember something Nina had told me the night before my first day of middle school: If you're going somewhere where you feel like you might not belong, the only person you need to work to convince is yourself. Everyone else is easy.

I stand up a little straighter and walk toward the door. *I'm not a groupie. I'm friends with the band. They'll be thrilled to see me.* When I get to the door, the big guy is holding it open while a little guy walks through with a giant amp. I look the big guy straight in the eye and smile my biggest Nina-est smile.

"I'm here to see Monster Hands," I say.

The guy just stares at me.

"I'm friends with them," I smile again, bigger this time.

"Sure you are, honey." He shakes his head and lets go of the door.

"I'm serious!" I say.

"Well, I'll tell you the same thing I told Tits McGee over there." He motions to where the girls in the gray dresses are standing by the bar doing shots. "The boys in the band didn't tell me about any special guests tonight, and until I hear it from them, you're not getting backstage."

"Well, then go ask them!" I say. "Tell them . . . tell them Nina Wrigley is here to see them. They'll be happy to see me. I'm positive."

The guy looks at me again and tips his head to the side.

"Seriously, they'll be really upset if they find out I was here and they didn't get to see me. I'm the girl who tattooed Ian's stomach!"

"Alright, alright, I'll go and ask them."

The guy disappears behind the heavy metal door and reappears a few minutes later, smiling and looking a little embarrassed.

"Sorry 'bout that, Nina. We've just had a string of crazy fans trying to get back lately so I've just had to be kind of a jerk about it. They're really excited you're here, they said to send you in. Go all the way back."

And then he winks and steps aside. I'm inside looking down a crowded hallway lined with guitars and amps and a dozen or so people are hanging out drinking beers. A guy in a charcoal gray suit is standing in front of a doorway at the end of the hall yelling "this is not a negotiable issue" over and over into his phone, emphasizing different words each time. "This is *not* a negotiable *issue, this* is not a *negotiable* issue." I walk past him into the room.

It's strangely quiet, as though all the noise of the hallway died at the entrance. The two red-haired guys are sitting cross-legged on the couch eating bowls of cereal. The black-haired guy is standing by an open window, shirtless in a pair of pajama pants with kittens printed on them, smoking a cigarette. They all look up when I walk in.

"Who the feck are you?" the kitten-pajama guy says in a thick Irish accent. He's smiling.

"You're not Nina," says one of the guys on the couch. He sounds very disappointed. I recognize him from the picture, he's the one who had his arm around her. "Where's Nina?"

"You here for some cereal?" asks the guy on the other side of the couch. He has a short red beard, and a tiny milk mustache. He's smiling. "We've got Cinnamon Toast Crunch and Lucky Charms, which I realize as I say it is a somewhat ironic cereal choice for us. You'd think a real Irishman wouldn't want them."

"Don't offer her cereal," says Kitten Pajamas. "She lied to big Jimmy. She's a Nina impersonator! She could be a crazed fan here to kill us!"

"We're not famous enough yet for that, Ian," says Milk Mustache.

"Like hell we're not! So, I would like to restate my previous question, who the feck are you?"

"I'm Ellie Wrigley," I say. "Nina is my sister."

Ian narrows his eyes. I hold out her passport.

Kitten Pajamas takes it, holds it up to his face. He looks at the picture, then at me, then at the picture, almost like he doesn't believe it. "This is really her." And then nods some more. "Peter, you want to see this." He holds the passport out to the guy on the couch. Peter's the one who had his arm around Nina in the picture.

"Well, would you have a look at that," Peter says. He puts his bowl of cereal down on the floor and holds the passport with two hands. "Jaysus." He shakes his head. His mouth drops open a little bit. He was in love with her. I can tell just from looking at his face.

"You alright?" Milk Mustache says. He wipes the mustache off his face.

"How's she doing?" Peter looks up at me.

"I don't know," I say. "I haven't seen her in two years, which is why I'm here."

Peter just shakes his head.

"So you guys did know her then," I say. "And you knew her pretty well?"

"Not as well as he would have liked," says Ian.

"I knew her," Peter says. "Or at least I thought I did." He looks up at me. There's tension around his eyes, like he's in pain but trying not to show it. "So she's your own sister and you don't know where she is then?"

"She disappeared two years ago," I tell them.

"We kind of figured something was up with that girl," Ian says. "Why'd she go?"

"Don't know," I say. "I'm looking for her now. And I saw a photograph of you all standing with her at Bijoux

Ink, or, well, I stole it actually. And then I saw a drawing she did that someone told me is going to be on your new album."

"And whoever told you that?" Ian asks. But he looks amused, not annoyed.

"A really big fan of yours," I say. "Well, two actually."

And Ian just shakes his head smiling. "Ah, the mad redheads, I presume?"

I nod.

"Well, that's not a surprise, I don't suppose, although I have a hard time imagining you associating with the likes of them. Then again, now what's this you said about stealing from Bijoux?"

"Um." I look down at the floor. Perhaps I shouldn't have mentioned this part, but it's too late now. "The woman who worked there said she didn't even know Nina, but I could tell that she did and then I got into the back room and when I saw the picture of you guys with my sister . . . I just took it and hid it under my shirt and snuck out."

Ian looks at me, and then at his bandmates, and they all burst out laughing. "Good on ya then," Ian says. "God love her but Eden deserves something like that, now and again. Ah, Bijoux," Ian smiles. "Favorite tattoo place in our old hometown, well, our second hometown after Galway, Ireland. Bijoux is the site of my greatest shame." He stands up. "I bet Peter and Marc here I could toss eight balled-up napkins in the trash without missing one. I was sure I could do it!" He pulls his kitten pajamas down slightly; there on his stomach is a picture of the two other guys' faces, inked in black. "Turns out I couldn't."

"Now whenever a young lady so happens to be spending time down there," Milk Mustache, aka Marc, grins, "she's staring me and Peter in the face!"

"So far I haven't had any complaints," Ian says.

"Well why would you?" Marc lifts his cereal bowl to his lips and drains the last of the milk. "We're gorgeous!"

Ian adjusts his pajama pants. "If I won, they were going to have to get my face on their arses."

"You should consider yourself lucky to have that," Peter says, and then looks at me. "Your sister was a genius. A true artist."

"Nina was only in Denver for a couple of weeks," Marc says. "But poor Peter fell in love with your sister straight away. Wrote a song about her and everything, but never had the balls to tell the girl."

"He's shy," says Ian.

"We were younger then and he didn't yet realize that being a big famous rock star means you can have any girl you want," Marc says.

"That's enough, boys," Peter says, shaking his head. "She just wasn't interested, alright?" He looks down at his lap. It's sort of insane to think that this is the same guy who was doing handstands on stage only a few minutes ago.

"I think she had a boyfriend," I say. "I thought maybe she left with him."

"Well, not when we knew her she didn't." Ian says. "Or if she did, he certainly wasn't with her when she left with us."

"What do you mean?"

"She hitched a ride with us out of Denver. Poor Peter was so excited when she asked if she could come." Ian sits down cross-legged on the floor, staring at the kittens dancing on his knees. "She was only with us for a few days, though. She left us when we got to Big Sur."

"Why there?" I ask.

"Dunno," Ian shakes his head. "She had us drive her up to this big house. She said she had to say good-bye to someone there, but we never found out who or why. And then that was it. My last memory of her was her standing in front of this giant house holding her little overnight bag and this giant snowboard, waving."

"Why did she have a snowboard?" Something clicks in my head suddenly. The other charge on her credit card bill, Edgebridge Sports. I'd almost forgotten.

"To go snowboarding, I assumed." Ian shrugs. "She was a mystery, your sister. And not too fond of questions. We asked her to get in touch but she never did. She left that drawing behind though, the one on our new album cover."

Peter leans over, reaches into a brown box, and pulls out

a record and hands it to me. "Our label thought it would be cool to release a proper vinyl record. And this is it," he says. "This is an advance copy they're mostly just sending out to radio stations." On the cover is Nina's drawing, the one Jamie-girl showed me yesterday. "She never even got to see the album," Peter says. "Never even knew that we put her drawing on there, actually. Will you take this and give it to her when you find her?"

"Of course," I say. And hearing him phrase it like that, *when*, not *if*, *when*, makes me smile. "Is there anything else you can tell me about your time with her? Anything she might have said about what she was doing or where she was going or . . . anything?"

"Well, like I said, we dropped her off at a big house in Big Sur," Ian says. "I bet you Peter remembers. He made us go back a couple months later on the way back to Denver."

"It was on our way," Peter says. "Sort of . . ." Peter picks a green notebook up off the floor and pulls a pen out of the spine. He tears out a little sheet of paper and scribbles on it. "There," he says, handing it to me. "That's the address. Don't know how much good that'll do you, though. When we went back the place was all deserted-like except for this lonely looking groundskeeper fella who was wandering around trimming the hedges. Said no one had been there in months."

"It's worth a try at least," I say.

"Do you want a bowl of cereal?" Marc has stood up and is pouring himself another bowl. "I'll rinse a spoon for you and everything!"

"I should go back out there." I motion toward the door. "But thank you."

"She was a lovely girl, your sister was," Peter says. "When you see her, would you give her this, too, for me?" Peter scribbles something else on a piece of paper and hands it to me, looking ever so slightly embarrassed. I look down. It's his phone number.

"I will," I say.

"And if you're ever in a pinch," Ian calls out after me, "you could always sell that album on eBay!"

twenty-five

Back out in Spit Pavilion, the music is softer and no one is dancing. There's a girl onstage in a baby blue dress with a flower pot balanced on her head, singing along with her acoustic guitar. And I am wandering through the quickly thinning crowd looking for Sean. I let the questions swirl through my head as I walk. So if Nina was single, then who exactly is J? And what happened with him? Did they run away together, and then break up? And why didn't she just come back then? Or did they break up and then get back together? Is she living with this guy somewhere?

And while we're at it with the questions, *Where's Sean?*

I look back at the stage where a couple is pressed against the wall, limbs entwined. The guy has short dark hair and a dark T-shirt, jeans. Just like Sean. The girl's hair is blonde. My stomach burns with hot liquid jealousy. The guy turns his head to the side, as though he can feel me staring at him. Not Sean. I feel a flood of relief.

"Ellie?" I hear someone calling my name, loudly, over

the music. "Oh my God, Ellie!" It's not Sean's voice. It's higher. A girl's. "*There* you are! I've been looking everywhere for you!" I turn around.

Amanda?

She wraps me in an expensive-hair-product-scented hug. My arms hang limply at my sides. She leans back, lets out a little squeal, and then hugs me again. "I got here a little late and I was worried maybe you'd *left!*"

I just stand there, staring at her face. The sound of her words and the motion of her mouth seem slightly out of sync, like she's been badly dubbed.

"Ellie?" Amanda says. She leans back again and looks at me. "Hello?"

I'm just not sure what to say. I'm too confused to say anything.

"Aren't you happy to see me?" She grins. But I can't answer because I honestly don't know.

"I went to visit you at work yesterday and Braddy said that you were going to see this band in Arizona, and I thought, wouldn't it be so fun if I just surprised you? I mean, it's summer, we both know it's not like I do that much at Attic, anyway. So I decided what the hell! I have money to burn, so why not just get a plane ticket!" She throws her arms up over her head. "So, SURPRISE!!!!"

She lowers her arms and then claps her hands together. It's like she's trying to rewrite a story that we were both part of and thinks somehow I won't notice that she changed it. Does she not remember the weirdness of the last few days? Her calling me over and over? Me not picking up?

But before I have a chance to decide whether I want to express any of this, I feel a warm hand on my arm.

I turn. Sean.

"Hey," he says. His voice is soft and low, the way he says "hey" makes it sound like it's a secret he's been saving just for me. The Sean from last night is back.

"Is this him, Ellie?" Amanda puts one hand on her hip. I can tell she's trying to sound perky, but her voice has an edge.

Sean looks at me. Our eyes meet. I feel that jolt of connection. "Who's your friend?" he asks.

I take a deep breath.

"Sean, this is Amanda." I look at him. Surprise flashes across his face and his jaw tenses.

"Amanda, this is Sean." I look at her. She's looking at him. I try and imagine what she sees, dark hair that's flopping in his face, black T-shirt, big intense eyes. Does he look the same to her as he does to me? His eyes, warm and full of a deep understanding, his lips, serious and playful at the same time. Kissable. An image pops into my head, his lips approaching mine, his hot breath on my mouth, his tongue about to slide in.

He's watching me. I blush.

"Hey, Sean," Amanda says. "Nice to meet you."

"Hi, Amanda," he says. But he's still staring at me.

And then we all just stand there. I want to tell him about everything that happened backstage, but I can't do that in front of Amanda. Not anymore.

Amanda glances down on the floor, in front of her is her big cherry-print LeSportsac. She's wearing a pair of high-heeled strappy leather sandals. Her toenails are painted bright pink. It's as though she dressed up special for this occasion, but she doesn't fit in here.

"Amanda came to surprise me," I say to Sean. "Brad told her I was here seeing a band."

Sean doesn't say anything. Just stands there looking uncomfortable.

"So where are you guys staying?" Amanda says.

Sean reaches out and puts his hand on my lower back. "We don't know yet." I can feel the heat of his hand soaking through my shirt. "We were going to find a place after this."

Amanda glances down at Sean's arm. A look of deep discomfort flashes across her face, as though she is suddenly realizing what she's gotten herself into. For a second I feel sorry for her.

"This'll be fun," Amanda says, but it sounds so forced, not one of us believes her.

twenty-six

In a parallel universe, Ellie2 is having the best night of her life. She's in a hotel room in the middle of downtown Phoenix, with her best friend and the guy she likes. They're laughing. They're making jokes. She leaves the room to go to the bathroom and overhears them talking about how great she is. How much they love her. They want to plan a surprise party for her! She gets back. They order room service! They jump on the bed! They take hilarious pictures of the three of them with a digital camera and post them on the new website they've created, devoted to just how much fun they're having!

But in the regular universe, the one I unfortunately happen to inhabit, things are going rather differently. I am in a room at the Golden Oasis Suites in Phoenix with my best friend and the guy I like, but instead of laughter and proclamations of *how much fun we're having!* the room is filled with so much awkward energy I think I'm going to puke. If one could, y'know, puke from a thing like that.

We checked in fifteen minutes ago, and right now Amanda is standing by the door of our enormous, gorgeous room, with her hand on her hip and a towel over her shoulder saying, "Come on, Ellie. Let's just go!" Sean is sitting on one of the queen beds, looking uncomfortable. And I am standing in between the two of them, with no idea what to do. Amanda lives for pools, no matter where we are, if there's a pool there, she wants to go in it. Ordinarily she can be a little bit prissy—about what bed she'll sleep in and what shower she'll use, but she'd swim in a dirty bathtub filled with soup if someone put a sign that said *Pool* in front of it. And there just so happens to be one here at the hotel, on the roof, and it's open all night.

"I don't have a bathing suit," I say. Sean has flipped the TV on and is now lying back on the bed watching an Animal Planet show about elephants.

"I brought an extra one," she says. "The navy blue boy shorts one that you wore at my house that first night it got warm back in May. Remember, Eric's friend Dylan kept staring at your ass all night?"

I glance at Sean who seems really engrossed watching two little elephants spray each other with water. Sean smiles at them and absentmindedly scratches his stomach through his shirt. The blood rushes to my face. I remember how it felt last night when I was leaning on him, our stomachs pressed together, my cheek on his chest, his hand in my hair. Was that really just last night? Amanda crosses her arms and starts tapping her foot.

"Are you sure you don't want to come?" I ask Sean.

"Nah, I'm tired." Sean shakes his head. "I think I'm gonna hang out here with my buddies." He motions to the screen where the two elephants are now nuzzling.

"Let's just go, Ellie," Amanda says. She sticks her hand out, the navy blue straps dangling from her fist. "Go into the bathroom and change."

And even though I don't want to, I'm not sure what else to do at this point. So I do what I'm told.

I change in the bathroom and then Amanda and I head out into the beige and cream colored hallway, thick hotel towels slung over our shoulders.

The second the door clicks shut behind us the smile leaves her face. "What the hell is going on?"

I stop, adjust one of my straps. "With what?"

"Um, I don't know, how about you randomly disappearing on some road trip without even telling anyone first? And then avoiding my calls? And then playing boyfriend/girlfriend with el freako back there? I mean, I know things were a little weird the last couple times we talked to each other, but just because we get into a fight doesn't mean you have to run off with some creepy loser."

"Stop it," I say, "you don't even know him." We walk toward the elevator. I push the *Up* button. About a second later the gold-and-glass elevator arrives and we get in.

"Neither do you," she says. She reaches out and pushes *R*. The elevator begins to rise. A few seconds later the doors open and we step out into a lush desert oasis—there are dozens of multicolored cactuses in terra-cotta planters, a half-dozen wood patio tables shaded by dark green umbrellas, and four cream colored canvas cabanas draped in hundreds of twinkling white lights, all surrounding a crystal blue swimming pool that's lit from underneath.

I turn to my right where Amanda was standing, but all that's left of her is a pair of flip-flops and a towel in a pile on the ground.

I hear a splash and watch concentric circles spread themselves out over the surface of the pool. A moment later Amanda's wet head appears in the center of it. Even though it's after midnight, it's still at least ninety-five degrees out. I dip my toe in, the water is pleasantly cool. I close my eyes and jump.

I can see the golden glow of the pool lights through my eyelids as I sink all the way down to the bottom. It's so quiet down here, so peaceful. I stay until I feel my lungs burning, then I push my legs against the floor of the pool and rise back up to the top. When I finally open my eyes again, Amanda's right there in front of me.

"Look, all I want to know is this." Her face is lit from underneath, all lines and sharp angles. "Since when do you go off on vacations with random guys you've just met?"

"We're not on vacation," I say simply. And as soon as

the words leave my lips I regret them. I know what's coming next.

"So then what are you doing here?"

I pause and take a deep breath.

"We're looking for Nina," I say.

Amanda stares at me. The water suddenly feels cold. I hear sounds, people moving around near the edge of the pool, but the lights in the pool make it hard to see outside of it. I swim over to the ladder, turn around, and lean against it. Amanda doesn't follow.

"I don't even know what to say to you," she says. She sounds so disappointed, like I've just told her I'm planning to become a junkie or start a homemade porn site.

"I didn't ask you to say anything." My voice sounds sharp, and I'm glad.

"I'm worried about you," she says. "I can't watch you do this to yourself anymore. I mean I came all the way out here to make sure you're okay . . ."

"And what *exactly* are you worried about?" I say. "That I'm actually going to find Nina? That someone else is helping me who isn't you?" Even *I* am shocked to hear myself say this. But the words are out now. And I can't take them back.

"No, Ellie, what I'm worried about is that you've lost touch with reality and you somehow think driving hundreds and hundreds of miles with a freak you don't even know is a perfectly normal thing to do."

"Who cares if it's normal?!"

Amanda swims over to my side of the pool.

"Do you really think it's a good idea to be here with that Sean guy? I mean, what do you even know about him? What is he even doing here?"

"He wants to help me," I say. "And at this point he is the only person in my life who is willing to."

"Are you sure about that?" says Amanda.

"About what?"

"Are you sure that his intentions are really so pure? That he just wants to help you?"

"What else would he be here to do?"

"I think all he wants to *help you* with is taking your pants off."

I just shake my head. I don't know what to say to this, but I know I don't want to be in the water anymore. I swim over to the side of the pool, get out, and wrap myself in my towel. I can feel Amanda watching me. I turn around.

"Helen's nephew said he was a total stalker freak!" Amanda's arms are crossed over the side of the pool.

"Don't talk about him like that!"

The wind blows and I feel goose bumps rise on my wet skin. I wrap the towel tighter.

"So what happened *exactly*? You met him at the party and you told him you don't know where your sister is and he just said, 'Great, okay, girl who I don't know, I'm going to volunteer to drive you across the country with no ulterior motive whatsoever?' I mean, who does that?"

"Someone who understands," I say.

"Oh, so he 'understands' you? And how is that exactly?"

"Because he's just like me!" I'm yelling now.

"You're nothing like him!" She's yelling, too. "He's a freak!"

"No," I say. "He's not. And he gets what it's like for me, with Nina, in a way no one else does."

"And what makes him so special?"

"His brother is dead," I say. My tone is cold now and I'm speaking softly. "That's why he's here and that's why he's helping me. Because he understands what it's like when someone is there one day and the next day they're not. And how that's not something you can *get over*. So if you think he's *weird* or you think there's something *creepy* about him, it's only because *you* don't understand. And lucky for you that you've never had to." And then I stop. I can just barely make out Amanda's face across the water. I can't see her expression.

"And you believe him?" she asks. She doesn't sound ashamed the way I figured she would, or even the slightest bit sorry in fact.

"What?!" I say. I spit the word out, hot bitter acid right at her face.

"How do you even know he's telling the truth? How do you know this isn't just some dramatic story he made up to get close to you and to get you to go on this insane road trip with him? Let me ask you a question, did he tell you about his dead brother before or after you told him about your sister?"

I don't say anything.

"And what did he say this brother of his died of?"

"I didn't ask!" I don't know why I'm even still answering her.

"Well, I bet he made it all up," she says. "I bet he never even had a brother."

"Shut up!" I shout. "Shut up. Shut up. Shut up. SHUT UP!!" And when I stop, she is silent. I hear the sound of footsteps behind me, someone running toward the elevator. I turn and see Sean's back. He's pressing the button on the elevator and then stepping inside. A look flashes across his face, just as the doors are closing, a look of such anguish tears spring to my own eyes in response. "Sean!" I call out. But he's already gone.

"What the fuck did you do?" I turn toward Amanda.

And she just opens her mouth into the shape of an O. I run toward the elevator. I hear her behind me.

"Ellie, wait!" she calls out. "Ellie, wait!" I just keep going.

There is a stairwell next to the elevator. I push through the door and start running down the stairs, taking the steps two at a time. I hear Amanda behind me, panting. Down, down, down we go. Around and around. My legs are burning as my wet bare feet slap against the floor. Finally, thirteen stories later, we are there. We both emerge panting into the hallway. The door to our room is cracked open. We enter.

The room is dim, illuminated by one tiny bedside lamp. Sean is crouched on the floor, leaning over his black leather bag, his back to us.

When he hears us enter, he closes the bag and clicks the lock shut. He stands up slowly. He's holding something in his hand. He walks over to the desk near the doorway and drops something on top, a square of newspaper, slightly yellowed. Then he stands back.

"I would never lie to Ellie." He doesn't sound angry, just very sad and very, very tired. And the three of us just stand there staring at the desk. "Go ahead," Sean says. "Read it."

Amanda looks at me, then looks at him, and walks forward. I'm behind her. She picks up the newspaper article and I read the headline over her shoulder.

"Elm Falls Teen Dies of Drug Overdose."

Early Thursday afternoon, just one day after celebrating his 18th birthday, Jason Cullen was found dead in the home of his mother and stepfather in Elm Falls, Illinois, by his stepbrother Sean, 14.

I hear Amanda's sharp intake of breath. Tears spring to my eyes. I look at Sean who is standing silently by the bed. Our eyes meet. I raise my hand to my lips and then look back at the article. *Memorial services were held late Friday at Our Lady of Grace, in West Edgebridge. "He was the kindest person I've ever known," said Max Davies, 20. "My family moved around a lot my entire life, Tennessee, Florida, Pennsylvania, but moving to Chicago was the first time I actually felt at home. And that was because of Jason. He was my first friend and my best friend. The fact that he's no longer alive isn't going to change that."*

His family could not be reached for comment. Authorities have yet to determine whether the overdose was accidental or suicide.

To the right of the article there's a picture of Jason, smiling in a graduation hat. Strong jaw, wide mouth. He looks happy. I feel like I've seen him somewhere before. He has that kind of face.

Sean is standing by the desk, looking down. I go over, lean against him.

"Hey," I say. He looks up and smiles a small sad smile that says, "well, so now you know." It hits me like a brick in the chest. What must it have been like for him? I can just imagine—fourteen-year-old Sean walking into his brother's room to say good morning, to see if his brother wants some breakfast. Jason is lying in his bed, maybe Sean thinks he's asleep. Maybe he always sleeps late and this is a familiar scene, or maybe he usually gets up early and the fact that he's not up yet is already odd. He's lying in bed. Is he dressed? Is he wearing pajamas? His eyes are closed. Maybe Sean says good morning, calls him a dickhead or a snotwad or whatever it is brothers call each other. Sean waits for his brother's response, but it doesn't come. Maybe Sean thinks this is a joke at first, or maybe he thinks his brother is just sleeping extra heavily. Calls his name again. He still doesn't answer.

And again. And again. Exactly how many times does Sean call his brother's name before he realizes something is wrong? Does he shake him? Does he check his breathing and take his pulse? Does he run out of the room? Does he start screaming? Call 911? Does he still have hope or did he know right away? And how does he live with a memory like that floating in his head, polluting and darkening all the others?

I turn to Amanda, who's still staring at the clipping. And she just has this look on her face, maybe it's shame? Maybe it's horror? I don't know. I don't care.

"It's time for you to go now," I say to her.

Amanda reaches out, trying to grab my hand. I move away.

If it is time to pick sides, I am choosing. I have chosen. I lean against Sean. Amanda looks up, her mouth open. "Just go." My voice is cold, hard. Amanda flinches. Things will not be the same after this.

twenty-seven

The moment the door closes behind Amanda, everything changes. It's like she took all the bad air in the room, packed it into her cherry-print LeSportsac, and took it downstairs with her to catch a cab to the airport. And now that she's gone, Sean and I can finally breathe again.

I am about to apologize for what happened, for everything Amanda said, but before I can even start, Sean is turning toward me, a sweet dreamy smile on his lips. "Thank you," he says. He puts one hand on either side of my waist and pulls me toward him. "Thank you." He holds my head against his chest and whispers into my hair. "Thank you, thank you, thank you, thank you." And although I'm not even entirely sure what he's thanking me for, I nod and hug him back. His T-shirt is warm against my skin.

He puts one hand on the side of my neck and brings my face toward his, brushing his lips so gently against my cheek I can barely feel them. He kisses me again, right next to my mouth, again on my chin, my forehead, the tip of my nose, again and again all over my face. When he finally presses his lips against mine, my insides turn to liquid. "Come," he says, and leads me toward the bed. He lies down and pulls me on top of him, arranging my body like a doll's, my head on his chest, my arms around his neck.

"This is fate," Sean whispers. "This is fate, Ellie."

I know there are things I need to tell him, about meeting Monster Hands, what they said about Nina, about the house in Big Sur, and I know I need to call Brad, and maybe my mom, too, but when I look up and see Sean's face, so close to my own, sweet and peaceful, I decide all that other stuff can wait. For the first time in a long time, I'm happy exactly where I am and I'm exactly where I know I need to be.

twenty-eight

At some point during the night, I am jolted awake by motion and noise. Sean kicks at the blankets, his arms are around my shoulders, tightening, releasing his fingers, scratching at my back. He's sweating, his skin hot against mine. I can just barely see him by the moonlight that's coming through the window. His eyes are closed. His face is contorted in pain. Strangled animal cries escape through his clenched teeth.

"Sean," I whisper, and then louder. "Sean!"

He's trying to say something, but the words come out garbled like he's just now learning to speak. "Indint safe-im, Indint safe-im." He's thrashing around.

"You're having a nightmare," I say. I wrap my arms around him. "Everything is okay. You're having a nightmare. Shhhhh." He puts his arms around my waist and clings to me, his head against my chest. I move slightly to adjust the pillow under my head. "Mmmmmm," Sean says. And he shakes his head, like "don't go away," like "stay here with me." Like he's scared I'm going to leave. I stroke his hair. "I'm not going anywhere," I say. And I just lie there with my arms around him. I lie there like that until the cool blue light of morning starts coming through the window. And only then do I finally fall back asleep.

twenty-nine

I wake up with sunlight streaming through the window and my face in Sean's armpit. When I lift my head up, he smiles, and he kisses me on the lips. "Morning, sunshine," he says. "You're an awfully gorgeous thing to wake up to." And he kisses me again.

"Hey," I say. My mouth is dry. I start to get up out of bed.

"Awwww." Sean pulls me down on top of him. "Not yet." He gives me a squeeze. I feel a rush of warmth course through me.

I lean back against him. "Those were some crazy nightmares you were having last night," I say.

"Nightmares?" Sean looks confused. "I was?"

"Yeah," I say. "What were you dreaming about?"

Sean frowns. "Don't remember. And it doesn't matter anymore, anyway." He pulls my head back down and presses it against his chest. I can feel his heart. My phone starts buzzing on the nightstand. I grab it and glance at the screen, the caller ID says *Mon Coeur*.

I look at the clock on the nightstand. 11:17. I was supposed to be at work over two hours ago. Hundreds and hundreds of miles away. "Ooops," I say. I flip open the phone.

"Braddykins! Oh my goodness, I am *so sorry*." But I am smiling because I know as I tell him about me and Sean, he'll be so excited, he won't even care.

"Hey, Ellie," Brad says. He doesn't sound terribly happy.

"I completely forgot to call you!" I say. "I should have asked for today off, too. I'm so sorry! I somehow didn't think of it when I was talking to you on Sunday." I untangle myself from Sean and start to stand up. He grabs my wrist. I smile and blow him a kiss, and then pull away and walk toward the bathroom. "But you won't be mad when you hear where I aaaaaam! I'm in a hotel room with . . ."

"I know," Brad says.

"You do?" I glance at myself in the mirror. My hair looks insane. I try and de-knot it with my fingers.

"I saw Amanda earlier." Brad's voice sounds strained. "She got in at like ten this morning and came by on her way home from the airport."

"Oh?" I freeze.

Brad doesn't say anything for a minute. "Look, Braddy, whatever Amanda said isn't true. And she was a real bitch."

"El." Brad's voice softens. "You know I love you, but Amanda sort of freaked me out a little bit this morning when she was here. She was really worried about you."

"She's not really worried, she's just jealous," I say.

Brad sighs.

"What did she say?" I ask.

"Just that the guy you're with might be . . . a little weird."

"Amanda thinks *everyone* is weird!"

"Well, you have a point there." I can hear Brad smiling through the phone. "When are you coming back?"

I think about the address Peter gave me that's still in my pocket, and I think about Sean back in the bed. "In a few days?"

"Oooookaaaaaay," Brad says. He's trying to sound begrudging, but I can tell from his voice that he's happy for me. And that is why I love him. He *wants* to be happy for other people. Unlike Amanda, who just wants to be controlling and dramatic.

"Thank you, oh Braddiest," I say. And then I pause. "I think he might be my Thomas."

"Well, I think I will have to be the judge of that!" Brad says. "Bring him in to meet me *for real* and then we'll talk."

"Okay!" I say. I rinse my mouth out with water and then start walking out of the bathroom. I hear a beep and look at my phone. The red battery icon is flashing. "Shoot, Braddykins, my phone is out of batteries. I don't have my charger with me so it's about to hang up."

"Okay," Brad says. "I expect stories when you get back! Kissies!"

"Kissies!" I click the phone shut and wander back into the main room.

Sean is still in bed. "Hey, who are you giving kissies to that isn't me?!"

"Brad, from work," I say.

"Well, don't use up any kissies on him that are rightfully mine!"

I smile. "Hey, would it be okay if I used your phone for a second? I'm out of batteries and I should call my mom, I guess."

"Go crazy." Sean tosses me his phone. I open my phone and punch my mom's number into Sean's phone right before my phone powers down. I don't even know my own mother's phone number without my cell phone. How sad is that?

She works the overnight shift on Monday nights, and now it's Tuesday, which means she'll have turned her phone off and she'll be sleeping. I dial her number, it goes straight to voice mail: "Hello, you have reached Jane Wrigley. I'm unavailable at the moment, leave a message and I will call you back as soon as I am able." I can hear the stress in my mother's voice, the lack of joy. It somehow seems even more obvious now than it used to. Maybe because I haven't heard it in a few days, maybe because I'm suddenly so happy. "Hi, Mom," I say. "Just wanted to let you know I've been at Amanda's house these last few days, which you probably assumed. And I'm still here. Anyway, okay. Hope work is going okay. Bye!" I hang up. A tiny part of me feels the tiniest bit guilty for lying, but what's the alternative?

Sean reaches up and grabs me around the waist, pulls me down into bed with him.

"I was supposed to work this morning. And I totally forgot," I say.

"Oh, what a terrible shame," he says. He nuzzles my neck.

"It's okay, though, Brad's not upset." I sit up.

"Cool," says Sean. "But, y'know, you don't have to have a job anymore if you don't want to."

"Huh?"

"Well, as you know, I have plenty of money, and I hope this offer won't make you feel weird or anything." Sean blushes. "But you could just have some."

I can feel myself blushing, too. "That's really sweet," I say. "But I'd . . ."

"Wait, wait, wait," Sean says. "Get that *no* look off your face. I'm just saying that if we decide we don't want to come back for a while, if we just want to go on a road trip somewhere else, maybe drive over to my family's vacation house and just relax there for a while, you shouldn't feel like we can't because you have to go back to work, that's all I'm saying." Sean smiles again. "Maybe we *should* go to the vacation house. It's really beautiful up there and I haven't actually been in like two years. Or we could go visit, I don't know, anyone. We could just pick some random person on the Internet and then ask them, 'Hey, can we come over for dinner?' and then we can just drive to wherever they are. We can bring a pie! Or we could go to the Grand Canyon. Have you ever seen it? Not just a big hole in the ground! Makes a person feel tiny in the best way possible."

I smile. "That all sounds really wonderful . . . but there are some things we haven't even talked about yet!"

"Oh!" Sean says. "Of course. I should have brought it up already, I'm really sorry about that."

"It's okay."

"No, I mean it, I'm sorry. I swear I wasn't hitting on her, things were just so awkward between you and me then and I wasn't sure what you were thinking and I didn't want to pressure you about anything. I was just trying to be friendly to that girl, but I can see how that would have been awful for you. If it'd been the other way around, I would have been so jealous. And don't worry, I'm not mad about that dude."

"What dude?"

"The one from last night, the one you were dancing with," Sean says. "None of that matters now. That feels like so long ago, anyway."

"I was talking about Nina," I say. "And me meeting Monster Hands."

"Oh," Sean says. "Right, of course." He shakes his head. "Tell me."

I repeat the story and show him the record. "And that guy Peter wrote down the address of that house they dropped her off at." I take the tiny slip of paper from the pocket of my jeans.

I hand it to Sean.

"Thirteen seventy-two Ledgeview Pass, Big Sur, California," he says very slowly, very deliberately. "This is where they dropped her off?" He sits down on the bed, his back to me. He coughs. The tips of his ears are turning red.

"Yeah," I say. "So I guess that's the next stop!"

Sean coughs again. "I don't know." He shakes his head. I walk over to the bed and sit next to him. "Didn't you say Monster Hands already looked for her there?"

"But no one was at the house." My voice sounds weird. "I just figured it'd be worth the trip just to check the place out, because that place obviously meant something to her, she definitely went there once . . . I mean, y'know, like the rest of the places we've been going." I'm suddenly very confused.

Sean takes a deep breath. "Are you *sure* you want to? I mean are you sure you want to just keep going like this?"

"I don't know what you mean."

"Just"— Sean breathes out through his nose —"well, I've been thinking about it, and I wonder if *this*"— he moves his hands back and forth between us —"is the reason you found that drawing of Nina's. Not so you could find Nina, but so we could find each other." He puts a warm hand on my arm, and looks me straight in the eye. I feel that flash again, the one I felt when I first met him. Only now for some reason it makes me nervous.

"But what about what we talked about?" I say. "About how it's impossible to just get over a thing like this? About how . . ." I stop. He's staring blankly at the wall. My face grows hot. What's going on here? I turn away.

"Hey, heeeey." Sean's voice softens. "Oh shit! I'm sorry. I'm sorry, Ellie." Sean sighs and shakes his head. "I'm not trying to keep you from searching for her. Forget what I said, okay? We'll go to Big Sur and look for her." He wraps his arms around my waist. "We'll leave right now, okay?" He squeezes me tight. I can feel his heart pounding hard through his shirt. This is Sean, sweet, wonderful Sean.

I nod, and then I smile as relief washes over me. "You'll love her," I say. "When you meet her, you'll really love her."

Sean doesn't even smile back this time. He just steadies my face with his hands and looks me straight in the eye. "I couldn't love anyone else now," Sean says. "Because I already love you."

thirty

According to the clock, we've been driving for an hour, but it feels like it could have been a minute or a week or a year. Time doesn't matter anymore.

And for that matter, neither do words. We're immersed in silence, not the cold jagged silence of yesterday, but a different kind, like warm liquid. Everything we need to say we communicate through our hands clasped together between the seats, through the tiny gentle motions of finger against finger, palm against palm.

And all I can think is *This is it, this is what it's like to be falling in love.*

Sean pulls off at an exit for a rest stop. "We need snacks," he says. "And gas, too." He drives for another minute and then parks. He stares out at the parking lot, and I try to interpret the look on his face. He looks a little anxious. I squeeze his hand and smile. He smiles back. "I'm just going to run in here," he says. He unplugs his phone from the car charger, squeezes my hand, and gets out of the car.

I lean back against the seat and watch him walk across the parking lot. I love the way he walks, shoulders squared, head hanging down ever so slightly. I put my bare feet up against the dash, the cool air blows against my legs. Over the soft hum of the air conditioner I can hear the muted blend of sounds from outside. Laughter and shouts and cries and car horns. Sean disappears into the rest stop.

I watch a couple in matching khaki shorts and matching white baseball hats walk toward their car, drinking sodas. A mother is walking in, carrying a screaming little boy who is tossing french fries onto the ground. A group of college-age girls stand near the trunk of an old Toyota while one of them changes into a pair of flip-flops. If it were a week ago I might have felt nothing for these random strangers. But now, in this moment, I love them all, and at the same time I feel sad for them, because none of them could possibly be feeling what I'm feeling now—the bliss that comes from being with someone who loves you, whom you are starting to love.

I always thought it was so silly the way Amanda's friends were always meeting guys and then a week later claiming to *looooove* them. I always figured they were just caught up in the moment, being immature, and not understanding Real Life. But I realize now, Real Life is lots of things, not just the hard stuff but the wonderful stuff, too. I guess *I* was the one who really didn't understand. And now, because of some sort of crazy miracle that I can only barely comprehend, I think I'm starting to.

A minute passes, and then another one. And I stare anxiously at the door. And I feel a gnawing in my stomach and I realize something so silly it makes me laugh out loud — I miss him. Sean has been in the rest stop for all of four minutes and I *miss* him. I laugh again. I will tell him this when he gets back. He will love this. He will laugh, too!

And then we will drive to Big Sur where I very well might, no, scratch that, where I *will* find a clue that will lead me to Nina. And then my life will be perfect. Then my life will be absolutely complete.

I watch the door. Four guys emerge with McDonald's bags. The woman with the screaming kid is walking out with a ketchup-stained shirt and a pile of napkins. And then there's Sean walking through the door; he's so beautiful, so incredibly beautiful. I remember the first moment I saw him, back at the Mothership. Back then, if someone had told me what he would end up meaning to me only four days later, I never would have believed it. How could I have? How could I have even begun to understand?

As he gets closer, my heart pounds harder. I smile, giddy with anticipation for the moment when he opens the car door, for the moment when I'll get to touch him again. He's close enough now for me to see his face clearly. He's staring at the car window, at me. But he doesn't smile. He has this crazy look on his face that I don't understand.

He walks past the driver's side door, around the front of the car. I roll down the window. "Hey? What's going on?" My heart is pounding. Did he lose his wallet or some-thing? He doesn't answer. Just keeps walking until he's standing right in front of the passenger side door. "Hey?" I reach out and put my hand on his arm. "Is everything okay?"

Sean doesn't say anything. He just takes my hand and gently, puts it back inside the car. He opens the car door and reaches and unbuckles my seat belt and wraps his arms around me. He holds me tightly against him. His skin smells warm. "Oh, Ellie," he says. He leans back. Takes both of my hands and holds them in his. He raises my right hand to his lips and kisses it. And then does the same thing with my left one. He looks like he's about to cry. My heart is pounding now. I can feel the adrenaline rushing up and down my spine.

"Ellie," Sean says. "I have to tell you something."

I look up at him. "Okay?" A horrible thought flashes into my head—he has a girlfriend. Oh God. Amanda was right. I start to turn away. "Ellie, please look at me," he says. "Please." I stare into his eyes.

"My family knows this private investigator, okay? My father hired him for something once, a few years ago, some-thing for his company." He pauses. Takes a deep breath. "This guy is pretty much the very best there is. He's an ex-FBI agent and has contacts everywhere. If a person exists on this earth, he can find them."

"Uh-huh . . ."

"So when I first met you and found out about Nina, I thought, maybe I was meant to meet you to help you with this, to help you find her. I called him when we stopped at that first rest stop on the way to Nebraska."

I nod.

"I didn't want to get your hopes up in case he didn't find anything, so that's why I didn't mention it before."

I nod again.

"Anyway, yesterday when we were at the show, when you were dancing with that guy, I went outside and called him to check in." The tears in Sean's eyes look like they're about to spill over. "He had some information."

I feel my heart pounding. It's pounding so hard and loud that I can barely hear Sean anymore.

"This morning, when I was saying how I thought maybe we should stop looking . . . I"— Sean's voice cracks —"it's because I had talked to him before and the stuff he said did not sound good and . . ."

"Did he find her?" I hear my voice ask. I sound so quiet, like I'm far, far away from myself. "Did he?"

"Ellie," Sean says. He looks down. And looks up. He opens his mouth, his lips are moving. But, the weird thing is, I can't hear anything. It's like the world has gone mute. He's motioning with his hands. He's nodding. But *I don't hear anything,* except for the beating of my own heart, like someone pounding on a drum inside me. Pounding over and over and over. And I'm frozen. Sean puts his hands on my shoulders. And shakes them gently. I hear a gurgling, like water rushing past my head. And then suddenly the sound comes back, loud, too loud. Cars honking. People laughing. One of the college kids calling out to her friend something about some onion rings.

"I'm sorry, I didn't hear you," I say to Sean. And I smile. Because it is awfully strange to suddenly go deaf in the middle of a parking lot. So strange it's funny, really.

"That investigator found out about Nina," Sean says. "She died." Sean looks at me again. "She's dead, Ellie."

And I nod. Because turns out I guess I did hear him after all. But I can't think about any of this right this moment because someone is screaming, a high-pitched, bloodcurdling, ragged shriek of a scream. A scream so loud that everyone turns in the direction of the scream. And it makes it hard to think, all that screaming. And then I realize something: It's not just someone screaming. It's me.

thirty-one

I remember one night when I was seven, lying in my bed, scared and confused, listening to my parents fighting. They always fought, but that particular night it was so loud that I could even make out actual words: my father yelling that he was leaving, and my mom screaming that he should stop threatening and just get the hell out already.

I was young enough then that hearing my mother say "hell" shocked me and made tears spring to my eyes.

After hours of turning over and over in my bed, my door creaked open and Nina crept in. It must have been right around midnight. I remember the way she looked, standing there in her pajamas, backlit by my night-light. Without saying anything, she took my hand and led me out into the hallway, then into the bathroom and shut the door behind us. She flipped on the lights. She was wearing her fluffy orange earmuffs, and she was holding my green ones in her hand. She put them over my ears and then she turned on the shower. But my parents' shouts were so loud that we could still hear them, over all of that, we could still hear them.

So then with her earmuffs on, the water pounding against the bath mat, she turned toward me and began to sing:

HAPPY BIRTHDAY TO YOU,
HAPPY BIRTHDAY TOOO YOOOOOOOU

It was late September and my birthday was in February, but Nina had always said "Happy Birthday" was the best song in the world because it was the only song everyone would sing just for you. And even if it wasn't for you, if you were hearing it you'd probably get to eat some cake soon.

HAPPY BIRTHDAY, DEAR BELLLYYYYYYYYYY . . .
HAPPY BIRTHDAY TOOO YOUUUUUU

She grinned at me and then started again.

HAPPY BIRTHDAY TO YOU
HAPPY BIRTHDAY TOOO YOUUUUUU
HAPPY BIRTHDAY, DEAR BELLYYYYYYYYY
HAPPY BIRTHDAY TOOOO YOUUUUUUU

I remember feeling the confusion and sadness lifting. And then she started a third time.

HAPPY BIRTHDAY TO YOU
HAPPY BIRTHDAY TOOO YOOOOOOOUUUU

By the time I joined in, I was smiling, too, and the world was starting to make sense again. So my parents were crazy. So what? It didn't matter because I had a big sister, *a big sister*! And she would take care of everything, just like she always did.

HAPPY BIRTHDAY, DEAR NIIIIIIINAAAAAAAAAA

HAPPY BIRTHDAY TOOO YOOUUUUUUU

We sang as loud as we could, for all we were worth, while the bathroom filled up with steam.

HAPPY BIRTHDAY TOOO YOOOOOOOOU

We sang it over and over and over until our voices were hoarse and the fibers on our earmuffs were wet with the steam. Over and over and over and over, smiling at each other the entire time.

After what felt like the millionth verse, we finally stopped to catch our breath. We could no longer hear any screaming. Nina opened the bathroom door a crack just to make sure. The cool air rushed in and steam escaped out into the dark silent hallway.

But Nina just looked at me then and grinned and closed the door. And we just kept on singing.

thirty-two

I am outside of my body now, watching as Ellie, who has just found out her sister is not alive anymore, sits back up and wipes the vomit off her chin.

This is how Ellie reacts when she finds out her sister is dead: She screams for a while and then she barfs on the pavement.

Ellie wants to ask questions, but it is hard at this particular moment for her to remember what words are and how to form them with her mouth. She closes her eyes until eventually a word drips down from her brain and pops out her mouth.

"How?" Is this the word she meant?

Sean reaches out and puts his hands on Ellie's shoulders. She can't even feel it. "Are you sure you want to hear this right now?"

Ellie says, "Yes."

"She was killed," Sean says. And then he winces, as though wincing for Ellie who is just sitting there perfectly still. "She was living in Las Vegas and working in a club as—" Sean looks hesitant "—as a stripper. She started dating a guy who was a big poker player. He was known for making really insane bets. Sometimes he'd win a couple hundred thousand dollars in a night. And other times he'd lose it. He had a losing streak once, a serious one. And he borrowed money from some really bad people and then he couldn't pay it back. And one night the guy he borrowed money from started beating him up, really badly, out in the parking lot of the club where Nina worked. He'd come to pick her up and the guys he owed money to found him there. Nina was upset. She got involved. There were guns. And . . ." Sean pauses again, as though he's scared to tell the end of the story, as though if he just doesn't say it, it won't have really happened. He takes a deep breath. ". . . She got shot and then that was it."

Sean looks down, and then back up. His mouth twists itself into a grimace of pain. He probably feels worse than Ellie does, because, truthfully, she doesn't feel much of anything at all. To her it sounds like she is hearing about characters in a story, a story that has nothing whatsoever to do with her. She knows she is supposed to feel something now, or supposed to do something now, but for the life of her she cannot remember what that is.

"Oh," she says. And she sits there, unsure whether she is frozen in one moment or if time is still passing. "When?" Ellie asks. "How long ago?"

"Just over a year ago," says Sean.

And Ellie nods as though, well, yes, of course that's when it would have happened.

"I need to talk to the investigator," Ellie says calmly. "Can you call him back please?"

Sean nods. Ellie waits as he dials. After a moment or two Sean shakes his head. "Voice mail," Sean says. "He told me he's on assignment when I just talked to him, so he's probably not able to answer his phone." And then back into the phone he says, "Hey, Doug, it's Sean Lerner calling again. We just spoke a minute ago, but we need to ask you some more questions, please give me a call back." And then he closes the phone and looks at Ellie. "We'll try him again later, if he doesn't call back in a couple of hours."

Ellie nods, as though she understands. But here's the most perplexing part. For an entire year Ellie has been living on a planet that her sister is not a part of, for an entire year, and somehow *Ellie didn't even know*. Ellie stares out the window at the people in the parking lot, walking places, holding things, talking to one another, eating. All those people have managed to survive all the many different things in the world that could kill a person, all the different times they were in danger, all the different times they could have died, they didn't.

And Nina did.

I pop back into my body then, to share this thought with

myself: *The world doesn't make any sense at all.* People tell you it does, try and pretend it does. But I know now what kind of place this is, what kind of world we live in. And my breath catches in my throat, and my heart rips apart not just for me, not just for Nina, but for all of us.

thirty-three

It doesn't take long for me to remember how to cry. I lean over in the front seat, my arm against the dashboard, my head against my arm, the sobs coming out of me as though all the holes in my face lead to an endless supply of tears. The images cycle through my brain like a photo slide show with my crying as the soundtrack:

Nina blowing up a hundred balloons and filling my room for my ninth birthday. Nina drawing a little cartoon about my socks and leaving it in my sock drawer as though my socks drew it themselves. Nina driving us to 7-Eleven the day after she got her license, flirting with a guy in the parking lot until he bought me a Slurpee and her a six-pack of Amstel. Nina coming back home at five in the morning after having snuck out five hours earlier, a mischievous smile on her face, putting her finger to her lips and winking as she slipped back into her room.

But then the other images come, invading my brain, without warning or permission. Nina running out into the parking lot of some strip club, a jacket on over high heels and fishnets. Her boyfriend lying on the ground, a large hulk of a man over him, kicking him. Nina taking a leap, flying through the air onto his back. The large man stumbling forward, then backward. Shaking her off him. Her falling to the ground. And then what? I squeeze my eyes shut and wince. I do not want to think about these things. I can't stop myself. Does she see the gun? Is she scared? Does he hold it over her and pause, make her apologize before he shoots? Or is it a surprise, a single bullet in the back of her head, the hot pain searing through her with no warning, her dying thought a question: What the *hell* was *that*?

I can't believe this is real. It is too much. It is just too much. The tears come harder now.

We are driving again. It's later. I'm not sure what time it is. Or where we are exactly. But what does it matter? No matter where I go, this will be the truth. No matter what time it is, this will be the truth. I cannot escape from it. I will never be able to.

I cry for a while more and then I pass into a weird place of calm, an empty bubble of blank space in between all these tears, and lift my head up. In front of us is the highway. This is what the highway looks like to me after I know my sister is dead. This is what it feels like to sit in the car after I know my sister is dead. This is what it feels like to breathe after I know my sister is dead.

I turn toward Sean, he's chewing his bottom lip, like he wants to say something but isn't sure he should. "Go on," I say.

Sean takes a breath. "Do you wish I hadn't told you? I thought about not . . . I thought maybe if I convinced you to give up looking . . ." Sean pauses. "Would it be better if you didn't know?"

But now that I know, it's hard to even imagine what it was like when I didn't. I feel like I have aged a hundred years since this morning, since an hour ago. I feel sorry for that poor innocent Ellie of earlier today, who so naively believed that everything was going to be fine. I shake my head. "The only way it would be better is if it hadn't happened," I say. And hearing myself say these words, the crying starts again.

Sean reaches out and squeezes my knee. "I've been through this," Sean says. "I will go through this with you, Ellie. You won't be alone. I promise you won't be alone."

And I nod, grateful at least for that.

thirty-four

We're at a motel now, the Grand Canyon Cactus Lodge, a group of wood buildings surrounding a parking lot. It's nothing like the fancy places we were at before, it's not even touristy, it's the type of place people go to sink into anonymity, the type of place people go to hide.

I am sitting on a bed, my bare legs against a faded scratchy Aztec-print comforter, leaning against a chipped plywood headboard. I am having another one of those strange blank moments. My head feels like it's stuffed with thick cotton that somehow cushions my brain from all my thoughts.

"Are you hungry?" Sean asks. He is next to me, holding my limp hand, looking at me with such concern. I am grateful to him for being here, for expecting nothing from me. But I don't have the energy to express this right now.

I shake my head.

"If I get you something, will you eat it? I think I saw a

pizza place near here. I could call information and find out the number." He pats his pockets like he's looking for his cell phone. He makes a slightly confused face. "Or we could eat brownies out of the vending machine."

And then I start crying again. Nina loved vending machines.

"What am I supposed to *do* now?" I say.

"You don't need to think about that," Sean says. "I'll do all the thinking for both of us. You cry it out. And I will take care of you."

And I lean back against the pillow. I am holding my phone limply in my hand.

"My battery died," I say. And I feel the tears slipping down my cheeks now. "I can't call anyone, because I don't even know anyone's number."

"You don't need to call anyone," Sean says. "You don't need to tell anyone."

And I want to believe him. I try to believe him, but I know that no matter how long I wait, at some point I will have to be the one to call my mother and tell her her daughter is dead. And Amanda, I will have to tell her. And Brad. And . . . I am crying harder now. How can I exist in a world that I know Nina is not in? And do I even want to?

Sean puts his arms around me and pulls me toward him, pressing my face against his chest.

"We don't have to go back," Sean whispers. "We don't have to ever go back."

All I can do is nod. I can feel the tears spreading out, soaking through his shirt, until my entire face is wet with them.

thirty-Five

Sean is in bed asleep, his cheeks flushed, his hands curled into fists around the edges of the scratchy brown blanket. He is smiling, just slightly. And I am awake watching him.

I do not think I will ever sleep again. The limp wet sadness of earlier is gone, having been replaced by a hard nugget lodged in my center, its sharp jagged edges piercing my insides, filling me with a thousand questions. Who was the man that killed her? And where is he now? Is he alive? Is he in jail? And what about this boyfriend, this boyfriend she died for? Where is he? And who is he? And what about Nina? Did someone have to go identify her at the hospital? And why didn't anyone ever call my mom? And where is her body buried? *Her body.* Her body that she is no longer in. Her body that is just meat now.

The fact that I've just had this thought fills me with such horror I gasp. I bring my hand up to my mouth. I take my hand away. The faint outline of a monster face remains on the inside of my wrist—the stamp from the Monster

Hands show. The album. It's in the car. Nina's drawing. I have to get out of here, get out of this room. I can't breathe. I get up and walk across the beige, water-stained carpet. Sean's jeans are neatly folded and lying on top of the dresser. I reach into his pocket and get his keys. I wrap my fist around them to keep them from jingling. I glance at Sean one last time, and slip out.

I walk through the parking lot toward Sean's car. Stop, stare in the window. The album is sitting on the cupholder between the two front seats. My heart is pounding hard. I unlock Sean's car door and climb in, sit down, reach for the album. I remove the plastic shrink-wrap and take out the record—dark gray grooved plastic with large, even darker gray fingers printed on the side, as though a giant gray hand is trying to grab it. Something flutters to the floor. The lyrics printed on a delicate sheet of rice paper in dark gray ink. I read the first song.

"Wherever Nina Lies"
Her face changes when she thinks you can't see her.
Staring out the window, always watching, someone's
> *chasing her.*
She twists her hands, draws pictures on her wrist,
> *bites her lips.*
Ask a question, she just shakes her head, won't answer it.
She cries at night, always cries at night, she thinks you
> *can't hear it.*

*Try and tell her it's okay, but you know she can't
   believe it.*
Ask her why and she only shakes her head no.
She says one day she'll go as far as she can go.
She says one day she'll go as far as she can go.

And I feel my lips curving into a smile. I know just what this last line means, even more than whoever wrote it did: When Nina was fifteen, and I was eleven, we got kind of obsessed with the weird local commercials that would come on late, late at night on cable. Sometimes when our mom was working the overnight shift, we'd stay up until one, two, three in the morning just waiting for them to come on. We loved the ad for Hammer Jones's Hardware featuring "Hammer Jones himself," and a spot for a local hair salon showing a woman with a bunch of foil on her head whom we recognized as the cashier at the drugstore. But our very favorite was a very silly ten-second ad for Covered Wagon Shipping in which a trucker dressed in colonial clothing said, "Whatever you need shipped, I'll personally drive it myself from just across the street"—flash to him driving the truck across a street—"to clear across the country. *That's as far as you can go!*" Flash to him driving past a piece of poster board onto which someone had written, *Welcome to San Francisco* in orange marker. Nina and I absolutely loved this commercial and it became a long-running joke for us. For years all one of us had to do was say, "I'm going about as far as you can go!" and the other one would crack up.

I can just imagine the guys from Monster Hands asking Nina where she was headed and Nina reciting this line. Maybe laughing a little to herself. Maybe thinking of me while she did. I smile, for a second, just for a second before I remember that figuring out the song lyrics is not a triumph now. This is not the next clue. This is not anything.

I look out over the empty parking lot. All the motel windows are dark. I clutch the song lyrics to my chest. It is so quiet out here. I feel like I am the only person in the world.

But the silence is interrupted by a buzzing coming from under one of the car seats. I lean over. A tiny red light is blinking between the seats. Sean's cell phone. I reach down and pick it up. It's 3:16 A.M. *Unavailable* is blinking on the screen. It's probably another one of those wrong numbers.

I am suddenly filled with such deep anger at whoever is calling, for interrupting me, for being alive when Nina isn't. I answer the phone.

"She gave you a fake number," I say. "Whoever you think you are calling, this is not them. This is SEAN'S PHONE," I say. "Sean. A boy." I pause. "You do not know him!" My heart is pounding. No answer. "Hello?" I hear breathing on the other end. And then there's a voice, very quiet, barely more than a whisper.

"Get away from him, it's not safe for you there."

My heart starts pounding. This is obviously just a wrong number, some stupid kid playing a prank probably. Or maybe Amanda is somehow involved in this.

"Who is this?" I say. But they've already hung up. I don't want to be in this parking lot anymore in the dark. I put the phone down on the seat next to me. I don't want to touch it. I just want to go back inside the motel. I'm scared.

There's a tapping on the window. I turn to the right. A hand. Big eyes. A face. There is a face, someone watching me through the window. I open my mouth and scream.

The door opens and a pair of strong arms wrap around me.

"Hey, hey, hey, hey, it's okay, baby." It's Sean. "It's just me. It's just me." He rocks me back and forth. "I woke up and you weren't there."

"I couldn't sleep," I say.

"What are you doing out here?" he says.

"I wanted to see that Monster Hands record," I say. "I just had this feeling that I needed to see it that . . ."

"Oh, Ellie." Sean's sweet face is creased with concern. He shakes his head.

"But you don't understand," I say. I look down at the lyrics in my lap. "I know where she was going. This song is about her. And this part, about going as far as she can go, that's about going to San Francisco. It's a joke we had when we were younger. That's where she wanted to go. That's where she would be if she hadn't . . ." My voice breaks then. I can't even bring myself to say it.

"I think it's time to let go now," Sean says. "It's time to let go."

Sean's phone starts vibrating again. He snatches the phone off the seat and hits *Ignore*. He slips the phone in his pocket. And then he takes both of my hands in his and puts them up against his chest, so I can feel his heart through his shirt. "That part of your life is over now," he says.

Back in the room, I drift in and out of a thick heavy sleep that paralyzes my limbs and fills my head with crazy dreams. Fast flashes of brilliant colors interspersed with slow-moving images, almost white, like a video made on a too-sunny day. Real memories and made-up ones mixing themselves together—Nina and I at a birthday party eating cake with our hands. Nina and I trying on dresses at Attic. Sean and Nina playing tag. Sean and I in bed in the hotel. Sean standing on a chair in this very hotel room, pushing something in between the blankets at the top of the closet, looking down to make sure I'm not awake to see him. Nina and I toasting each other in a fancy restaurant. Nina and I running away from home. Nina and I in France. Nina in a car with Sean's brother, driving away from the house we grew up in, waving, waving, waving good-bye.

thirty-six

I do not have the luxury of forgetting. There is no moment of blank calm, no moment of peace before reality catches up. I wake up as the sun rises, remembering exactly where I am and exactly what has happened. I'm crying before I even open my eyes. This is the first morning I've had to know it. Yesterday seems hazy, like a dream, a dream full of paranoia and denial and trying to convince myself that reality was not reality. But this morning I have woken up with a clear mind at the bottom of a well. Now this is real. This is all completely real. And now I have to deal with it.

It is time to tell my mother.

I can hear the sound of water coming from the bathroom. The shower is on.

I get out of bed. There is a beige plastic phone on the bedside table. I pick up the slightly sticky headset and hold it to my ear. How will I find her number? I called her on Sean's phone, when was it, two days ago?

Sean is singing in the shower. Loudly and terribly. His phone is blinking on the desk.

I flip it open and go to the call log. There's my mother's number right there. I hold it in my hand as I dial 7-7-3-5-5-5-7-6-4 . . . I am about to dial the last digit when I realize something strange. Something so strange my heart starts pounding before I'm even done processing. The call log. There's the incoming call from Unavailable that I answered in the car last night. And before that there's a call to voice mail. And then there's my call to my mother on Tuesday morning. And before that, there's a number Sean called on Saturday a few hours after we started driving to Nebraska. The number looks weirdly familiar.

But there were no other calls made on this phone between my call to my mother and the call I made last night except for the one call to voice mail at around four-thirty yesterday. Which is right around when Sean told me Nina was dead.

One call to voice mail when Sean said he was calling the investigator's number.

So when did Sean talk to the investigator exactly?

I am sure there is a reasonable explanation for this. I'm sure there is. There has to be.

My heart is pounding harder now. The phone starts blinking in my hand again. The unavailable number is calling again. And I don't think. I just pick up.

"Hello?" I whisper. I don't hear anything for a moment. And then a voice, whispering back.

"Are you alone?"

I stare at the bathroom door. I don't think I hear the rush of the water anymore. I think the shower has been shut off. Sean will be back any second.

"Are you alone?" the voice says again.

"Yes," I whisper. My hands are sweating. "Who is this?"

"Is this Ellie?"

My heart stops at the sound of my name. "Who is this?" I ask again.

"You called me the other day," the voice says. "You were looking for your sister. My name is Max and I know her . . ." The bathroom door opens a crack, a trail of steam escaping. It looks like smoke. ". . . and Sean did, too."

"Wh. . ." I start to say. But before I can get any words out the bathroom door opens.

I snap the phone shut and toss it onto the bed just as Sean emerges from the bathroom, his hair damp, a white towel wrapped around his waist, another one hanging around his neck.

"You're up," he says. He takes the corner of the towel around his neck and dries his face. It's flushed with heat.

"I'm up," I say. Panic courses through me. But somehow I manage to twist my face into something resembling a smile.

"Well, you look like you're feeling a little better this morning," he says.

"Yeah," I say. "Maybe a tiny bit."

My mind races. Max. The guy I called from Attic, the guy whose phone number was written on the drawing, is the same guy who just called me on Sean's phone. But how did he get Sean's number? It was his number I called. I reach out, grab my jeans off the floor, fish the cardboard credit card out of my back pocket. The number on the drawing *is the number Sean called on Saturday a few hours after we left my house!*

What the hell does all this mean? It means Sean is hiding some things and probably lying about some things. Does this mean . . . *Sean could have lied about Nina being dead?*

With that simple thought, I can feel something happening inside me. Hope is bubbling up. The guy on the phone said he *knows* Nina. Not *knew* her. *Knows* her. Like she is around to know. I feel my mouth curling into a smile and quickly stop it.

Sean walks over and stands in front of me, his chest dotted with beads of water.

"What are you looking at that for?" Sean asks. He's staring down at the cardboard credit card clutched in my hand.

"I don't know," I say. I look up.

"I think it's time to let this go now, Ellie," he says. Sean snatches the card from my hand. The little sketch Nina drew of me is staring back at me. I look scared.

Sean walks toward the bathroom.

"Wait!" I say.

"I'm doing you a favor," he calls out

"WAIT!"

He closes the door behind him, a second later I hear the toilet flush.

Sean comes back into the bedroom. "After Jason died there were certain things I held on to, things that reminded me of him, and I couldn't move on until I let them go." He smiles at me, reaches out to stroke my face. "I think it will help you not to have that around," he says. Then he takes the towel from around his neck and starts rubbing his damp head. I stare at him. Who *is* this person I have spent the last five days with? Who I have shared a bed with? I suddenly feel like I've never seen him before in my life.

His left arm is up behind his head, the skin between his elbow and his armpit covered in those thin white scars. I remember tracing them with my fingers three nights ago when we got drunk in the hotel room. I remember thinking they were somehow beautiful in their chaos. But as I stare at them now, they start to look different. They are not chaos at all, there's an order to them, a pattern in the jumble.

Letters. They are letters. Carved in and then covered over with hatch marks, as though he was trying to hide them. But when you know what to look for, they come through. Four letters. Carved into his skin.

N I N A.

I can't breathe.

I want to be imagining this. But now that I've seen it, it's impossible to un-see it. Her name, there it is. It was there all along.

My brain is spiraling out of control. I feel my lips parting. I can't breathe. Sean is staring at my face. I look down.

"I think I'm going to take a shower," I manage to say.

"Okay," Sean smiles sweetly. He reaches out to put his arms around me. His skin is warm but touching him gives me chills. Over his shoulder, I see the blankets up at the top of the closet. I remember my dream last night, which maybe wasn't a dream at all . . .

"Could you go and get us some food?" I say. "I mean, while I'm in the shower."

Sean smiles again. "You're hungry?"

"I'm suddenly starving."

"What do you want? Name anything and I'll go and get it."

"A salad," I say. "A really giant salad, with a lot of things in it."

"For breakfast?"

I nod.

"Okay, whatever you want," he says quickly. "I'll have it for you when you get out." He sounds so pleased then, pleased that I'm asking him for something, pleased that it's something he's able to do for me.

I nod, and force another smile. I manage to keep my knees from buckling until the bathroom door is closed safely behind me. I turn the water on and wait, my ear pressed against the door until I hear the outside door slam shut. And only then do I let myself scream.

thirty-seven

There is no time to think.

I drag the heavy desk chair over to the closet, climb up, and stick my hands between the scratchy beige blankets on the top shelf. Only a few inches in, my hands hit leather. *So I wasn't dreaming after all.* I reach in further, it's a handle. I grab it and pull out Sean's leather messenger bag. It feels warm, alive, like whatever's in here has a pulse of its own.

I jump off the chair and crouch down on the floor.

The bag is locked with a five-dial combination lock with letters where you'd normally find numbers. I tug on the lock. There's no way I'm going to be able to break in and the leather of the bag is definitely too thick to cut through.

I'm just going to have to try and unlock it with a guess. I rotate the tiny dials as fast as I can:

N-I-N-A-W

No.

J-A-S-O-N

No.

A-N-G-R-Y

No.

A-B-C-D-E

No.

I need to get into this bag.

S-E-A-N-L

Damn.

N-O-S-A-J

Shit.

W-A-N-I-N

Fuck. Now what?!

I take a deep breath and a thought pops into my head. That bathroom wall back in Nebraska. Nina's graffiti. Cakey ♥'s J. CAKEY.

I turn the tiny dials one by one. I am all sweating palms and pounding heart.

C-A-K-E-Y

I hold my breath and pull down on the lock.

It pops right open.

I breathe out. Breathe in. Breathe out again. Once I see what's in here, there will be no going back.

I lift open the top of the bag and dump the contents on the floor. The newspaper article about Jason, a pile of envelopes, a drawing, and a photograph. I pick it up. It's of Nina and someone else . . . I bring the picture closer to my face so I can get a better look. *Oh shit.* It's Sean's brother, Jason.

In the picture Nina and Jason are sitting behind a giant wooden dining room table with their arms around each other, smiling these giant glowing smiles. The table in front of them is covered in the remnants of a party: wrapping paper, a big pile of what look like pink Hostess Sno Balls, beer bottles, etc. Also on the table is a snowboard covered in ink drawings of the two of them, with a bow on top. They're sitting in front of a silver wall with a black rocket ship painted on it.

I've seen this wall, at the Mothership. I flip the picture over. In Nina's handwriting: *I love you J.*

J as in Jason.

Oh God.

I move on to the drawing.

I smile for the briefest of seconds despite everything that's going on. This is just so *Nina.* Only now I'm completely baffled because . . . Nina drew this for *Sean*? No wait . . . no she didn't.

He changed it. Sean took a drawing meant for Jason and *he changed the name* so he could pretend it had been drawn for him. My stomach tightens and I feel like I'm about to puke.

I let the paper fall from my hand and look down at the letters. There are dozens of them.

I pick up the one on top. My hands are shaking. The letter is dated June 24, the night Nina disappeared.

Dearest Nina,

I understand how hard all of this must be for you, but I hope you know that I truly meant everything I said at Jason's funeral. I am here for you now, to lean on, to talk to, for whatever you

need. I am here for you with all my heart, and I will always be here. No matter what. I don't actually know where I'm going to send this letter because I don't know where you are right now. But I'm sure you'll be back soon so I guess I'll just keep this for you. I want us to go through this together Nina. We need each other now more than ever.

With love,
Sean

Oh my God. I flip through the stack.

Nina,

I went to the Mothership again looking for you today. I don't understand why you'd leave and not tell me where you went? We need each other now. We are supposed to be going through this together!! No one else can understand you the way I can. No one else can be here for you now the way I can be. Why won't you let me?

Nina, I went to the Mothership last night. Some guy said he thought you'd been staying there but that you were gone now. He hadn't seen you in days. Where are you? Where are you? Where are you? Where are you? I need to find you. Nothing makes any sense anymore. You need me now. YOU NEED ME! Why don't you understand that?

Nina, the police came to my house today to ask me questions about where Jason might have gotten the heroin. I told them that

I had no idea. But where would they have gotten the idea that I would?

Nina,

I called your house today looking for you. Your mother got angry and told me to stop calling. It's been almost two entire weeks since Jason went away. I've been trying not to sleep, because when I do the screaming starts inside my head and it doesn't stop. I can't get you out of my head. I feel like maybe you have an idea what I did. But anything I did, I only did for us. You must know that. Come back to me.

I flip a few letters ahead.

It's been a month now. Where are you? Every night, when I lie down, he's back and he's begging me not to do it. But time is all funny and really the decision has already been made. I try and tell him that I had to...for love! But he doesn't understand and in the dream I don't understand, either. When I wake up, it makes less sense than it used to. Where are you? Where are you, sweet Nina? We are supposed to be going through this together. If we're not, _THEN WHAT WAS THE POINT?_

I feel sick now, most of the time. It has invaded all my thoughts and everything I do. I can't get away from it. You are the only person who could make me forget, who could make me remember why this is okay, why I had to do this.

I go places where I think you'll be and wait for you to come *back. This is all I can do now: Wait. Wait to pass the time and write you these letters, which I'll show you when I finally find you. WHERE ARE YOU!?!?!?! I want to believe you are lost, and I can help you find your way home. I am trying to have faith, but it is hard to have faith when you're alone. I am trying.*

WHY ARE YOU DOING THIS TO ME?? WHY WHY WHY WHY WHY! I can't take it anymore. I can't take it. I can't be without you. WHERE ARE YOU? I am sick every night and every day. I know you love me! I know you love me! I know it I know it. But why can't I feel it anymore? Something is fading. When the love is gone other things rise to the surface. Things I can't think about. I will never be able to stop without you.

My hands are shaking so hard the pages are rustling. I breathe in sharp gasps. There are too many letters here, too many for me to read them all. I flip to the last page in the stack. Five words. Stark black. All alone:

I DID IT FOR YOU

I let out a cry and raise my hand to my lips. No no no no no no no. This is not possible. This can't be real. This can't be real. How can this be real?

I pick up the newspaper clipping about Jason's death and I look at the date. I can't believe I missed this before: Jason died the day Nina disappeared.

I need this not to mean what it seems like it means.

This must be a joke of some kind. Or a creative writing exercise. Or something. Or anything! I think back to the party at the Mothership. To everything Sean ever said to me there. To his willingness to help me. His insistence. The mask he wore to the party. So no one would recognize him? Oh my God. Oh my God. Oh my God. I think of him gazing into my eyes. Telling me how much I looked like her. Oh God.

I hear the sound of a car pulling up outside. Sean is back. The letters are all over the floor. I run to the door and lock it with the chain. I grab the letters in handfuls and stuff them all back into the bag and then lock the lock. I can hear the sound of a key in the door. I climb up, lift the bag overhead. The doorknob is turning. I push it in between the blankets, lean back slightly, almost topple off the chair. The door is opening.

Please someone tell me what to do now.

"Ellie?" Sean's voice is calling from outside. I get off the chair and without breathing drag it back to the desk. "Ellie?" Sean's hand reaches in between the door and the jamb. He shakes the chain. My heart is pounding. "I can't get in!" Sean calls out. "Are you still in the shower? Ellie?"

The shower. I tear off my clothes and run into the bathroom. I turn the water on. I can hear Sean outside calling my name. "Ellie! Ellie! Ellie! I'm locked out! I can't get in!" The water feels like ice. I drench my head, my face. When my whole body is wet, I jump out of the shower. I hit my ankle against the side of the tub. Hard. My eyes tear up. I wrap one of the flimsy towels around myself. I turn the water off. Run back, dripping.

"Sean? Is that you?"

"Yeah, Ellie, I'm locked out!"

What can I do? What can I do? There's nothing I can do. But he doesn't know what I've seen. So I just need to keep it that way.

"Sorry!" I yell. "I'm opening it!"

I take down the chain and pull the door open. Sean is standing there, holding a clear plastic container out in front of him. "Hey, you!" he says. "I come bearing salad!"

"Hi!" I say. I try to sound normal. I'm shouting. "Were you waiting long?"

"Not too long, but why'd you lock the chain?"

"I was scared." The water is dripping off my body onto the floor, pooling around my feet. My ankle is throbbing. "When you left, I just, I don't know, I got freaked. Because of Nina, I guess," I say. "I lost track of time in the shower." I try and smile. Am I acting normal? I don't even remember how normal people act.

"Aw, sweetie," Sean says. He walks inside, closing the door behind him. He puts down the salad and a pink vitaminwater. "I'm sorry I left you alone for so long. Don't worry, I won't do it again."

He presses his body against mine, holding me to him. It takes everything in me not to push him away. "You're shaking," says Sean. He rubs my arms.

"I'm cold," I say.

I lean back and look at Sean's face. Everything that was beautiful about him looks different to me now. His intense gray eyes are filled with something dark and sick. His sculptured cheekbones look too sharp. His lips too wet.

"Do you want to get dressed?" Sean says. His voice is soft and gentle, like he's talking to a child. And all I can think is, *How am I going to get out of this?* I will go into the bathroom and put on my clothes. And then what?

And then what?

"And then you can come and eat your salad," Sean says.

I nod. Just because you're trapped in a hotel room with a guy who is stalking your sister and killed his own brother, that's no excuse for not eating your vegetables.

I gather my clothes, bring them into the bathroom. I watch myself in the mirror as I slip my shirt over my head, pull my pants up. I smile at myself in the mirror. I look terrified.

When I come back out, Sean is standing by the desk, the salad is laid out and next to it is a plastic fork on top of a paper napkin. The vitaminwater sits next to it. He's taken the cap off for me.

"For you, my love," he says. I walk over.

His phone starts vibrating. He reaches into his pocket and stops it. I stare at his hands. He grabs the back of the chair, pulls it out from under the desk. I sit. I stare down into the plastic bowl—limp lettuce, bloated red tomatoes, rubbery cucumber slices, corn, covered in a slick of sour-smelling vinegar. I stab the fork into a piece of tomato. A piece of corn is stuck to the side, like a small rotting tooth. I gag.

"You okay?" Sean says.

"Yeah," I say. I put the tomato in my mouth, chew the cold flesh. Flesh. I gag again. I taste bile. Sean is standing over me, staring down. He puts his hand on my shoulder.

"I understand," he says. "I couldn't eat for almost a month after my brother died, but it will really make you feel better." I nod. My thoughts are zipping around inside my brain, collecting speed as I remember different things he said, things he did that I'm now understanding in a new way.

"It's hard," I say.

"I know it is, baby." Sean reaches out and strokes my hair. "I'm just so glad I can be here for you now. I'm just so glad I can be here." He crouches down so his head is level with mine and he puts his hands on either side of my face, forcing me to face him. "You are in my heart now, Ellie." He looks me in the eyes. "And that's forever." He leans in toward me, his lips parted, his breath hot against my face. And then, I can't help it, I flinch, ever so slightly.

He leans back. "Oh God," he says. He raises his hand to

his mouth, his lips part. "That look you just gave me." He stands and stumbles backward. "You know."

"What?" I'm shaking my head. "What are you talking about?"

"You *know*," he says.

His face is changing now, in slow motion, his mouth turning down, opening, closing, and opening. He's blinking. His eyes are clouding. It's too late. It's too late.

"No, no, no, no, no, no, no," he says. "Oh God, I'm so stupid. I should have known . . . you went into the bathroom to shower with all your clothes on, but when I came back, your clothes were all around the room. And you'd locked the door and . . . "

He walks slowly over to the closet, reaches up into the blankets and takes the bag down. He stares at the lock, his back to me. ". . . and these are not the letters I left the lock on." He stares at me. I look down at the limp lettuce, at the bloated tomatoes. "Do you know how I know?" He waits for me to answer. I am silent. "Because I left the lock turned to Ellie."

I can hear Sean's footsteps, soft on the carpet. Approaching.

I should get up. I should run. But I am frozen in my seat.

I feel his hand on my shoulder. My stomach drops.

It's too late. He turns me around in the chair, bends down, gathers me into his arms, squeezes me, tighter, tighter, and tighter. He pulls me off the chair until we're crouched facing each other. It hurts how hard he's holding me.

"Oh, Ellie," he says over my shoulder. He sounds like he's crying now. I think I can feel his body shaking. He strokes my hair, hard. "Do you love me, Ellie?"

I swallow. "Of course I do," I force myself to say. My heart is pounding so hard I can feel it throughout my entire body.

He mashes our faces together in some sort of approximation of a kiss. His tears run down my cheeks.

"No, you don't." He leans back.

"I don't know what you're talking about," I say. "Of course I do." But it sounds like a lie, even to me.

"It's so unfair. So incredibly, terribly, horribly unfair. One mistake! I made one mistake in my entire life, and it ruins everything! I guess that's the funny thing about a mistake like that, you can't take it back. Even if you want to. You just can't ever take it back. And here's the worst part, it wasn't even my mistake! Nina made me do it for her. I didn't want to do it. She set it up so that I'd think I had to! I loved her and she knew it, and I know she loved me. Or at least she could have if she let herself. But then he wasn't around and she still wouldn't be with me!" His eyes are filling up again. "She tricked me!"

He clenches his jaw, a vein throbs near his temple.

"It's going to be okay," I say.

"No," Sean says. A tear escapes his left eye and slides

down to his chin. "It's not." He walks around behind me and grabs my wrists. "I don't want to do this." He lets out a choked cry. "Please just know that I really, really don't want to!"

He pushes me forward and wrenches both my arms behind my back. I try to pull away. I can't.

"What are you doing?" I say.

I feel something being wrapped around my wrists and tied tight to the back of the chair. His belt I think. "Don't go anywhere," Sean says, as though I actually could. And then he is out the door, running through the parking lot. I pull against the belt as hard as I can. "Help!" I shout. "HELP!" But no one comes.

Sean's phone starts vibrating again on the desk. I lean over and with my chin, I knock the phone to the floor where it continues to vibrate. I stretch out my leg, pull the phone toward me with my foot, and flip it open with my toe. "HELP!" I shout toward the phone. I look down, pray it's Unavailable calling again, but there on the screen is a random number I don't recognize. "Hello?" I hear a faint voice coming through the phone. "Hello?" The voice calls again. My heart explodes in my chest. Is this . . . Could it really be . . .

Sean is back, I kick the open phone under the desk just as he enters the room.

"Do you want to know something, Ellie? Something I've never told anyone before?" He's not even looking at me. The tears are falling faster now, an unreal amount of them, as though someone has turned on a faucet inside his face. He has one arm behind his back. "He didn't just go to sleep." Sean shakes his head and wipes his nose with the back of his hand. "That's how I thought it would be for him, y'know? Just like going to sleep. But it wasn't. I went into his room and I held him down. He was a really heavy sleeper and didn't even wake up when the needle went in. But at the last second, he opened his eyes and looked at me. He had this look of *horror* on his face, Ellie. His last moment on this earth was spent looking his own brother in the eye and *knowing* what I did to him." Sean takes a deep breath and takes his arm from behind his back. There's something in his hand. Stark black barrel, shining dully under the motel's fluorescent lights. Cartoonishly menacing. A gun. Sean looks down at it, then back up at me, then down at the gun again. "I got this for myself," Sean says. "For, y'know." He raises the gun to his head, jerks his head to the side, and then sticks out his tongue. "It's supposed to be hard to get a gun, but if you have a lot of money, it's not really hard to get anything, I guess."

And he looks up and smirks, as though he expects me to laugh. "At first I couldn't take it, the guilt, you know. And Nina was gone and I couldn't handle it alone. Then, Thanksgiving break, a few months after it happened, I came home from boarding school. Normally we would spend Thanksgiving at our house in Big Sur, which, hey, you'll think this is funny, that's actually the house where that band dropped your sister, but anyway, we didn't go that year because it was like my brother's favorite place on earth and my dad and stepmom thought it would be too hard to be there without him. So it was just the three of us at my house sitting at that giant table, staring at our plates, at all this food the cook made that we weren't eating. And I just . . . I *missed* him, which was so crazy. I just started thinking about how different dinner would have been if he was there. And how cool he was and how funny he was. It was like that was the first time he really felt like a brother to me and it made me sick, so I excused myself, which no one really minded. And I went up to my room and I got the gun out of this box in my closet. I wasn't even sure I knew how to load it right. I'd just read this tutorial on the Internet but it's not like I really had any chances to test out shooting before. So I did what the website had said and then I held the gun up to my face and I was about to squeeze the trigger when suddenly it was like someone was talking to me directly inside my head. I don't know if it was God or my brother's ghost, but the voice told me not to do it, not to kill myself, because that wouldn't make things right. I wasn't really the one at fault there, see. I wasn't even the one that killed him, they were my hands, but doing what *she* wanted. Your sister was the one who did it to him." Sean looks to the side and presses his lips together. "It was her fault and I was the only person on earth who knew that. Before that I'd been looking for your sister for months. But after that moment I stopped looking and I just waited. I knew if I waited long enough, I'd get a chance to make things right because it was fate that I should. It was hell, all that waiting. But I never lost faith and I never gave up hope and then when I finally saw you at that party that night at the Mothership, I knew my wait was over and that you'd been sent there for me, to lead me to her, to help me make things right. But then I started falling in love with you." Sean tips his head to the side and smiles like he's telling a story about something beautiful. "I thought that maybe *that* was the reason I was at that party, not to find Nina, but to find you! So I thought if I could just let the past go, then it would all be okay. That's why I told you she died, so we could move on . . . together."

Sean looks up at me then, staring me straight in the eye. "Stop looking at me like that," he says.

I don't move.

"Do you know what I've been through, Ellie? Can you even imagine? You think you have suffered for love? *I have suffered for love* and so there I was, waiting for the love I've earned to come back to me. And then there you were. Dear, sweet, beautiful you who looks so much like her, only you look at me differently than she ever did, and then when you told your friend to leave I knew she had never loved me the way you do. You are the reason I knew it was okay to let her go. Because I had you now. Someone to look at me the way you did. But *you are not looking at me like that anymore.*"

Sean's nose is practically touching mine. I can see the muscles twitching in his jaw.

"I'm sorry," I say quietly.

"Look at me like that again." He is begging me. There's a vein throbbing in the center of his forehead. "Please, Ellie, just look at me like that again, the way you did before."

And I try. I try with every fiber of my being to look at his face and see what I saw before I knew the truth.

But I just can't do it.

"You look disgusted," Sean says. His breath is hot on my face. "I didn't have a choice, Ellie." He takes a quivering breath. "Tell me." His voice is quiet now, barely a growl. "Tell me you understand why I had to do what I had to do. TELL ME!"

"I understand why you had to do what you had to do," I say.

"And tell me you understand why I have to do what I have to do next," he says. There are tears in his eyes, he's nodding slowly.

My whole body goes cold. "What is that?"

"You already know," Sean says. "I already told you the story."

"The story?"

"The one about Nina in the parking lot."

"But that didn't actually happen!"

"That didn't actually happen . . ." A tear drips down each cheek. "Yet."

My mouth drops open. I cannot speak.

"I don't want to do it," Sean says. He stomps his foot on the ground. "I mean, you know that, right? I'll do you here first so you don't have to watch, and then head off to San Francisco on my own after you're . . ."

"Are you talking about . . ." My voice is just a whisper now. ". . . killing me?"

Sean looks down at the floor. "Well, when you put it that way, it sounds so harsh." Sean smiles this funny little smile. And then he bursts into tears. He sobs in ragged gasps, his shoulders shaking. And I just watch him. He picks his head back up; he wipes his eyes with the heel of his hand. "This is what I have to do now. I wish I had a choice . . ."

"But you do!" I say. "You always have other choices!"

"No," Sean says. He waves the gun back and forth like an extension of his finger. "I could never just let you go." He's shaking his head. "You'd tell people and then I'd never be able to make things right." Sean is pointing the gun straight at me. He stands up and steps back. "And even if you didn't, you don't love me anymore and you think I'm some monster. And I just couldn't live knowing that you think such terrible things about me. I couldn't stand it." His arm is shaking. Clear fluid is running out of his eyes, his nose. I strain against the belt, but it's tied too tightly. I can't move. I stare at the gun. I cannot believe this is real. I cannot believe this is real.

I cannot believe it ends like this.

"I have to just get this over with." His voice is calmer now. He's talking to himself. "I just have to do it and get it over with." He walks forward, wraps his arms around my shoulders, and squeezes me tight. I can feel his heart pounding. "Just please," he whispers. "Keep your eyes closed, okay?"

Ten seconds left on earth. He lets go, kisses me on the top of the head, squeezes me again, hard. Five seconds.

"Sean, wait!"

Four seconds.

"I can't."

Three seconds.

"WAIT!"

Two seconds.

"I'm really sorry, sweetie."

Sean takes a deep breath. He cocks the trigger.

One second.

"Close your eyes," he says.

thirty-eight

"SEAN, I LOVE YOU!"

Sean freezes, his arm stuck straight out in front of him. He blinks.

"What?"

My whole body is shaking. "Sean, don't kill me," I shout. "I love you! Do whatever you want to Nina. I don't care! I don't care, I only care about you."

Something flickers across his face.

"You're just saying that," he says, "to get me to let you go." But he wants to believe me, I can tell he wants to believe me.

"No," I say. "I don't *want* you to let me go! *I want to be with you.*"

"Then why . . . then why were you acting like that? Why were you looking at me like that before?"

"I was jealous! When I saw those letters, it made me feel sick! Because I was jealous and I wanted you to be able to love *me* that much."

Sean frowns. "But why did you go into my bag then?"

"Because I love you!" I say. "Isn't that obvious? I was

feeling insecure." I pause. "And I was worried that maybe that person who calls you all the time and hangs up really *is* another girl and just the idea of it makes me want to vomit and I just want you all to myself! I wanted to make sure there was no one else!"

And Sean is staring at me, wrestling within himself. I can see it on his face.

I go on. "I don't care about Nina or your brother or anyone! I understand why you did what you did! It was only because you're so passionate, because you really know how to love people. Because you really love with all your heart! So I don't care what you do to Nina because I love you and that means you're my family now. And I am your family, and we don't need anyone else."

Sean leans forward.

"You really love me?" He sounds so desperate.

"More than anyone I've ever known."

He lowers the gun and leans in even closer. Our foreheads are touching.

"I'll still need to go to San Francisco and take care of Nina, you understand that, right? I don't think I'll be able to move on until I do. It's not fair for her to be alive when he isn't. And I won't be able to go on and live a normal life until everything is even. Until I make it even." He sounds so calm now, like he could be talking about anything.

"Of course," I say. "She deserves it. Whatever happens to her, she brought it on herself."

He leans back. "So you'll come with me? You'll help me find her?"

I nod. "I'll go anywhere you want," I say.

"You think she'll still be there?"

"Oh yes," I say, and then in my loudest voice, "She's definitely still in San Francisco. And I know just where to start looking for her when we get there, too. Right on Haight Street. We'll find a clue as to where she is, right on Haight Street. So we'll be there in about twelve hours, I guess. Or maybe thirteen. And we'll go right there to Haight Street."

Sean leans back. He's not crying anymore, his eyes look huge, oddly beautiful, in that way sick things can be.

He stares at me. I stare back.

This is my last and only hope. I slow my breathing. Inside I am screaming, but my face is calm. I just stare into his eyes, trying to radiate love.

Time creeps by. One minute. Two minutes. I don't even blink.

Finally, Sean lets out a huge sigh and his mouth curls into a strangely sweet smile. For a moment he looks about ten years old. "I love you more than I ever loved her," Sean says. "You don't have anything to worry about. That was just a fantasy, but this . . ." His lips are over mine, his breath is hot, his teeth knocking against me. It takes everything I have in me not to gag. He pulls back and strokes the side of my face with the gun. ". . . this is real."

thirty-nine

I shift in my seat and press my face against the glass, gazing out at the soft blue arc of the sky stretching for miles in every direction. We're two hours closer to San Francisco on a mostly empty highway, driving fast.

Sean reaches down and takes his extra-large iced coffee out of the cupholder. His third of the trip so far. "I was supposed to go to San Francisco once, a long time ago," he says. His voice is soft and gentle, like he's telling me a bedtime story. "My mom was going to take me, but we never quite made it there." He holds the straw up to my mouth, offering me a sip because my hands are duct taped behind my back. I shake my head. "It's kind of a funny story actually." He raises the straw to his own lips and sucks. "So we were staying at my family's house in Big Sur. This was when it was just me and my dad and my actual mom. My mom didn't like to ski but my dad was out skiing every day, and I guess my mom was getting bored and lonely or maybe she was just mad at my dad, I don't know. But one night at like three in the morning she just woke me up and told me we were going on vacation, just her and me. She told me to get in the car because she'd already packed and everything and we needed to leave before traffic got bad. So, I mean, I was five at the time so I didn't think much of it, other than that it sounded fun, so I just got into the car in my pajamas with my pillow and my blanket. After she started driving, she told me she had friends in San Francisco and that we should go and visit them because she hadn't seen them in twenty-five years and she wanted to show them how cute I was. So we drove along for a while, stopped at an all-night mini-mart for ice cream sandwiches and then kept driving. I don't remember anything else after that except at some point later we were surrounded by about fifteen cop cars with their sirens and lights on. Turns out my mom had never mentioned her plan to my dad, so when he woke up the next morning and found the house empty, he freaked. She hadn't been taking her medication for a couple of weeks so she ended up back in the hospital for a while after that, and then about nine months after *that* she went away for good. My favorite part of the story, though, is that later the maid was unpacking the bags my mom had put in the trunk and you'll never guess what was in them." He pauses. "Try and guess."

"Clothes?" I say.

"For me she'd packed nothing but this tiny winter jacket that I'd worn when I was about two, a bunch of action figures and a bunch of mini juice boxes. And for herself all she brought was," Sean starts laughing then. Laughing so hard he has to stop and take a breath. "A bag of . . . floor-length . . . black-tie . . . gowns!" Tears are filling his eyes, he's laughing so hard. "These custom-made designer gowns, probably worth a total of about a hundred thousand dollars." He reaches down for his coffee and takes another sip, hic-cups, and wipes the tears off his cheeks. He takes a deep breath. "In my dad's version of the story, when the police finally found us, I was curled up in the backseat of the car, scared out of my mind, covered in ice cream. But that's just not how I remember it. I think it's probably my very favorite memory of my mom actually." Sean turns toward me and smiles. "I guess we didn't pack that well, either, come to think of it. But anything we need we can get while we're there, since I figure we'll want to go . . . Hey, you know what we should do? We should go on a big shopping trip after . . ." Sean stops then, reaches down for his coffee. He turns toward me and smiles this sweet sheepish smile, like he's just slightly embarrassed by what we're on the way to do.

The sun is high up in the sky now and the road is filled with other cars. We are not talking anymore, just driving. Sean has one hand on my knee, as though to make sure I'm still there, to keep me from floating away.

*　　*　　*

They say that no matter what life throws at you, there's always a lesson to be learned, and I sure have learned some important things in the last eight hours while we've been on the road, such as exactly what it feels like to spend the better part of a day sitting in a Volvo with your wrists taped together, and that I am, as it turns out, capable of pulling my pants up and down that way, too, to go to the bathroom. Also, I learned that I am probably the most talented actress the world has ever known, too bad my best and only performance is taking place in a car in front of an audience of one.

The sun is setting now. Sean pulls over on a long stretch of highway surrounded on either side by giant fields of waist-high grass that no one has touched for years. "I'll be right back," he says. He gets out of the car, walks fifty feet into the middle of the field, and holds the gun straight up over his head. There's a loud *CRACK*. It echoes. A delicate whisper of smoke curls from the barrel of the gun up toward the sky. Sean walks back to the car, gets in, and shuts the door.

"I just wanted to check," he says, "that it would work."

Sean starts the car again. We will be there soon.

*　　*　　*

I'm staring out the window at the early evening sky, at the swooping red cables of the Golden Gate Bridge lit by a thousand tiny lights and the sparkling ocean beyond it. It looks like a postcard that we just so happen to be a part of.

"It's beautiful," I say.

"Yeah," Sean says, the tension is back in his voice. Maybe it's the nine extra-large iced coffees. Maybe it's just that what he's about to do is finally sinking in. "Haight Street?" Sean says. "That's where you said you think we'll . . ." Sean stops, for the last twelve hours he hasn't, not once, actually directly referred to what we've come here to do. "That's where you think we should go?" He turns toward me.

My organs, my bones, everything inside me, has dissolved into a pool of molten hot liquid panic. But I smile calmly. "Oh yes," I say. "Haight Street, I'm sure of it."

Sean reaches into his pocket, then behind him into his seat, then leans down and sticks his hand between the seat and the door.

"Everything okay?"

"Yeaaaah," Sean says slowly. "I'm just trying to find my phone and I'm not sure where it is."

"How weird," I say. "I hope you didn't leave it back at the motel."

"Me, too," Sean says. "I wonder what happened to it?"

I shrug. "I guess it's just a mystery." I close my eyes and picture that phone, exactly where I left it. And I have to turn my face toward the window because at this moment it is impossible for me not to smile.

Forty

To everyone else out here we're just another young couple enjoying an evening stroll on Haight Street. No one can see the loaded gun shoved down the front of Sean's jeans. And the red marks on my wrists where the duct tape was ripped off. Or the fact that Sean is crushing my fingers with his own, as though to keep me from running, as though he never plans on letting go.

A girl in a tiny plaid skirt and fishnets walks past us and smiles at Sean. When she gets a few feet away she turns around and looks back. Is this . . . ? Nope, just some girl who thinks he's hot. She sees what most people see when they look at him, just a seventeen-year-old kid, with floppy skateboarder hair and a heartbreakingly beautiful face. I used to see him like that, too.

"Whatcha looking at?" Sean asks. His hair falls over one eye and he pushes it away, anxiously.

"I'm just glad we're here is all," I say.

He tries to smile but he's too nervous. His teeth are chattering. "Me, too," he says.

We keep walking up the steep hill—we pass a fancy home goods store, a store that sells handblown glass bongs, a tapas restaurant, a place with psychedelic posters stuck up in the window.

We keep going. Sean squeezes my hand again. I can feel his heart beating through his fingers. Or maybe that's my own.

Everything we pass seems somehow meaningful. A man in a pair of too-yellow pants walks by, struggling with grocery bags filled with too much fruit. A girl in a maroon hooded sweatshirt is very deliberately looking for something in her pocket. A man drops a bottle of water and the water splashes on his shoes. He looks up, we make eye contact for just a second. He looks away. Two men in tuxedos are walking arm in arm.

"Hey, dude, can you spare a cigarette?" We turn to the right, look down. There's a girl and a guy sitting cross-legged on the sidewalk behind a cardboard box with a few coins inside, and *Why Lie? We Want Beer!* written on it in pencil. The girl has short bleach-blonde hair and a steel bull-ring through her nose. "Or some change?"

"Sorry," I say. I look at her again . . . is she? No. She's not even looking at us anymore. Sean and I keep walking.

Finally we reach the top of the hill, the street ends at the entrance to Golden Gate Park. There's a grassy area in the front, and behind it a paved pathway winding back. A young couple is leaning against a brick wall kissing. Three guys are kicking around a Hacky Sack. A half-dozen people are sitting in a circle, drinking out of paper bags, listening to a girl playing guitar. Sean gasps suddenly, he grabs my upper arm, squeezes it.

"Ellie," he whispers. "Ellie." I can feel his hand shaking. He motions toward a little group standing just a few feet away, a girl with long dark hair, a big guy with red hair, a smaller guy with blond hair, and a girl with a blonde pixie cut. They're all looking around, like they're waiting for someone. The girl with the long dark hair is smoking a cigarette. The big guy glances at his watch.

And all of them are wearing identical T-shirts, white V-necks with a graphic drawn in the center. A sweep of a jawline, the arch of an eyebrow, the crescent of a crooked smile.

It's a face: mine.

Sean leans in close. "Bingo," he whispers.

We walk forward. The girl with the long dark hair takes a final drag of her cigarette, tosses the butt on the ground, and grinds it out with the heel of her boot. She watches us approach.

"Hey," Sean says. "I really like your shirt."

"Yeah?" The girl tips her head to one side. She has giant eyes rimmed in gold eyeliner. Her friends are clumped together behind her. The blonde girl behind her is staring at me. Our eyes meet. She holds my gaze a second too long.

"Yeah," Sean says. "It's really fucking cool."

"Thanks." The dark-haired girl grins. "This local artist makes them."

The big guy steps forward. He's about six-five, with giant arm muscles bulging under the thin white fabric of his T-shirt, which is almost exactly the same as hers, except my face is a little distorted where it's stretched across his massive chest. "We each got one."

"Awesome," Sean says, nodding. "Really cool." He pauses. "You don't happen to know where I might find the person who made the shirts, do you? We're from out of town and these would be great to bring back home."

"I do indeed," the guy says. He turns around. He points to his back over his shoulder.

NINA WRIGLEY DESIGNS:

Custom-Made Hand-drawn T-shirts.

1414 Avery Square, San Francisco, CA

"She sells them out of her apartment," the guy says. "You can just go there right now, I bet she'll be there."

"Thanks, man," Sean says. He squeezes my hand. "Can you tell me how to get there?"

The guy glances at me, and then back to Sean. "I'll do you one better, I'll take you there myself."

Sean starts shaking his head. "Nah, that's okay, man. You don't need to do that."

"Oh, I don't mind," the guy says. "Let me!"

"No, seriously, you can't," Sean says. "I mean . . . we're not going to go tonight. We'll just probably go tomorrow or the next day or something."

"Okay," the guy says, slowly. "Okay. Okay." He reaches into his pocket and takes out a little notepad and a pen. He starts scribbling down the directions. Sean is watching the guy. The girl behind him is still watching me. When our eyes meet again something flickers across her face. The guy hands the directions to Sean.

"Cool," says Sean. "Thank you."

"No problem," the guy says.

"Good luck," says the girl.

We turn, and start walking. Sean is holding on to my arm, his entire body shaking. "Let's just get this over with," he says. "We'll just go now, no stopping, no thinking. We'll go and then we'll find somewhere to sleep and then when we wake up tomorrow morning, this will all be behind us."

"Yes," I say to Sean. I am walking beside him, breathing in and out and in and out, reminding myself to have faith in her. To keep walking. And when the time comes, to be ready. "By tomorrow morning everything will be different."

Forty-one

We turn right and walk up a steep hill on a narrow street, surrounded by tall skinny houses on either side. It's pretty and peaceful. Not the setting you'd expect for something like this. But really, what is?

Sean's hand is on his stomach, holding on to the gun through his shirt. "This has already happened," he whispers. "All of this has already happened."

We're both panting. We turn right, then left, then right again. I think I hear footsteps behind us, but I'm too scared to turn around. My heart is pounding.

Sean whispers, "I can't wait until this is all over." "Me, neither," I whisper back. We keep walking. The sky is dark. Our only guides are the yellow light coming from the cracked street lamps and the faint white glow of the moon.

Finally Sean stops walking in front of a narrow gray house, with a heavy brass *1414* hung upon the blue front door. "This is it," he says in a voice that no longer sounds like his own. Sean grabs the doorknob. He turns it. The door is unlocked. Sean whispers, "Fate."

He opens the door. There's a skinny staircase leading up with a yellow paper lantern dangling above it. Sean takes the gun out from under his shirt with shaking hands. He whispers, "Go." And I start walking slowly up the stairs.

Right foot.

Left foot.

Right foot.

Left foot.

"Call her name now," he whispers.

I take a deep breath. "Nina," I call out.

"Louder," he says.

Right foot.

Left foot.

Right foot.

"NINA," I say again.

"That wasn't loud enough," Sean says.

Left foot.

Right foot.

"NINAAAAAA!" No answer. "NIIIIIINNNNNNNN-AAAAAA!!!!!"

Left foot.

Right foot.

Left foot.

"Belly?" We hear a voice coming through the door at the top of the stairs, very quiet, barely more than a whisper.

My heart stops. "Belly? Is that you?"

Sean's breath catches in his throat.

I squeeze my eyes shut and I inhale deeply. I smell sweetness and spice. Oranges and ginger. Nina. I'm not scared anymore.

We reach the top of the stairs and push through the door. We're in a large living room—dark wood floors, big fluffy couches, framed drawings covering every last bit of wall space, and there, standing by herself in the center of the room, is my sister.

My sister.

Looking both exactly like and completely different from the person I remember.

Our eyes meet just for a moment, and I feel a warmth spreading outward from the middle of my chest. When she sees me she starts to smile, but then she looks behind me, at Sean, and stops. Her jaw drops, her lips pull back. It looks like she's screaming only no sound is coming out. I have never in my life seen Nina afraid before. But now, she is terrified.

She is not supposed to be terrified.

My heart pounds painfully in my chest. Icy sweat springs out of every pore in my body.

She is not supposed to be fucking terrified!

That final call that came in on Sean's cell phone back at the motel, the one that I answered with my feet, *I thought that was Nina.* I thought I heard her voice saying hello through the phone. And I thought she had been listening to everything Sean and I were saying after I kicked the phone under the desk. I thought she knew we were coming to Haight Street. And I thought she was leading us to her. I thought she was going to save us.

But I was wrong.

Everything I thought was wrong.

"Nina," I hear Sean's voice over my shoulder. I turn. He's staring at her, his nostrils flared, his eyes glowing. He barely even looks human.

"Sean," she says. "What are you doing here?"

Sean reaches for the gun inside his shirt.

"I think you already know that," he says. "This is for what you did to me . . ." He sounds like he's reciting lines from a script he rehearsed in his head a thousand times over. "This is for what you made me do to him."

He raises his arms, the gun clutched between his shaking hands.

Nina just stands there, frozen, staring.

The gun is pointing straight at her.

This is it.

This is it.

This.

Is.

It.

And then, an explosion. Not a bullet out of the gun, but something within me:

Nina is not the only one who can save us.

Suddenly I am flying through the air screaming, "LEAVE MY SISTER ALONE!!!"

I stretch out my arm, catching Sean right under his chin, snapping his head back, hard. And then I slam both my shoulders into the middle of his stomach with everything I've fucking got. We tumble down to the floor. Sean lands on his back, a wheezy whistling noise escapes from his lips. The gun is knocked from his hand and slides spinning across the wood.

And for a moment we are all silent and completely still. I don't think a single one of us can quite believe what I've just done.

"FREEZE! PUT YOUR HANDS ABOVE YOUR HEAD!" I look up. Five uniformed police officers have materialize out of the shadows. They stand over us, their guns cocked and aimed at our heads. Sean turns to the side, the expression on his face one of such complete and utter bewilderment that for a second I actually feel sorry for him.

But just for a second.

"What's going on!?" he says. "Ellie? Ellie?!"

All I can do is shake my head.

A police officer yanks his arms behind his back and cuffs him. Another one starts to read him his rights. Two others lift him up, his body limp like a doll's, his head hanging down. His feet just barely brush against the ground as he is carried backward toward the door.

But right before he is pulled through, he looks up, and

there is a hint of something else on his face. Something that looks an awful lot like relief.

And then he is gone.

I look up. The wall behind Nina is covered in drawings, photo-realistic scenes from our lives growing up—the park where we used to play, our aunt's house at the beach, even a little picture of the guy from the Covered Wagon Shipping commercial. And right in the center is a framed portrait of our mother. In the picture she looks different than I've seen her in a long time, soft and pleased and proud as though this is how Nina's been remembering her.

I look back at Nina, standing right there in front of me. It took two years and two thousand miles, but I am finally here with her. Her bottom lip is shaking. Mine is shaking, too.

We run toward each other, Nina and I, crash together into a tight hug, a hug that feels like any of the thousands and thousands of other hugs we've shared in the last sixteen years, but also completely different because of all that it took to get here, because we almost didn't get to have this one. Neither of us says anything because words just do not exist for this kind of moment. We just stand there hugging until the tears are pouring down both our faces.

Forty-two

What happens next is a blur, but there are certain details I know I will never forget—the sour human smell in the back of the police car, a mix of a hundred people's anxious sweat, the sound of my mother's voice on the phone when they call her from the station, because I can tell she's crying, the buzz of the bright fluorescent lights in the room where I tell Detective Bryant a four-hour-long story about every single thing that happened in the five days since I've met Sean. But more than anything I know I will never forget the look on Nina's face when Detective Bryant comes into the waiting room where Nina and I sit on scratched-up wooden chairs to tell us that Sean confessed. To everything. "We barely even questioned him," Detective Bryant says. He shakes his head. "That happens sometimes." And Nina just turns toward me, her lips pressed together, her eyes watering, her entire face contorted with such pure relief, I know I cannot even begin to understand the hell that preceded it.

"It's over," Nina whispers. "It's finally over." And she squeezes my hand.

"I'll take you home now," Detective Bryant says.

So we stand up and we walk outside. The clear early-morning sunlight shines on our faces. I can already tell it's going to be a beautiful day.

Forty-three

Everything out the window shrinks as we rise higher, houses, cars, people, mountains. My ears pop. I press my face against the glass.

"Wait, wait, wait, Belly," Nina says. "Don't move for just ooooooooooone more second . . ." She holds her pen up to her lips and then brings the point back to the napkin she's been sketching on. "Your face is more angley than it was the last time I drew you." She holds the pen to her lips again. "More cheekboney."

I smile. "Maybe," I say. I glance at the napkin onto which she's sketching the outline of my face.

"No, definitely," she says. "You look older."

"Well . . . time will do that to a person, I guess," and I try to make my tone light and jokey but it doesn't come out that way. The problem is this: After two years of wondering, my brain doesn't quite know how to stop. I've reminded myself that now that Nina is safe and I can see her, that nothing else matters, that nothing else should matter. But what we tell ourselves and what we deep down believe, those are two different things, I guess.

"I can't believe Mom's taking the day off just to come meet us at the airport," Nina says. Out of the corner of my eye I can see her shaking her head slowly. She looks at me, down at the napkin, back up at me. "I mean, when's that ever happened before, right?" She's smiling. I don't say anything.

The unasked questions sit heavy in my mouth like marbles, and everything else I try and say has to work its way around them. "I don't know," I say. After what my sister's been through, it doesn't feel fair. It doesn't feel fair to make her explain anything. But my brain just won't stop wondering.

"Oh, Belly." Nina sighs and puts down her pen. "Please, just ask me, already, okay? I know you need to ask me and it's okay. Just . . . ask me."

"How did you know . . ."

"We're sisters," she says simply. "That's how." And she turns toward me and smiles this bittersweet smile.

We're sisters. There's someone here now who can say that to me.

I take a deep breath. "I just need to know why," I say, very quietly. I look down at my lap. "And I know it's selfish to ask because of everything that you went through."

Nina lets out this wry little laugh and then shakes her

head. "I'm not the only one who's been through something here, Bell. Need I remind you?"

I shake my head.

"Look, you need to know, so I need to tell you." Nina takes a deep breath. "So here it goes. Three years ago I went to a party at this crazy house called the Mothership. It was the middle of summer, but it looked like the middle of winter in their backyard because someone had somehow gotten ahold of an industrial snowmaking machine and they just turned that sucker on and left it running for two days straight. When I got to the party, everyone was outside going nuts, some girls were building an igloo and there were snowball fights everywhere and some guy was making this insane snowman that actually looked like a person. So I had had this idea to make this sort of fuzzy pink dress for myself and dye my hair light pink, and be a Hostess Sno Ball. So I did, and that's what I wore to the party, but everyone just kept asking if I was cotton candy or a pink pom-pom or something.

"And then this guy came up to me, really cute, carrying this snowboard. And I'd noticed him before doing these insane snowboard tricks on this ramp they'd set up. Anyway, he just turned to me and, I'll never forget this because it was the very first thing he ever said to me, he said, 'Someday I'll be telling our grandchildren how when I met their grandma she was dressed up like a snack cake.' And I know that could sound like a cheesy line or something but because of the way he said it and because it was about snack cakes, it didn't feel cheesy, it was just funny. And then I looked at him and I was like, 'Well, you know, by the time we have grandkids it'll be way in the future and snack cakes might not even exist anymore,' and he was like, 'Well, if that's true we should probably start stockpiling now, don't you think, sweetheart?' And that was the first conversation we ever had." Nina turns toward me and smiles.

I smile back.

"That was kinda it for me. We were just together after that. We didn't have to talk about it or wonder about it, we just . . . were. So, one day Jason starts telling me about his stepbrother and how he was kind of messed up and how he got sent away to boarding school and how really deep down he was a good kid." Nina shakes her head. "Jason saw the best in people. Which wasn't always so good for him, I guess." She looks back down at her napkin. "Jason said his stepbrother was going to be in town on break from school and he wanted me to meet him. And I was excited, actually. I mean, I had no idea where all this would . . ." Nina swallows hard. "I had no idea where all this would end up. But anyway, so I met Sean. I remember thinking right when I first met him that there was just something really, I don't know, different about him, I guess. But I kind of liked that about him. You know what I mean?"

I nod. "I thought the same thing when I met him." And I smile wryly, because it's all so ridiculous.

Nina smiles wryly back. "He was really charming some-times. Charming and weird and I thought, well, good for him for doing his own thing. And to be honest, at first I really liked having him around, it was nice having someone to be a big sister to." Nina tips her head to the side. "I missed *you* then, Belly. But you were always so mad at me around that time."

"I'm sorry." I nod. "I just wished you were around more then, I guess, and I didn't really know how to express it."

"I know that now," Nina says. "What I'm trying to say is just that I was thinking of him like a little brother. But he didn't see it that way. He got this crush on me. Right at the beginning I thought it was just kind of innocent and sweet," Nina takes a breath, "it didn't take too long to realize it wasn't.

"He started writing me these letters from school, like really, really, really long letters, full of all this stuff about how one day we'd be together, and how we were soul mates and how much he loved me. And no matter what I said or did, he couldn't be convinced otherwise. It's like the more I told him we were never going to be together, the harder he tried to impress me. He bought some heroin this one time. I don't even know where he got it, but he had it with him when he came home for winter break. I remember when he showed it to me, he was just so excited about it, like I was going to be so impressed." Nina looks at me and shakes her head. "I wasn't.

"Fast forward to the next summer, two summers ago, right after Jason and I both graduated. It was Jason's eighteenth birthday, and his best friend, Max, was in town staying at the Mothership, which is where he always stayed when he was visiting, and so we were having a little birthday party there for Jason. It was just me and Jason and Max and a few other kids hanging out. And I had gotten this snowboard for Jason that I knew he would love. It was expensive though, I had to get a credit card so I could pay for it. And I knew he'd never let me get him such an expensive present unless he had to," Nina smiles, "so I drew all over it so there was no way he could bring it back. And I'll never forget his face when he opened it, his eyes just got huge and he couldn't stop smiling and he got a little choked up even, like, in front of his friends and everything." Nina smiles, pressing her lips together hard like she's trying not to cry. "He said it was the very best present he'd ever gotten and asked if I would take a trip cross-country with him for our one-year anniversary, which was in about a month, at the end of July. He said we'd just pack up his old blue Volvo and hit the road, crashing with friends on the way, and then we could stay at his stepdad's house in Big Sur and he'd teach me to snowboard and we could give his present its first trip down the mountain together."

"Wait, Jason had a blue Volvo?" I tip my head to the side.

"Yup," Nina says. And then she tips her head to the side,

too. "Oh shit, that's what Sean was driving when . . ." Our eyes meet and I nod. Nina sighs and shakes her head.

"Go on," I say.

She continues. "It was around three-thirty in the morning and Jason and I were getting ready to leave the Mothership so he could drive me home, but we were both being really slow about it, I think because neither one of us wanted the night to end. I mean, it really had been just the most wonderful, perfect, amazing night. And that's when Sean showed up, acting all casual like it was the most normal thing in the world for him to be there. Except the Mothership was about twenty miles from their house and Sean had walked there. To see me. Jason wasn't mad or anything, because he never really got mad, he was just worried about Sean and didn't want him to get in trouble for sneaking out and wanted to get him back home as soon as possible. At that point I felt like it would probably be better if I wasn't even in the car with them, so I said I'd just stay over at the Mothership. I always tried to make sure I was back home by the time the sun came up, but that night it seemed like the only other choice was a really bad one. So Jason came over and said good-bye and that he'd come back and pick me up in the morning and he'd get the snowboard then, too. And then he just gave me a quick hug and we didn't even kiss or anything because Sean was like just standing there glaring at us. They walked out waving. And then at the last second Jason stuck his head back in the door and said something about how we could get waffles in the morning, and then he mouthed 'I love you,' . . ." Nina looks down, "and that was it."

"So that was the last time you . . ." I start to say. I bring my hand up to my mouth. I can't even bring myself to finish the sentence.

Nina nods. And takes a deep breath. She wipes her face quickly with her hands, because she's crying a little, and I wipe my face with my hands because as it turns out, I am crying a little, too. "The next morning I called Jason and he kept not picking up his phone and I was figuring he left his phone on vibrate or something. So I just kept calling and calling. And then finally his mom answered."

Nina looks up at me. My heart squeezes in my chest. "She sounded really weird on the phone, it was like I was talking to this robot or something who'd been programmed to sound like her. I was trying hard to be extra friendly because I always had the feeling she didn't like me. I was saying something about the wallet she'd gotten for Jason for his birthday, how nice it was and everything but she just cut me off. And she just asked me if I'd seen Jason the day before and I said yeah, that I had. And that we'd had a birthday party for him. And then she said, and I remember, these are her exact words, she said, 'Well, Nina, your little birthday party killed him.' And at first I somehow didn't even think she meant literally, I thought she just must have meant she thought he was really hungover or something, which didn't even make any sense because he'd been driving and he would never drive if he'd had anything to drink. But then she started saying all this stuff about the preliminary autopsy reports and how they suggested a heroin overdose. And it was obvious from the way she said it that she thought it was my fault."

"But how could she even think that at all!" I say. I feel my face growing hot. I'm getting mad now.

"Her son had just died, Belly," Nina says. "I'm not sure you can blame someone for *anything* they're thinking in a situation like that."

And I stop and I nod, because I suddenly remember that I've had the tiniest taste of what that might feel like when I thought Nina was dead, and I don't think I'd even begun to really feel it yet.

Nina goes on. "So here was Jason's mom telling me he was gone, and I still somehow didn't even understand what she was saying. I kept thinking that they must have made a mistake and maybe he was just sleeping! And then finally she just said that she had to go and she hung up. My head basically exploded then and I don't remember much of what happened for a while. I stayed at the Mothership basically catatonic until the funeral.

"It wasn't until after the funeral was over that I started to think about some things. Like how I knew Jason would never, ever, ever, ever, *ever* have done heroin, and how Sean had gotten some up at school that time. And then I started thinking about how weird Sean was acting at the wake. I just had this vivid memory of him sitting next to me on the couch, rubbing my back, and telling me how he and I needed each other now that Jason was gone. And that Jason would have wanted us to go through this together. And even though I felt like something weird was definitely going on, I still couldn't even imagine that Sean would have done what he did.

"But then something else happened. There was this girl named Jeannie who I'd met at the Mothership. She was this funny girl from Texas with a thick Texas accent and was just in town for a few days. But she was there the night of Jason's party, and after Jason died, she came to his funeral. So she was hanging out with me at the Mothership the day after and the two of us were sitting out front and she was comforting me and I guess she had her arm around me or something. And I just remember looking up and there was Sean walking up the driveway, and he was just glaring at her with this *hatred*. The next day she was driving back to Texas and she got in a car accident and the insurance company investigator said someone had fucked with her brakes. Thank fucking God she was wearing her seat belt so she was basically fine, but *that's* when it all finally clicked in my head. When I found out about Jeannie, I suddenly realized what had happened."

Nina leans back in her seat. My heart is pounding. "So what did you do?" I say.

"Well, as soon as I realized what happened I went to the police. But all they said was that they'd 'look into it'." Nina makes air quotes with her fingers. "It was obvious that they thought I was crazy and weren't taking me seriously and probably weren't going to do a damn thing. So I went to his mom and stepdad and tried to explain but they wouldn't even talk to me. Meanwhile, I was still staying at the Mothership then. I didn't feel like I could leave or come home, I was just too messed up. Sean kept coming by to see me and finally I just hid in the basement so everyone would think I wasn't there anymore. But then I just kept thinking about you and about Mom, and how if Sean was capable of killing his own brother to get to me, and would slice some girl's brakes just because she had her arm around me, then what would he do to the other people I cared about the most? Wouldn't killing you guys make me *need* him? And isn't that what he wanted? So I decided the only thing I could do that would make everyone safe would be to leave . . ." Nina pauses. "So that's what I did."

She turns toward me, her eyes look wet. "I am so, so, so sorry for what you must have gone through. But I know you, Belly, and I knew if you had any idea about what was going on, you'd have insisted on trying to help me."

Nina looks at me.

"But I knew if you tried to help me at all, you weren't safe. So I decided it was much better for you to miss me and still be around to miss me . . . So before Max left and went back home, he'd invited me to come stay with him in Denver for a while if I wanted to. And I didn't know what else to do with myself, so I got on a bus and I went. I'd written his phone number down on this little cardboard credit card thing that I'd been using as a bookmark but then I ended up forgetting it back at the Mothership, so when I got to Denver I didn't even know where to go at first and I had no money and I lost my credit card on the bus and had to cancel it. I ended up at this tattoo place and I got this, in honor of Jason." Nina leans forward and pulls the neck of her tank top down slightly, revealing three tiny numbers inked in black right over her heart. "Jason's birthday," Nina says, tapping it. "The way he was on this day, *this* is how I want to remember him." Nina lets go of her shirt and takes a deep breath. "And then I ended up staying with the woman who owned the tattoo shop for like a week before I was able to get in touch with Max. After that I worked for her for a while. But it's like here I was in Denver, pretending my head was screwed on to my body when it was floating a hundred miles up in the sky. I'd wake up every morning and forget where I was and who I was and that Jason wasn't with me anymore. I just felt like I needed to *do* something, you know, like to really say good-bye. And I had the snowboard I'd given him with me, because I didn't know what else to do with it. So I thought about how excited Jason had been to bring the snowboard to Big Sur and give it a trip down the mountain and how he'd always wanted to teach me to snowboard, so I decided that was something I could do for him, give the snowboard just one run, and then go live in San Francisco because he and I had talked about living there together one day, and it seemed like a good place to start over. So finally I made it all the way out to Big Sur. And it was this really perfect gorgeous day and the snow was pure white, just like the snow on the first night I met him. And I stood up at the top of the mountain on Jason's snowboard looking down at all the trees I was somehow going to have to navigate my way around and I thought, I am insane, this is going to fucking kill me, I mean, I still had never even been on a snowboard before. But I said fuck it, and I just pushed off the top of the mountain, and I know this sounds crazy, but I swear, I could feel Jason with me, holding me up the entire way down. And by the time I reached the bottom, I felt him let me go. And I let him go then, too." Nina breathes out. She reaches out and puts her hand over her heart. "I went to San Francisco after that. And I've just been there ever since." Nina turns toward me again. "Belly," she says. She's staring at me. "Don't think for even a second that I ever forgot about you or Mom. I thought about you guys every day and every time Max went to check up on you I just asked him to . . ."

"Wait," I say. *"What?"*

Nina looks at me, like she's confused by my confusion. And then she nods. "Oh, right, I haven't told you that part yet," she shakes her head. "Max, Jason's best friend and the guy whose number you found, has been checking up on you and Mom. You'll probably recognize him when you meet him later."

I stare at her, blinking. "You had someone check up on us?"

"Every month for the last two years." She nods. "Max was surprised you didn't recognize his voice on the phone when you called him, actually. He said you've talked to him at least ten times."

I stop and look at Nina while I try and take all this in.

"So you really didn't forget about us," I say.

Nina shakes her head. "Of course not, not even for a second. And all along, I was planning on coming back, I just wanted to make sure I waited long enough that it would be okay for everybody. It's funny, because just a couple weeks ago I started thinking that maybe it was time. And then Max called me and he told me what was going on, that you'd called him. It wasn't until later that we realized who you were with, but by then it was too late. When I finally heard you talking to Sean in that motel room, that was the most relieved I'd ever been in my entire life, but then when I heard him almost . . ." Nina looks at me and just exhales deeply. "How did you pull that off?"

"It was open under the desk," I say. "I kicked it there and then tried to talk as loud as possible so you'd hear us."

"Well, it worked. As soon as I heard you through the phone telling him that you were going to look for me on Haight Street, I got my friends to go stand and wait for you guys at Golden Gate Park since I figured you'd have to end up there."

"Did they follow us? After they told us your address? When we were walking over I had this feeling someone was behind us the entire time . . ."

"Of course." Nina nods. "They followed you up the hill and then you guys came into my apartment and then, this guy pointed a gun at me and my amazingly brave little sister tackled him. And I guess you pretty much know the rest."

And then Nina nods and she collapses back into her seat, like someone who's been running and running for years and has just finally stopped.

I turn toward her. I have waited so long for this, for this story, for this moment, and I want to tell her I'm sorry, for ever doubting her reasons for leaving, for being angry, for not trusting her, for everything that she's been through. But when our eyes meet, she just smiles, this bittersweet smile, sad and wise, and I know I don't have to say anything at all because, in this moment I can tell she already knows. And I know something right then, too, this Nina, this person sitting next to me, is the sister I grew up with, but she's not quite the same person she was when she left. Then again, neither am I.

"Hey, Belly," Nina says. "I still want to hear *your* whole story, too, you know. I mean, there's a whole lot of what happened that I still don't understand." And then she stops and smiles. "But I guess there'll be plenty of time for that later."

"Plenty of time for that later," I say. And I smile, too.

Then Nina goes back to her drawing, and I go back to staring out the window. We'll be home soon.

Forty-Four

I see her before she sees us, my mom, standing by the baggage claim holding two bouquets of yellow flowers.

Nina spots her a second after I do. "It's her," she whispers. And then she takes off running.

"Mom!" she shouts. "MOM! MOM! MOOOOOOOM!"

Our mom turns when she hears Nina's voice and then her entire face just lights up. And she just stands there beaming in this light blue sleeveless dress and makeup and the little gold earrings Nina and I got her for Mother's Day like ten years ago. This is the first time in I don't even know how long that I've seen her in anything other than a nurse's uniform or a bathrobe and pajamas. She looks beautiful.

When Nina reaches her they throw their arms around each other, and there's hugging and crying and laughing and when I reach them I get roped in to the hug, too. Out of the corner of my eye I see that everyone who passes is staring at us and smiling. I feel like if we wanted to we could grab every single passerby, one by one, and pull them into our hug until the entire airport is sharing in our happiness. Such is the power of a moment like this one.

Finally, after a very long time we let go and stand there still huddled in the chilly airport air. Nina's eyes are twinkling, just the way I remember them doing before she ever left. And my mother is just staring at us, looking so soft and pleased and proud, it's like the drawing of her on Nina's wall is a portrait of her from just this moment. And then she glances down at her hands like she just realized she's still holding onto the bouquets of yellow flowers which have now been completely crushed by the fury of our hugs. She thrusts them out toward us. The remaining petals flutter to the floor.

"You're both grounded," she says. And the three of us burst out laughing.

Forty-Five

A week ago at this time is when it all began. I had just left Mon Coeur with a bag of broken cookies in my hand, and was about ten minutes away from finding Nina's drawing, and about four hours away from going to a party at the Mothership, and about seven hours away from leaning against a wall and meeting what I thought was just a friendly stranger in a mask. A week ago at this time, I could not have even begun to imagine all of the insane things that were about to happen. But now, sitting out here on lawn chairs on the sidewalk in front of Mon Coeur, I know that even if I could, I wouldn't change a single moment of the last week. Because if it had somehow gone differently, things might not be exactly the way they are right now.

"Shouldn't be too long now," Brad says. He squints at his watch. "The fireworks usually start ten minutes after sunset."

"*You* usually start ten minutes after sunset," Thomas says, poking him in the side.

Brad grins. "I have no idea what that means, sweetness,

but you're too cute to have to make sense." And he leans his head on Thomas's shoulder.

It's just the seven of us, stretched out on the best piece of sidewalk in all of Edgebridge, on the blue and white lawn chairs that Brad found in the back room. To my right, Brad and Thomas are messing with Brad's digital camera. To my left, Amanda is chatting with Adam, the new guy she's been seeing, and Adam's cute best friend Cody, who smiles shyly at me whenever he catches my eye.

And right there in the middle, Nina and I are eating the last bites of our ice cream sandwiches.

Nina licks her fingers, stands up, and tosses both of our wrappers in the trash. "I hope he gets here before they start," she says. And then she twists her head around, looking at the heavy crowds of people on either side of the street.

"Who?" I say. But she doesn't hear me because she's up on her tiptoes waving her arms and yelling.

"Max!" she calls out. "Maxie! We're over here!" A lanky guy, with red hair and an earring in each ear, is walking towards us through the crowd, grinning.

"Hey, girl," he says. He's laughing. "Hey! Hey! Hey!" They hug and he spins her around.

"Maxie," Nina says. "This is . . ."

"Hey, I know you," Brad says suddenly. "You come into Mon Coeur! You always order something quirky . . ." He starts snapping his fingers, trying to remember.

"Two Earl Grey tea bags in a small to-go cup with extra room for milk!" I say suddenly. This is Earl Grey!

"Girl deserves a raise," Max/Earl Grey says grinning at me. "Sorry I had to lie to you when you called me last week." I notice his slight Southern accent now. "That was, uh, kind of necessary at the time."

"No problem," I say, grinning back. "Just drop a couple bucks in the tip jar next time you're at Mon Coeur and we'll forget all about it."

"Wait!" Amanda says suddenly, disentangling herself from Adam's giant arms. She stands up. "You're the Southern guy, who we called from Attic! The one who used to date Deb . . ."

"Well, except there is no Deb," Max/Earl Grey says. He rocks back on his heels. "That was just some quick thinking on my part." He taps his temple and winks.

"I am *so* confused," Amanda says. And I look over at her and she grins at me like this-is-all-so-crazy.

"I'll explain later," I say with a wink.

To her right, Cody is smiling at me again, I smile back.

It's almost time now.

Women are putting little cardigans on over their dresses and couples are holding hands and leaning against each other. Directly across the street two little girls, one older, one younger, are running, running, running around their parents' legs.

I turn toward Nina. She reclines a little in her seat and something white falls out of her pocket onto the grass below. I can still just barely make it out under the fading light. It's the napkin Nina was sketching on during our flight home. There I am, curly hair curling in all directions, one dimple, and a crooked smile. And there she is, straighter hair, matching dimple, big smile that takes up half her face. I reach out for it, but stop myself. I will leave this one here for someone else to find.

"Belly." Nina pokes me in the arm. "Look up! They're starting!"

And I tip my head back just in time to see the dark summer sky fill up with light.